The Good Stuff

A NOVEL

By
Michelle Stimpson

West Bloomfield, Michigan

Acknowledgments

Giving first honor to God for the gift of writing that He granted me. I am elated, Father, at how You continue to work EVERYTHING for Your glory. When it's all said and done, I simply want to know You more.

My husband (Stevie) and my kids (Steven and Kalen) continue to be a source of strength and a reality check. I am grateful for your confidence in me and for the sacrifices you all make in support of my writing. I want you to know that I am acutely aware of how blessed I am to have a family that "gets" what God is doing through all of us.

To my "people" (my family) who continue to mention my books to everyone—and I do mean *everyone!* My mom (Wilma), dad (Michael), brothers (Michael and Tony), the Williams, Stimpson, Lenear, Music, and Smith families—thank you so much! I have run into so many people who have said, "Your mom/dad/brother/uncle/aunt/cousin told me about your book!" Thanks!

I am also blessed to have a circle of friends who laugh and consistently pray with me through all the drama of my life which, coincidentally, ends up in novels: Kim, Jeanne, Opal, and Shannon. To those who just send me an email or give me a call to let me know that you are looking out for me, including Shaundale, Miriam, Joycia, Della, Dollie, Carolyn, Michelle P., and my big Sister in Christ, Karen Bradford, thank you.

Ellen and Jayne, former coworkers—now forever friends— who lend their literary genius to my projects, big and small, by reading the drafts and giving feedback—I just love y'all. Mrs. Kimbrough, thanks for your insight as well!

To all the book clubs which have selected *Boaz Brown* and/or *Divas of Damascus Road* for reading and discussion, I mentioned many of you in the pages of *Divas of Damascus Road*. Let me add to the list: Sisters United to Read, Divas Read 2, Glory Girls, Oak Cliff Bible Fellowship Women's Book Club and Creative Tyme Ministry, Girlfriend 2 Girlfriend, Sisters With a Purpose, Sisters Sipping Tea, Literary Ladies, Chi Zeta Omega Chapter of Alpha Kappa Alpha Sorority, People Who Luv Good Books, the Women's Ministry of Greater Allen A.M.E. Cathedral of New York, and the many book clubs with which I convened by telephone and Internet. Also to the organizations and people who keep putting me out there: The Black Writers' Guild of Irving (Hey, Christina—future author!), MyFirstChapter.com (Shelia Benson), Region 10 Education Service Center, The Valder Bebee Show, Shaundale Johnson, Daniel I Am, The Antonio Johnson Show (KHVN Radio, Dallas, TX), Booking Matters, The National Coalition of 100 Black Women (Greater Miami Chapter), New Jerusalem Temple Church (Dallas, TX), Young Ladies Anointed and Chosen for Distinction, Emma Rodgers, and JoKac's African American Books—your support is priceless and I am *always* flattered! Please accept my gratitude! And if I left out a name, please charge it to my head, not my heart.

To all the women who shared stories about their marriages—the good, the bad, and the ugly—you know who you are, and I thank you for being so candid.

To all of the readers who continue to email me and sign my guest book—it is so nice to hear from you! This book was a long time coming, and so many times as I was ready to kick this project to the curb and start over again at square one, I got an encouraging email from someone. God uses us all to build each other up. Thank you!

For the wonderful writers whom I have encountered and who have been so open in sharing advice, contacts, etc., thank you. I have to give a special thanks to the authors of Walk Worthy Press, ReShonda Tate-Billingsley and Francis Ray. Shout out to my fellow Anointed Authors on Tour: Vivi Monroe Congress, Vanessa Miller, Tia McCollors, Kendra Norman-Bellamy, Shewanda Riley, and Norma Jarrett. You all are too funny and I'm so blessed to tour with you!

To my publisher, Denise Stinson. I have a growing appreciation for what God continues to do through you. You go, my sister! To Monica Harris—you are my kind of editor and I'm so glad to work with you! Thanks, also, to the Harrison House family.

Mrs. Irma K. Parker

Mrs. Irma K. Parker knows why every good romantic novel or movie ends with the engagement or the wedding. She'd be the first to say that by falling in love, "You really ain't done nothin'," because *falling* in love is the easy part. It's the getting back up, dusting off, getting nerve, forgiving again in love—that's the hard part. And after you learn to work through all that, well, *that's* when you get to the good stuff.

Throughout her service in the church and in cleaning homes, she'd seen it more times than she wanted to remember: the rise and fall of a marriage. Newlyweds sitting up on cloud ten, looking down on cloud nine, and things going well for a while. Then comes life. They decide to make some changes: go back to school, get a dog, have kids, move into a bigger home.

Now, Irma figured that if they added a few more chapters to those romance novels or a couple more scenes to the movies (at least past the honeymoon phase), that same couple would be getting up every day going to work, going to church, coming home, eating, going to bed, and then doing the same thing the next day and the next—only after a couple of years it's no longer a pleasant consistency. It's boring. The freshness of that other person's features is gone, replaced by a common image. Just like every new puppy, every new outfit, and every new car takes on new meaning when it comes to scooping up that poop, opening that credit card bill, and paying that car note every month.

Makes a woman wonder why she ever got married in the first place. Makes her wonder if she would have been better off with what's-his-name. Makes her wonder if the person she married was really the one God had in mind or if, maybe, she should have waited for somebody else.

One day she wakes up, rolls over, takes a good long look at the man lying next her and asks herself the question that 99.9 percent of all married women (including Irma herself) have, at some point or another, asked themselves: "Why did I ever get married?"

Don't matter how old, how saved, how rich, how poor, how beautiful, or how many times folks have already been married; fact is, every marriage loses its innocence at some point. People make mistakes, bad choices, or whatever you want to call them. Priorities change, interests change, people change—as they should. That's all a part of growing. And there's no set formula for how people grow. Some grow faster than others, some take off and then stop for a while before starting again. Some wait around and then sprint so hard their feet kick their behinds toward the end. In the meanwhile, hearts get broken, families split up, people move on for better or for worse.

To Irma, it seems a shame that women who have been through all of this and come out with stronger, longer marriages don't get much chance to sit down with the less experienced wives and show them the art of standing by a man. Not behind him like a mother, or in front of him like his father, or over him like he's her child, or under him like a doormat.

Beside him. Like his wife.

After 42 years of marriage, what Irma K. Parker knew that Sonia Gipson-Riley and Adrian Jacobsen *didn't* know (after a combined total of 12 years of marriage) is that failure is a part of success. It's *not* all or nothing when it comes to a marriage.

Sometimes, you need to just sit down and listen to the older women tell it like it T-I-Z.

CHAPTER 1

Sonia and Kennard Riley

Sonia found a good stopping point and shut down her computer. She rushed to the breakroom where she sliced and wrapped two pieces of cake to give to her kids, Kamron and Kelsi. Thoughts of the afternoon's retirement gathering for Renee Johnson ran through Sonia's mind as she carefully selected pieces that hadn't been touched. The impromptu party had been nice, with a moment or two of sincere regret for Renee's departure. Sonia had to admit, she would miss walking into Renee's office for a chat with the door ajar, or a sister-girl session with the door shut. Renee and her husband were looking forward to moving to the country and sharing their golden years together. Sonia didn't envy Renee, however, because Sonia couldn't imagine spending her golden years with her husband, Kennard. They'd be lucky if they made it to their next anniversary because, in the words of Atlantic Starr, it was a fragile situation that could fall apart at any time.

Instead of thinking about Renee's happiness, Sonia focused on the fact that she was the first runner-up for Renee's position as senior account manager. Though protocol required an official posting of the vacancy, it was no secret that Sonia Gibson-Riley was the best fit for the job. Renee herself had even made reference, during her good-bye speech, to Sonia's dedication. It was just a matter of time.

As Sonia finished wrapping plastic over the second piece of cake, she did think (for an instant) about getting a piece for Kennard, but decided against it. He would probably gobble it

1

down and then follow it up with one of his sarcastic remarks about her imminent promotion.

Sonia grabbed a sticky note and a pencil from the counter and left a friendly message letting the custodial staff know that they were welcome to the rest of the cake. Down in the parking garage, she packed her laptop and briefcase into the trunk of her late-model Lexus and prepared herself for the "third shift"—the work that working moms do after work. A list of things-to-do flashed through her head as she accelerated onto the highway.

Once she'd made it through the downtown Dallas mix-master and onto her side of the city, she stopped at Lil' Ones to pick up the kids. Lang, the center director, met Sonia at the door. She and her staff had cared for Kamron and Kelsi since they were five weeks old, and Sonia appreciated her relationship with Lang. Lang never charged extra when Sonia picked the kids up late, and she let Sonia take them in early when necessary.

"Kelsi and Kamron!" Lang called the children as Sonia crossed the threshold into the center.

In unison, the twins rose to their feet and ran toward their mother. It was a picture worth taking—both twins missing their two front teeth and smiling like there was no tomorrow. Kamron with his shirttail flapping, Kelsi with her pigtails bouncing wildly. "Slow down," Sonia said for the sake of propriety, secretly thankful that her children seemed to live for the moment that she picked them up from daycare. It was nice to be missed.

"Mommy, did you get the new job?" Kelsi asked.

"Well, I told you, Miss Renee retired today. Mommy won't know about the new job for a couple of weeks at least," she curbed Kelsi's curiosity. It was amazing how much that girl could remember. A casual conversation a month earlier and Kelsi was right on top of it like white on rice.

"Are you getting a new job?" Lang asked.

2

"I'm applying for a promotion," Sonia downplayed the question as she secured the twins' backpacks on their shoulders.

"I'm sure you'll get it. You're a great lady. They would be crazy not to promote you." Lang gave her a smile loaded with genuine support.

"Thank you," Sonia said, tilting her head to the side. It was all she could do to keep from crying. *How is it that my day-care provider can be more excited about my opportunity than my own husband?* "We'll see you Monday."

"Good-bye, kiddos!"

"Good-bye, Mrs. Lee," the children chimed as they walked to the car.

After Sonia was sure that Kelsi and Kamron were safely strapped in, they headed home. She turned off the radio so she could talk with them about their day at school. First grade had been pretty good for Kelsi. Kamron seemed to be having a bit of trouble with reading, but his teacher, Mrs. Scott, was certain that Kamron would catch on in time. "We can't all be Kelsi," she'd remarked with laughter. Since that time, Sonia had taken the initiative to read to the children almost every night and, though he still didn't read as well as Kelsi, Kamron improved significantly.

The canopy of trees overhead always produced "oohs!" and "aahs!" from the children as they approached their quiet neighborhood via the back roads. The back roads took them out of the way, but Sonia needed the calming effect just then. Her thoughts drifted back to Renee's position; taking over would be a challenge. Maybe even more trouble than it was worth. But she couldn't imagine *not* moving up. After all, that was the purpose of the M.B.A.: career advancement, more money, more for the kids, more for retirement.

A cheer came from the backseat forward, filling the car with delight. "We're going down the tree-top way!" Kamron announced, air swishing through the gap in his teeth with every word. It didn't take much to please them.

They rounded the last few blocks and then pulled into the garage. Once the car was parked, Kamron bounded out of his seat belt and ran to the front yard, chasing a flock of birds across the yard. Kelsi, six going on twenty-five, remarked that it was foolish for him to be chasing birds. "He won't never catch one," Kelsi said as she grabbed both backpacks from the seat.

Sonia joined her daughter at the rear of the car and together they walked down the driveway's slope to the mailbox. "How do you know he won't *ever* catch one?"

"'Cause the birds are too fast. They can fly."

Sonia pulled one of Kelsi's long, brown ponytails playfully. "Me-Maw says that you should never say never. Sometimes things that seem impossible happen."

"What does impossipull mean?" Kelsi asked.

"When something is impossi-*ble,* it means that you don't see a way for it to happen. You think it's impossible for Kamron to catch a bird, don't you?"

She nodded matter-of-factly. "Have *you* ever caught a bird?"

"No, Kelsi, I can't say that I have." Sonia laughed at her daughter's question—an obvious challenge. "But I have seen some impossible things happen. When the impossible happens, we call that a miracle."

"Ooh," Kelsi smiled, "there's a girl in my class named Miracle."

"That's a pretty name." Sonia smiled back.

Kamron gave up his bird chase and followed them into the house, panting and begging for water. Kelsi pushed him away from the refrigerator, insisting that he allow her to get it for him. Kamron obeyed, taking a seat on a stool and waiting for his sister to serve him. Kelsi pulled a cup from the dishwasher, inspected it, and then proceeded to prepare the water for her brother. At the refrigerator, she pushed the lever, allowed a minimum number of ice cubes to fall into the cup, and tiptoed so that she could visually monitor the depth of the water. She rationed just enough to cover the tip of the ice.

Kamron wiped his forehead as Kelsi brought him the cup. When she placed it on the table before him, he thanked her. She gave a half "you're welcome" and turned her back to him, heading for the fruit basket. She grabbed two apples, said "Here's you go," and plopped a Granny Smith down before him. She watched him gulp down the water and waited for him to lift the apple to his lips and take a bite. Satisfied that Kamron was in compliance, Kelsi took a bite of her own.

As Sonia watched Kelsi's interaction with her brother, she couldn't help but notice how close *this* apple had fallen from her maternal tree. In Kelsi's six short years of life, she'd watched Sonia walk into a room, size up the situation, and take immediate action without consulting any of the parties involved. Kelsi could be overbearing, Sonia knew, but there was never a worry about anybody pushing Miss Kelsi Danielle Riley around. She would be a strong black woman, in the tradition of those before who kept going through tough times, even when men were trippin' or absent or both. Black women had survived and were stronger for it. Sonia had to admit, she was proud of her daughter.

The house smelled of Pine-Sol and bleach. Irma Parker, their housekeeper, had come and gone after her biweekly routine. Sonia threw on a pair of jeans, a black T-shirt, and a pair of fluffy house shoes—the kind that should have been thrown out a long time ago—and then walked the first floor, inspecting the bathrooms, the living area, the kitchen, and the master bedroom. She had never had a problem with Irma's work, but it was Sonia's habit to double-check things. On the second floor, she examined the children's bathroom. Every scrap of toothpaste they had managed to slap around the sink was gone. The spots where Kamron missed the toilet were gone. In the children's bedroom, linens were changed and furniture dusted. And even though Sonia had told Irma that she didn't need to worry with straightening up the kids' toy room (that was their job), Sonia could see that Irma had gone behind them and perfected their six-year-old efforts.

As always, Sonia gave Irma a call to let her know that she had done a good job. It was not what most people do with their housekeepers, but Irma was a dear. Sometimes Irma left an encouraging card on the refrigerator or a cheerful note on top of the mantel. It seemed a shame to Sonia that for all that Irma had done to keep the Riley household running smoothly for the past six years, the two women rarely got to see each other.

"Hello, Miss Irma, it's Sonia Riley. How are you?"

"I'm blessed of the Lord. How 'bout you?"

"I'm fine, too. Just wanted to let you know that the house looks great."

"I tell you, those twins are sure growing up! I put in a load of laundry before I left—I see they're up to a size seven now!"

"Oh, Miss Irma, you didn't have to do that."

"Well, I finished a little early today and I figured I might as well." Sonia could hear Irma's sweet smile through the phone.

"Thank you, Miss Irma. I sure appreciate you."

"I appreciate you, too, sweetheart. Bye, now."

All appeared well in their four-bedroom, three-bathroom, three-thousand square-foot home in their master-planned community. When Sonia really thought about it, she was grateful for God's blessings. She had more than a lot of people, financially and otherwise. Her kids were healthy, and that was something she never took for granted after the rough time they had coming into the world. Twins are always a risk. "Thank You, Lord," Sonia exhaled.

After the kids finished their snacks, Sonia sent them off to their rooms, reminding them that because it was Friday, they would be going to Me-Maw's house.

"Get your suitcases. They're on your beds."

Kelsi had already taken the liberty of going through her luggage. "Momma!" she called from her upstairs bedroom.

"What?"

"I want Me-Maw to see my pants with the glitter on them. Can I pack those, please?"

"I told you—those pants are for special occasions," Sonia yelled back.

"But I don't like the pants you packed. They look like *boy* pants."

"Those are *not* boys' pants. I bought them...." *Earth to Sonia. Am I really having a debate with my six-year-old about clothes?* "Kelsi, you are wearing the clothes that I packed for you. Now, if you don't want to wear those clothes, you can just stay home." Sometimes, Sonia had to catch herself with that girl.

Sonia shook her head and walked back into the kitchen to thaw out a few chicken breasts for herself and Kennard. With the children gone, they would need only two or three. Maybe not even that many, depending on what he had planned for the night.

A few minutes later, the children arrived at the foot of the staircase, luggage in tow. They were so strong and healthy now, nothing like the little helpless, unstable babies they had been at birth. "We're ready," Kelsi spoke for the two of them.

"Oh, I almost forgot—I've got a special treat for you two."

"What is it?" Kamron asked with wonder in his eyes.

"I got some cake today at work," Sonia announced as she unfurled the top to the breadbox, revealing the cake magician-style. Both children squealed with joy and followed Sonia to the table.

"Where did you get this cake from?" Kelsi asked as she took the plastic off her piece and dove into it.

"Well, it's the cake I got from work. Miss Renee is retiring, so...."

Kelsi abruptly stopped eating her cake and asked, "Did you get a piece for Daddy?"

"No," Sonia said without offering an explanation.

Kelsi slid her fork down the center of the corner piece she had left on her plate. "I'm gonna save this half for Daddy."

Sonia mustered every ounce of Christian love within her and gave Kelsi a grin. She prayed silently for the strength to refrain from telling her daughter the truth: that he wouldn't have done the same for her.

As good as that cake was, Kelsi rewrapped her daddy's half and placed it back in the breadbox. "When will Daddy be home?"

"I don't know, but I'll make sure he gets the cake," Sonia assured her daughter.

Satisfied that her father would be taken care of, Kelsi threw her fork in the sink and joined her mother and brother again at the table. As Kamron finished his cake, they all rose and headed for the car and Sonia's mother's home. It was a short drive back into Dallas since they were on the lighter side of traffic. The kids entertained themselves with songs and a game of I-spy, and in no time Sonia was parking in her mother's driveway, ready to drop off the kids and make way for peace and quiet.

"Hey, y'all!"

"Hey, Me-Maw," the children echoed as they ran toward their grandmother. She received them with hugs and kisses.

Then Clarice kissed her daughter on the cheek and held back the screen door so that Sonia could enter the home she used to call her own. With the way Clarice baked for the sick, shut-ins, and bereaved, the house always smelled like bread. The members at Gospel Temple always said that the best thing about being sick was Missionary Gibson's homemade rolls. Though Sonia had stood by her mother's side and watched her mix, knead, and bake countless dozens, she never could make those rolls quite the way Clarice did. "You gotta put your foot in it, girl," Clarice would laugh.

The twins went off to the guest room to put their things away, while Sonia and Clarice detoured to the kitchen. "You want some prune juice?"

"No, thanks," Sonia said, taking a seat.

"Keep you regular." She poured herself a tall glass.

"I *am* regular."

"You talked to your daddy?" Clarice forced a sore subject.

"Not in a couple of weeks."

"Well, he's down in Louisiana for the rest of the week. You should try him on his cell phone. I talked to him just the other day. Says he might be home by Monday, depends on if he wins or not."

Sonia tap-danced on her mother's nerves. "Why doesn't he just stay there?"

"'Cause I'm his wife and I'm here. *That's* why. You know, the Lord works in mysterious ways."

It was beyond Sonia how her mother could claim to be married to her father, 'Buddy' Gibson. For as long as Sonia could remember, her parents had lived two totally separate lives; her mother in the church, her father in the streets. Throughout Sonia's childhood, Buddy kept a steady job Monday through Friday. He provided a roof over their heads, but that was the extent of his paternal presence. Now that Buddy was retired, the only evidence that he resided with Clarice was his name on the deed.

"I got some fresh bread in the oven. You want some?" Clarice switched gears.

Sonia laughed at her mother's offer. "When have you *not* had fresh bread in the oven?" They both laughed while Clarice busied herself with fixing a plate of rolls for Sonia to take home.

Sonia looked around the kitchen and counted the same one hundred and thirteen stripes on the wallpaper that she'd been counting all her life. Then she watched her mother from behind. Clarice moved slower now, her back rounded ever so slightly. Her mother was getting old. Sonia wondered if she should stop trying to make her mother realize that she was married only on paper. Maybe Sonia should just let her mother take this fantasy to the grave because, aside from Sonia and the kids, Clarice didn't appear to have much left.

As for Clarice, she saw a younger version of herself when she looked at Sonia: mocha skin, brown eyes, big puffy lips, and a behind to match. Sonia had those two-tone microbraids that all the busy younger women seemed to be wearing these days. She'd twisted the braids around and secured the base with some kind of clip and left the ends of her hair to swing with every step.

Clarice placed the rolls in front of her daughter and sat down at the table with her. She watched her daughter sink her teeth into her hot, buttered roll and remembered the good old days, when Sonia thought the world of her and these rolls. Back then, Sonia didn't question where her daddy was or why he didn't come straight home after work. She just let it be.

"I'm gonna keep the kids 'til Sunday morning. We're having our youth day and I was going to take them to rehearsal with me tomorrow and have them sing on Sunday morning. Is that alright?" Clarice had obviously rehearsed this speech.

"Kamron's got a lot of reading to do," Sonia twisted the words out of her mouth.

"What's more important— readin' Jack and Jill or the Bible? Servin' the Lord pays off after while. And only what you do for Christ will last. That's what's wrong with kids now...."

And she's off! Clarice got up from the table and grabbed a washcloth, wiping spotless counters as she fussed. As crazy as it was, Sonia appreciated hearing her mother go off on these tangents. It was nice to be up under somebody again, to have Clarice tell her what to do instead of everybody just assuming that Sonia knew everything all the time, because she didn't.

"When was the last time *you* been to church?"

Now was Sonia's chance to redeem herself and let her mother know that she was not a heathen. "Sunday."

Clarice fussed as she folded a wet cloth in half and placed it across the faucet. "And here it is Friday. Almost a week since you set foot in the house of the Lord. I know I was glad when they said unto me, let us go into the house of the Lord. Ooh, I tell you, me and your daddy raised you better than that."

Sonia felt a *no-she-didn't* rising up in her throat. Aside from an occasional reference to "the Man upstairs" or attending somebody's funeral, Buddy didn't have anything to do with the Lord or church. Sonia moaned defiantly.

"We need more young folks to take part in the church," Clarice continued. "Seems like Gospel Temple is dryin' up. Folks is leavin' for these big, flashy churches with singles groups and conferences and bookstores and durn near professional football teams." She stopped and stared at Sonia. "Y'all still got Wednesday night service at your church?"

"Yes, ma'am. I didn't get to go this week, but I can get the CD on Sunday and listen to it in the car through the week when I'm driving back and forth to work."

She relented. "Well, all right. The truth will set you free. Did I tell you Gospel Temple might be closing?"

"Yes, you told me."

"I don't know what I'm gonna do if the church closes," she said as she rolled her lips between her teeth and shook her head.

"You can come join my church; it's not too big and you said yourself that you like Pastor Butler's teaching."

"I said I like his *teachin'*, not his *preachin'*," she said as she gave her daughter a self-righteous snarl. "He ain't got no get-up-and-holla in him like Pastor Williams. I ain't used to somebody just readin' from the Word and talkin'. That's dead."

"I know it's different from what you're used to, but different doesn't mean bad. Things are changing, you know. "

"Whoo! I'm too old to change. Guess I'll have service with just me and the Lord here at the house 'cause I ain't about to listen to no youth group come up and rap and dance in the pulpit. Lord'll have to take me on home to glory first. Won't be nobody there able to put me out."

Sonia decided to end this conversation. "I'm gonna get on back, Momma. The Lord isn't taking you anywhere just yet.

You've got two grandkids to help raise." She stood and kissed her mother on the cheek as the children rushed into the kitchen.

"You rested up?" Sonia asked as she slung her purse to her shoulder and grabbed her keys from the counter.

"Yeah, I'm always ready for my grandbabies." The twins rushed into the kitchen and grabbed Clarice's hands. They ushered her into the living room with promises of dazzling scenes from the Disney movies they'd packed.

On the way home, Sonia thought about all the things she wanted to tell her mother but couldn't. There was no use in trying to overturn Clarice's fantasy. Maybe this arrangement between her mother and father was okay for Clarice, but it wouldn't do for Sonia. Sonia wanted more.

CHAPTER 2

By the time Sonia got back from her mother's house, Kennard still wasn't home. *It's Friday. Who am I kidding? He could have hit half a dozen happy hours by now.* Sonia made salad for one and resolved to catch up on her best friend, Gina.

"Hey, girl," Gina answered the phone in her usual cheerful tone.

"What's up, Gina! Haven't heard from you in, what, a week now? I guess you don't talk to blacks no mo?" Sonia teased.

"Anyway!" Gina laughed. "Girl, this new job is kickin' Reggie's butt! He hasn't been home before eight any night this week! I'm just sittin' around here talking to myself. I need to get a part-time job or somethin', girl, 'cause I can't take this anymore."

"Oh, the woes of stay-at-home wives," Sonia teased with a hint of envy.

"Whatever! So, what's up with you and Kennard and the kids?"

"Same old, same old."

"Kennard still trippin?"

"You got it. He squeezes all the anger out of me like a sponge!"

"Okay, so have you talked to him about counseling?" Gina asked.

"Girl, he ain't tryin' to hear that. You know how brothers are—they think can't nobody tell them nothin'."

"Hmph. I've been talking to some of Reggie's colleagues' wives. Most of them are white, and let me tell you, I don't think this hardheadedness is a black thing. Some of them have the same issues with their white men."

Sonia managed a joke. "It's an equal opportunity thing, huh?"

"Seriously, this thing between you and Kennard has been going on forever. The kids are, what, six now? It seems to me that when they were born, you and Kennard stopped being married. You two need to get it together."

"Who you tellin'?"

"Go out on a date! It's Friday—doesn't your mom have the kids tonight?"

Sonia had to admit, "Yes, she does, but I don't even know where Kennard is."

"So, call him on his cell phone and ask him out on a date! Or, find out where he is and what time he'll be home and meet him at the door naked. How 'bout that?" Gina suggested mischeviously.

"You're trippin', Gina."

"I'm serious!" she laughed. "God saved sex for the relationship needs it the most. Take advantage of it!"

"Do you really think I can have sex with someone who hasn't had two kind words to say to me in the past two days?" Sonia asked.

"It don't take words to have sex, girl. Let your *body* do the talking."

Sonia knew that she was talking to a rabbit. Gina and Reggie were newlyweds and, let Gina tell it, they went at it almost every day. Sonia was up for sex just as much as the next woman, but she was no Gina. "It's not that simple for me. I'm having a hard time getting emotionally naked right now."

"Start with *physically* naked; maybe the emotions will follow."

How could Sonia explain this to someone who'd never been in her shoes? She loved Gina, but they were at different places in their marriages. Once past the honeymoon phase, a roll in the hay can't fix everything. Sonia couldn't explain her situation to Gina—and she didn't want to, either. *Why mess her up with my mess?*

"Look, Sonia, I'm not tryin' to tell you what to do. All I know is, y'all have to go to the Lord and then a counselor or a pastor or somebody. I love you, I love Kennard, I love the kids, but in all selfishness, I have to tell you: I miss your joy."

A lump rose up in Sonia's throat and she fell silent. Sonia missed her joy, too.

The hum of the garage door opening announced Kennard's arrival and set Sonia's sensors on alert. "Well, Kennard's home. I gotta go, girl. I'll call you back later."

"Okay. Bless God that he made it home safely, right?"

"Yes, bless God for that."

"And remember—think nay-ked, nay-ked, nay-ked," Gina chanted.

Kennard walked through the door and Sonia tried her very best to be nice with her clothes *on*. "Hey, hon."

He mumbled something inaudible and dropped his keys onto the entertainment center. "Did you call to renew the insurance on the cars?"

The question was simple enough, but Sonia didn't answer. "Did you hear me say hello?"

"I *said* hello to you, too," he snapped back.

"Is that grumbling supposed to be a 'hello?'"

"I ain't got time for this today, Sonia. Did you or did you not call about the insurance?"

Sonia lied, "No." He didn't *deserve* to know the truth, not with that attitude.

"Are you going to call 'em tomorrow?"

"Why don't *you* call," she suggested.

"I will," he sighed angrily. "What's the number?"

"Look it up." Sonia left him on his own to figure this one out. No doubt, he would be angry when he learned that she'd already handled this business of the insurance because she didn't want to drive around uninsured anymore than he did, but that was irrelevant at the moment.

It was little things like walking into the house and acting like you can't speak that got on Sonia's nerves most.

Kennard had some concerns of his own. Every time he walked through the door and smelled pine cleaner, he got upset. "Boy, you kill me. You gotta do everything like the white folks— got a black housekeeper and everything."

"Yes, I do have a housekeeper, but it has nothing to do with black or white," Sonia confirmed.

"They don't make wives like they used to," he shook his head.

"They don't make husbands like they used to, either," her voice chased after him as he proceeded on toward their bedroom in preparation for his own personal evening plans. "Husbands used to eat dinner with their families back in the good old days!"

No response. He simply disappeared behind the door and turned on the shower to let Sonia know that he wasn't listening anymore.

Minutes later, Kennard emerged from their master suite wearing a pair of boxers and a T-shirt. His six-foot-three-inch frame was straight-up eye candy. His broad chest gave a steady anchor for his shirt, with muscles that rounded like knots in bread dough. His rich, yellow, fluid skin flowed from the top of his bald head to the bottom of his solid feet. The elastic in his boxers was hardly necessary, as his perfectly shaped behind could have held that cotton up all on its own. Just below the hem, Kennard's muscular thighs gave testament to his years of running track from junior high on through his freshman year in college.

Nay-ked, Nay-ked, Nay-ked. Maybe Gina was right—at least for that night. "Do you want me to make the pineapple punch?" Sonia was the first to offer an apology, by way of his favorite beverage.

"Make whatever you want to make," he answered, reaching over her and getting a glass from the cabinet. "I ain't gonna be here to drink it."

"Okay, you just got home. Where are you off to now?"

"I'm going to the barber shop."

"Ain't that much hair-cuttin' in the world," Sonia sighed.

Kennard rolled his head to both sides and popped his neck twice, releasing the pressure that had built up between discs. Sonia couldn't *stand* it when he made that annoying noise. *Big 'ole turtle.*

"After I leave the barber shop, I'll probably go over to Victor's. He's having a get-together."

Victor was Kennard's friend from high school. Sonia knew him casually, and from what she knew, he was the typical bachelor. Rippin' and runnin'. The one good thing she could say about Victor, however, was that he had not reproduced. "I haven't seen Victor in a while. Is this a men-only event?"

"No, but I know you. You won't like the crowd."

"What makes you say that?"

"'Cause they smoke."

Sonia could already see herself washing the smell of smoke out of her braids. But she would do it, if there was a chance that she and Kennard might spend some time together. "I can stand a little smoke."

"This ain't no regular smoke," Kennard advised.

It took Sonia a second or two to figure it out, and then she laid into him. "Why would you even want to *be* around people smokin' weed?"

"Hey, Victor is grown. I can't tell that man what to do in his own house." Kennard raised his hands to his chest and took a step back. "It's not my place to judge."

"Obviously not, because you have *no* sense of judgment. What would you do if the police went up in there and smelled marijuana? What if you got arrested?" Sonia fussed.

"Dang, be quiet. You goin' jinx us. I ain't goin' to jail. I don't smoke cigarettes or weed, I don't do drugs. I'm just going to a party. You can come if you want to, but I don't want to hear you hollerin' about being ready to go at ten o'clock or how you don't like the atmosphere."

"Go on out there, if you want to. Don't call here if somethin' happens to you. Call your friends at the barber shop."

Kennard left in his usual funk, and Sonia stayed in hers. It never failed. Every time she tried to meet him halfway, he made her feel like a fool. "Why do I even try?" she asked herself. Maybe, ten years ago, she might have gone to that party at Victor's. But not now. Now, they had kids, careers, and financial responsibilities.

Sonia was resigned to the issue of the party and decided not to worry about it anymore. She would be content to read a novel that night. Besides, the issue wasn't really the party. It was more about Kennard's refusal to grow up and let go of things past. He was still living like a college kid. Sometimes Sonia wished that she could live like a college kid. Those were the good old days.

I'm only thirty-four years old, and I'm already feeling like my best days are behind me. Sometimes Sonia wished that she could take back the day she met Kennard and play it all over again. A simple trip to the post office, that's all it was. When he held the door open for her, as any gentleman would have, she made the mistake of looking into his eyes and smiling. He had told her he'd melted inside, charmed by her fluffy eyelashes and deep brown eyes. Sonia knew that she'd caught his eye, since she was no stranger to getting men's attention. Kennard had already dropped off his mail, but he got back in line behind Sonia and struck up a conversation. When he finally reached the counter, all he could say was, "I...need to buy a book of stamps." The postal worker, an older man who had seen this kind of thing happen more than once, glanced at Sonia and then back at Kennard.

Kennard met her outside of the post office and asked Sonia for her number. The rest was history.

Sonia used to remember that day fondly. She and her girlfriends actually had a nickname for Kennard: Mr. Stamps. They dated for a little over a year—movies, dinner, occasional parties, some church. Back then, Sonia had known that Kennard was rough around the edges. But she liked that. She wanted to help him smooth out those jagged corners. Refine him. He was a work in progress.

Now, Sonia imagined that her life would have been so much better if she had just gone through the automatic gliding doors instead. Then again, if things hadn't been exactly the way they were, her kids wouldn't be exactly who they are. There was no denying that Kelsi and Kamron were the deliberate handiwork of God.

By the time she got pregnant with the twins, Sonia and Kennard had reached a plateau in their marriage. It wasn't good. It wasn't bad. It just was. Call her stupid, but Sonia really thought that having the twins would be the positive change they needed to get their marriage moving ahead again. However, Kennard obviously never got the paternal telegram that things were a-changin'. Matter of fact, when Sonia really thought about it, Kennard never really comprehended the fact that he was married. He would still come home with a meal for one and make plans with the guys for Saturday night without so much as consulting his wife. It's not like he had to ask permission—just be considerate, that's all. Those little nuances only worsened after the twins were born.

Following their birth, Sonia and Kennard's sex life ebbed and flowed. Six years later, they'd had a whole lotta ebbin'. Now that the kids were older and Kennard was gone almost every night of the week, sex was one of the last things on Sonia's mind. Granted, Sonia's body had been sending her signals that it was time for a truce. But the thought of being intimate with Kennard in the midst of all this distance was not enticing.

Come to think of it, the last few times they'd made love, she'd felt...used. She remembered thinking, *How can he ignore me and treat me and the kids like we're liabilities all day and then expect me to roll over and play Happy-Wife at night?* She realized then that sex was beginning to feel more like a wifely duty than the Thank-You-Lord privilege of holy matrimony.

Kennard noticed it, too. "What's up with you?" he'd asked one night at the conclusion of their lovemaking.

"Nothin'."

"Why'd you make me do *all* the work?"

"You can't expect me to have this wonderful, sensual response when you haven't spoken to me all day." Sonia instinctively covered her bare breasts with the comforter.

"So what I gotta do? Have long, drawn-out conversations with you before we have sex?"

She chuckled at his observation. "Yeah. Pretty much. That's how it usually goes."

"I can't do all that no more," he said as his head hit the pillow in exhaustion. "I'm too tired from work."

"Well, if you're too tired to talk to me, then I'm too tired to have sex with you."

"Dang, what do you want from me, Sonia? What is it?" He smashed his face into the pillow.

"I want you to grow up, Kennard. I want you to stop hanging out with your friends and going to happy hours and playing video games all day," she rattled off the abbreviated version of his issues.

He looked up at her. "You gotta make up your mind. You don't want me at home, but you don't want me gone. You can't have it both ways."

"I want you at home or out doing things with *me* and the *kids!*"

"Things like what?"

"Things like baking cookies, reading books, going to museums together."

"Don't nobody want to do that corny white-folks stuff," he said as he shook his head.

You don't have to be white to go to a museum, you idiot! Sonia literally bit her tongue and let him have the last word on the matter. It was too late at night to be arguing.

Not much had changed since that night, roughly a month ago. Between a few fake headaches and an alleged extra long menstrual cycle, Sonia had performed her "wifely duty" only a few times since then.

She searched her bottom drawer for bedclothes and she noticed the stack of teddies, crotchless panties, and other enticing playwear. "No sexy lingerie tonight, either," Sonia said as she grabbed a pair of white, cotton granny-panties and closed the drawer. She hit the shower thinking that it was nice to at least be able to pray about things. If she had gleaned nothing else from her years in Sunday school, it was to have hope that better days were ahead.

That hope, however, was fading as surely as the water slipping through the drain at her feet.

CHAPTER 3

Adrian and Daryll Jacobsen

In the hour before Daryll got home, Adrian watched two court television shows and ate a bag of cheddar popcorn for dinner. Daryll could eat whatever he could find, so far as Adrian was concerned. She propped herself up just right: naturally nappy hair on the headrest, throw blanket covering every inch of her small frame except for the deep brown hand that reached for the popcorn on the coffee table. When Daryll came through the door, he'd see that she had not made any effort to prepare for his return. She had to teach him a lesson.

When Daryll's car pulled into the driveway, Adrian took the stage. She eyed the door-knob. When it turned, Adrian quickly switched her gaze to the television set. After dating through college years and being married three years, Adrian and Daryll had their way of *not* talking to each other.

The smell of grease reached her before she actually saw the brown paper sack in his hand. Big Momma's catfish and fries. *No, he didn't.*

Daryll passed by Adrian without a word and proceeded to the kitchen where he opened his plate of fillets which also contained green beans and a baked potato, fully loaded. Daryll took off his jacket, threw his tie back over his shoulder, and went to town on that meal for one.

Adrian walked past their dining room table on her way to dispose of the empty popcorn bag. "I see you picked up food for yourself *only*," she remarked.

"I need to learn to take care of myself, remember?" Daryll said with a mouthful of food. Adrian watched him as time slowed. The way his strong, golden hand matched the color of the fillets and the way his thick lips shined from green bean juice was intoxicating. Adrian could almost see the food travel down the center of her husband's muscular torso, nourishing his five-foot–eleven-inch frame from the top of his wavy college cut all the way down to his big, flat feet.

You old selfish, sorry cow, Adrian thought. She rolled her eyes at him one good time, but he didn't see her. She'd have to do it again when he was looking.

Later that evening, Adrian sat alone in their bedroom while Daryll held a lively telephone conversation with one of his friends. Adrian tried to be nonchalant about things, but when she heard her husband laughing loudly with his buddy, there was no denying her hurt feelings.

Truth be told, she missed her husband. Adrian hated the silent treatment. But what else was she to do after all the yelling and screaming? They couldn't keep arguing because that wasn't getting them anywhere. And neither was the silent treatment. Sooner or later, one of them would give in and say, "Okay, enough. What do you want?" Then they'd have a truce, a discussion, promises of improvement, indirect apologies, professions of love, and a few days of phenomenal make-up sex. Next thing you know, somebody would do something silly, they'd have a big blowup, and the cycle would start all over again. Up and down, up and down. Only now, after three years, it seemed that the arguments were more intense, the truces were shorter, and the silent treatments lasted longer.

This particular silent treatment had been in effect for four days and counting. The argument had started simply enough at the kitchen table as Daryll reviewed their joint checking account. "Don't make no sense to throw away over two hundred dollars a month on a housekeeper when you could be doing that work yourself!" he shouted. "Lord Jesus, I just wish I had me a Proverbs 31 wife!"

Adrian called to him from the living area. "The Proverbs 31 wife had *servants!* Besides, do you know how good it feels to sleep in on a Saturday morning after a hard week at work? Wait—the answer is yes for you, Daryll. You know what it feels like because you were still asleep on Saturday mornings when I was up cleaning."

"I cut the grass!" he shrieked.

Adrian walked into the kitchen for better firing distance. "Please, let's not even compare the workload of keeping a lawn in season to keeping a house year-round. As far as I'm concerned, Miss Irma gave me back my Saturdays. You can't put a price on time."

"I can. It's called an hourly wage," he said, writing the last few checks for the month's expenses.

"So, you gonna pay me for cleaning up on Saturdays?" she asked, inviting an unpleasant response.

He wrinkled up his face and picked up his pencil again. "Please, I ain't gonna pay you. That's what a *real* wife does. My momma cleans house *every* Saturday."

"I ain't cha momma," Adrian cleared that up. "Besides, your mother didn't work."

"My mother *did* work. She raised me, my brother, and my sister," Daryll said.

"And what a fine job she did," Adrian's voice swung with sarcasm. "What's her success rate? Thirty-three point three percent? And that's giving her credit for *you*."

"Your momma's only fifty-fifty," he computed.

"Fifty-fifty is seventeen percent over *your* mom. *My* mother was single and she held down *two* jobs. What's *your* momma's excuse?"

"Look, there's no reason why you shouldn't work. We don't have kids...." Daryll hit a sore spot.

"And whose fault is that?"

"It ain't my fault that your momma didn't teach you how to handle money," Daryll shrugged.

"Please, my grandmother ran four Laundromats. My family knows how to handle money," Adrian reminded him, standing up for the Millers.

"Well, that good financial sense must have skipped two generations 'cause nobody else in your family knows what to do with money."

"And what about *your* sister?" Adrian turned the tables. "She won all that money and now she got debt collectors callin' *our* house lookin' for her? What you call *that*?"

That was how they argued: pulled in mommas, grandmommas, aunts, uncles, dead or alive, past, present, or future. Adrian and Daryll went a few more rounds on the initial topic of the division of labor. Somehow they worked themselves on to other issues: cars, high school class rings, the Commodores, Anna Nicole Smith. In the end, they made a hostile declaration that it was every man for himself when it came to dinner.

Four days later, they still weren't talking.

To add insult to injury, Daryll didn't even eat all of his food. He'd never intended to eat it all. "I'm having company over," he announced as he closed the Styrofoam container and stored the catfish in the refrigerator at Adrian's eye level.

"What?" Adrian rushed from their bedroom to the living area to confront him.

"I'm having some people over tonight."

"Who?"

"The usual. My daddy, Antonio...probably Shotgun, too."

She interrogated him. "How do you know that I didn't have plans for the house tonight?"

Daryll knew his wife. She didn't bit more have any plans for their home at 9:30 P.M. "Do you?"

Adrian's neck settled into her shoulder blades with a bouncing motion. She didn't have any plans for the house, but she had to *act* like maybe she did. "I guess it wouldn't have mattered if I did, since you've already invited your people over."

Daryll made a smacking sound with his lips. "That's what I thought. No plans."

"I *wish* I had plans with you." Were it not for the crossed arms and attitude surrounding her statement, Daryll might have cancelled his impromptu gathering. If he had looked into Adrian's charcoal eyes, he might have seen how they softened despite her body language.

"Whatever!" Adrian stormed back to their bedroom.

No one would have guessed that this was the home of a deacon and his wife.

Later that night, Daryll, his father, his best friend Antonio, and an older neighbor took turns talking their noise out on the covered patio. Let them tell it, they'd all been star quarterbacks, class valedictorians, and ladies' men back in the day. *Whatever one day that was, Adrian laughed to herself.*

The smell of Daryll's special secret barbecue sauce smoking on the grill wafted all the way into the master bedroom and reminded Adrian of better times gone by. Daryll used to grill for her all the time when they first got married, and she'd complement his barbecue skills with baked beans, potato salad, and German chocolate cake. Back then they'd invite friends over for an evening of fun. Dominoes going on one table and Spades going on the other. Music playing on the stereo, a basketball or football game playing on the television. And after everyone went home, Daryll and Adrian would sit out on the covered patio and talk until the sun came up.

Over the years, people moved and had kids and didn't have time to sit outside all evening like they used to. The patio crew had whittled down to Antonio, Shotgun, and the Jacobsen men. Adrian's friend, Camille, had a man now, which meant that Adrian wouldn't hear from Camille again until the relationship ended. Truth was, since Adrian married three years earlier, her relationship with Camille had changed. They had tried to keep hanging, but one day while out shopping together, Camille remarked that Adrian's wedding ring was "good–man–repellant."

"When we're together, it's like don't-talk-to-those-two-women day," she'd explained, while tapping along in her sandals through the mall and swinging her long mane like a shampoo commercial. "They see you're married and they think I'm married, too—you know, that whole 'birds of a feather' thing," Camille had joked, but Adrian was bothered by Camille's flippant commentary.

Maybe it was just life—the changing of seasons. Either way, Adrian was the first of her clique to get married and she'd paid the price. Slowly, the relationships with her single girlfriends had become formalities, leaving her to rely on Daryll alone for companionship.

At a time when she should have been able to go to her "people" for companionship, she now felt almost like a fish out of water. Adrian's sister Nikki was too trifling to bear without a crowd of people to drown her out. Come to think of it, Adrian admitted to herself that her whole family was trifling. Adrian's life with Daryll was far removed from what she had known growing up. It certainly didn't help that she'd gone to college or that she worked for the state. As far as the Millers were concerned, Adrian had done something out of the ordinary by getting an education and holding down a steady job. Any one of them could have done it. They were poor enough to qualify for all kinds of grants, scholarships, and work-study programs. Adrian got through all four years without owing a penny. And it had been her experience that employers are more than willing to work with anybody who isn't afraid of hard work. For her efforts, Adrian always braced herself for her family's backhanded compliments.

Pleasant Hills, where she lived now, was one of those neighborhoods built for whites in the early 60's. But after desegregation, the whites flew out of there and upwardly bound blacks moved into the fine homes. Teachers, doctors, attorneys, pastors, politicians—every African-American community leader who had any kind of clout lived in Pleasant Hills. Those in Adrian's old black neighborhood, Groverton, rarely had occasion to mix with Pleasant Hills black folk, with the exception of funerals, church musicals, Juneteenth, and Black History Month observations.

Adrian and Daryll lived in Pleasant Hills in a home that his parents once owned. When they married, his father had given the deed to Adrian and Daryll as a wedding gift. Their original plan was to live there for a few years, move into their own place, and rent this one out. Three years later, Adrian had to admit that the home felt like theirs even with all of its squeaky doorknobs and the sound of the air swishing through those metal vents. Daryll was elated to live mortgage-free, and Adrian liked the floor plan of this charming one-story brick home. She was tempted, now and then, to look at new homes. Sometimes she even brought home a few brochures to share with Daryll, but they had yet to come across a model with comparable bedroom space in a neighborhood where people actually knew each other.

Juanita Jacobsen, Daryll's mother, was never really excited about the fact that Daryll had gone all the way to the University of Texas to fall for Adrian, a dark-skinned, holiness church girl from Groverton. For her part, Adrian's mother, Marsha, wasn't too happy about her marrying one of those snobbish high yellow Baptist Negroes from Pleasant Hills, either. "That's that church deacon's boy from Mt. Calvary, ain't it?" Marsha had asked.

"Yes, ma'am."

"That figures," she laughed as she pulled her swollen feet from a pair of thick-heeled nursing shoes. "You be careful foolin' with those Baptists. They ain't half saved, if you ask me. I done seen 'em standin' right on the church parking lot smokin' cigarettes."

"I know, Momma, but Daryll doesn't smoke," Adrian had defended the man she already loved.

"Well, the Baptists ain't the same as us. They ain't got the Ten *Commandments*, they got the ten *suggestions*," Marsha said just before she yawned, laid straight back on the bed, and fell asleep in a matter of seconds.

For the first few years of her marriage, Adrian thought that Marsha had been all wrong about Daryll. But recently she wished she'd listened to her mother's advice. Not necessarily because of the whole Baptist thing, but because…well, she never thought that she and Daryll would end up in a rut like this.

They used to love each other like the people in the novels. Smiling, touching, going places together. He used to finish her sentences. She used to anticipate his needs and desires. They used to lie on opposite ends of the couch and rub each other's feet while watching movies. They used to throw M&M's up in the air and catch them with open mouths. *Whatever happened to that?*

It would be just Adrian and the Lord tonight. Another scripture, another prayer, another night of blah. Adrian tried to get into the Word, but she was too distracted by the men's joking. It was torture knowing that Daryll's most cordial side seemed reserved for everyone except his wife. His rejection tasted like steel.

She watched television until they finished their man talk. After the guests left, Adrian tried to have a decent conversation with Daryll. It was time for a truce. "Did y'all have a good time?"

"Yeah," he answered with a pinch of irritation in his voice as he started getting ready for bed.

"I should have made some beans, huh?"

"The meal was fine, Adrian. Is that what you want me to say?" he snapped at her.

She got up and followed him to the bathroom. "I want you to *talk* to me, Daryll. That's all I'm asking for."

"Okay." He tapped his toothbrush on the rim of the sink, rushed out of the bathroom, and dramatically plopped himself down at the foot of the bed. "So, talk."

Adrian returned to her warm spot beneath the covers and asked, "How was your day?"

"It was fine; how was yours?" he answered in a sales-man's tone.

"Well," Adrian took a deep breath as Daryll squirmed. "Mr. Heath announced a reorganization today."

Daryll sat there with his arms folded, giving a patronizing nod. Then he stopped nodding. "What?"

"Now is when you ask me questions like, 'Who is Mr. Heath? What is his position? What does this mean for you, honey?' That kind of stuff," his wife informed him with great animation.

"Tell me more about Mr. Heath, Adrian," Daryll grumbled and slumped his shoulders.

"You know what? I don't even want to talk about it anymore." She opened her Bible again now and pretended to read, though her eyes never focused on one word. Despite the fact that they had been arguing as much as they always did, Adrian happened to be on the verge of a spiritual mission. Last Sunday, Pastor preached a message on the importance of spending quality time alone with God as the basis for a peaceful, productive life. In her quest to spend at least fifteen minutes alone with God each day, Adrian did find herself looking forward to that snippet of serenity. Actually, she decided that her time alone with God would be her time away from worrying with Daryll.

Daryll rose from their bed and said with a smirk, "You're the one who said you wanted to talk."

"You're not talking *right*," Adrian said in her most holy tone.

"How am I *supposed* to talk?"

"I want you to talk to me like you just talked to *them* outside. Share your life with me. That's what we're *supposed* to do." Adrian felt her voice climbing beyond her reach.

"You know about football?"

Her face was blank.

"Basketball?"

Blank again.

"*Any* sport *at all?*"

Adrian attacked, "There's more to life than sitting around reliving your high school fantasies through professional athletes."

"That's why I can't have that same conversation with you," he said. "Besides, you don't want to talk about the stuff *I* want to talk about."

"How about this topic: I'm ready to have kids," Adrian announced, as though she were putting this out on the table for the first time.

"Oh, please, Adrian. Not again." Daryll threw his hands in the air and disappeared behind the bathroom's French doors. Adrian could only imagine the sarcastic expression on his face as he yelled from the closet. "I already told you—we have enough money for me and you, but not enough for kids. We'd either have to move to a better neighborhood or send them to private school. Then we gotta think about college. We're not ready, Adrian, and I'm tired of talking about it."

"Is money all you think about?" she hollered loudly enough for him to hear.

"No, I think about *reality,*" he yelled back. "Every time I look up you've got a new pair of shoes. I can only imagine what you'd do if we had a child. You'd spoil her rotten and run up all the credit cards again like you do every time your sister goes out and has a baby."

Well, he was right about the shoes. Adrian had to skip those points completely. "I did *not* run up all the credit cards."

"Did you pay them off at the end of the month?" he asked.

"No."

"Well, that's what I call running up a credit card. Any time you can't pay it off at the end of the month, you best believe you overspent. Remember," and he repeated his father's motto with Adrian silently nya-nya-nyaing every word right along with him, "young and broke is romantic. Old and broke is stupid."

"So, let me get this straight. I'm twenty-seven years old, but I can't have kids because I might need the money when I'm eighty-five?"

"Precisely."

"So whose picture am I supposed to put in my picture frames—George Washington?"

He stepped onto the bedroom carpet and gave her a gotcha-grin. "Try Ben Franklin."

"Okay, I don't want to talk to you anymore," she puffed, half-amused by his wit. Daryll was a smart man. Adrian liked that about him, even if it worked against her sometimes.

"I told you, you wouldn't want to talk about what *I* want to talk about."

"That's because all you ever want to talk about is money." Adrian shook her head and looked up at the bare white wall, a testament to her husband's frugality.

"Handling the money is my job. That's what a real man does. And a real woman is supposed to follow her husband. You might want to read the fifth chapter of Ephesians, while you're sitting there holding that Bible in your hands—upside down!"

Adrian focused her eyes and quickly flipped the Word right side up. Inside, she laughed at herself. "I'm supposed to submit, and you're supposed to love me like Christ loves the church," she added.

"Hmm," he murmured as he turned off the bathroom light. They both felt the discussion winding to a surprisingly calm close.

Adrian sighed. "I think we need help, Daryll. We need some counseling. This relationship needs a lot of work."

"I work every day. I'm not trying to do anymore work. You're the one who needs the professional help." He pushed it all onto her plate. "You and this thing about having a baby."

"Since when is it so wrong for a woman to want to have a child with her husband? Be fruitful and multiply, Daryll. Genesis nine and seven."

"The Lord gives wisdom. Proverbs two and six. It's not wise to bring another liability into a situation when *somebody* doesn't know how to manage the funds they are already blessed with." He grabbed a pillow from their bed and tucked it beneath his arm, walking toward the door. He didn't want to discuss the issue of babies anymore. It was a hot button with Adrian, for sure, but it was even more touchy for Daryll.

"Where are you going?" she asked.

"Where does it look like I'm going?"

"Looks to me like you're running away from problems again."

"I told you—you're the one with the problem. Not me." He closed the door behind him, trying desperately to wash the issue from his mind.

That's all right. I didn't want you to be my baby's daddy anyway! Humor helped, but there was still the reality. Daryll wasn't budging. And neither was Adrian. When she thought about it, all she could do was pray and dab at the tears. Adrian got through only a few verses of her Bible-in-a-year program that night. It's hard to read the Word when your heart is sore. Instead, she pulled out her new spiritual journal and wrote:

Lord,

How is it that only three years ago, I said "I do" before You and witnesses, and now I can hardly stand to be in the same room with Daryll? I can't put my finger on it, but something has gone wrong. A mismatch. Is this what people mean when they say, "We grew apart"?

Your daughter,
Adrian

CHAPTER 4

It was the next night before Daryll decided to rejoin Adrian in bed again. Daryll didn't actually wake her with a kiss. It was more of a nuzzle, like a puppy trying to wake someone. "Daryll, if you want to make love, just say so," Adrian suggested, wondering if he'd ever come up with some new foreplay techniques. Candles and roses maybe.

Daryll rolled his eyes and surrendered to his hormones instead of his attitude. "I want to make love," he said, his eyes taking in her body.

Adrian peered at him, her eyes thinning to slits. The look said, "I can't stand you, but I'll tolerate you since you've got what I need." Nothing like the white-hot passion of anger.

When the alarm clock buzzed on Sunday morning, Adrian reached over Daryll and pressed the snooze button. He rolled from under her arm and sprang to his feet like a slice of bread popping out of the toaster. Daryll was a morning person if there ever was one.

It always took Adrian a few more minutes to get with the program. During the first few years of their marriage, Daryll might have coaxed her to consciousness with a kiss on her bare shoulders or by trailing his fingers up and down her spine. They'd missed many a Sunday school lesson on account of what Daryll started in those first few moments after the alarm went off. Now, he just hopped out of bed and started getting ready without her. Rather than argue with him about it again, Adrian grabbed her robe and headed for the kitchen to fry bacon and eggs. Then she took her turn showering while Daryll prepared his signature pancakes.

With the water running over her face and body, Adrian closed her eyes and prayed. Would today be the day that she and Daryll got back on track? Maybe there would be a song on the radio, a quote on some school's marquee, a Scripture in the lesson; some kind of railing to grab onto and rescue them both from this mudslide. Just two years ago, they had been so happy. She couldn't put her finger on exactly when things had begun to go awry. It was a combination of occurrences that individually meant nothing, but collectively they meant everything: rushing out the door without a kiss or a good-bye, working late at the office and skipping dinner, combination birthday-Christmas gifts, some nights of going to bed while angry with each other, passing up on opportunities to say "I love you" and "I appreciate you" because there's always tomorrow.

That particular morning, Adrian had posed mental flashcards of all the things she couldn't stand about her husband, from the way he snorted to relieve his sinuses in the morning to his outright refusal to parent a child with her. Everything that used to be temporary, trivial, or cute was now permanently and seriously ugly. Habits that she had once ignored were now in-her-face annoying, and those things that she'd hoped would change or at least improve with time had only gotten worse.

This Sunday morning, just as Adrian stepped out of the shower, the phone rang. "Adrian, telephone!" Daryll called, presumably too engrossed in some video game to come and get her like any decent human being with manners.

"Why are you hollering like crazy?" Adrian whispered angrily as she made her way to the living room wrapped only in a towel.

"It's just Camille, baby."

Embarrassed at Daryll's tone, Adrian grabbed the receiver from him and tried to cover her anger with a laugh. "Hello," her voice was easy and light.

"Hey, girl," Camille's friendly tone came through loud and clear, "what's up?"

"Hold on a second." Adrian walked briskly back to her bedroom and covered the receiver as she slammed the door for Daryll's sake. "Hello, stranger. You must be single again 'cause that's the only time I hear from you."

"Whatever! Guess what?"

"What?"

"I'm engaged!"

"What?" Adrian stopped breathing. She knew that Camille was dating some dentist, but *engaged?*

"I'm getting married," Camille sang.

"Did I miss something?"

"I told you about *Dr.* Sheldon Mumphries. We're going to tie the knot in Vegas next month. Isn't that wonderful?"

Adrian wanted to scream, "Don't do it! Don't ruin your life by getting married!" Instead she kept silent.

"So?" Camille prompted.

"I...I don't know," Adrian squirmed under the wet towel. "Are you sure you're making the right decision? How long have you been dating him?"

"Adrian," Camille went straight to the heart of the matter, "what is the problem? Why can't you just be happy for me?"

"Marriage is hard work, Camille." Adrian spoke words that she wished someone would have said to her. Not that she would have listened.

"We love each other very much..." and then Camille rattled on about how the Lord had answered their prayers with all this love, love, love. Adrian had come to the conclusion that current love has absolutely no bearing on future love.

"Adrian."

"Huh?"

"I asked you a question."

"I'm sorry, Camille. I guess I didn't hear it."

"What's wrong, girl? Wait a minute—this must be I'm-too-absorbed-in-my-own-problems day. What's up, girl?" Camille asked.

Camille didn't know the half of it because Adrian hadn't told her. Sometimes you just don't feel like telling anyone—not even the closest thing to your best friend.

"I don't know," Adrian skirted around the issue.

Camille pried, "Come on Adrian, spill it."

Adrian figured it couldn't hurt anything to tell Camille. "Sometimes I wonder about me and Daryll, you know?"

"Aw, Adrian, you know Daryll loves you," Camille said. "If he didn't, why would he put up with you?"

"Whatever!" Adrian laughed, lightened by Camille's ever-present sense of humor.

"I'm serious, Adrian. You know you're not the easiest person to live with. Remember that time we went to that women's conference together? Girl, I didn't think we were *ever* going to speak again," Camille laughed.

"That's because we're women and women weren't meant to live together."

"No, that's because *you* are a *diva*," Camille said. "But don't worry; I love you. And so does Daryll. Whatever the problem is,

I'm sure it'll get better. And if it doesn't get better by tonight, call me. We'll have a heart-to-heart, okay?

"I can't wait to settle down with Sheldon," Camille skipped back to joy. "Maybe we could start hanging with you and Daryll. I *have* missed you since you got married. Unlike *some* people I know, I'm not going to melt into my husband when I get married."

Suddenly angered, Adrian said, "I did *not* disappear into my husband. *You* stopped hanging with *me* when I got married."

"I didn't stop hanging with you," Camille denied. "*You* didn't want to hang with me because I was still mingling and you were like 'Camille, grow up and stop flirting so much,' and 'Camille, you need to stop with all this serial-dating.' That's what all you married people do, as though being married suddenly makes you more mature."

Adrian couldn't believe what she was hearing. Yet, she suffered the insult hoping that, if they cleared the air, maybe things could get back to normal between them because what Adrian needed more than anything was a friend right now. "Is that all you've got to say?"

Camille hesitated, then answered, "Yeah."

"Naw, come on, Cletus. Come on! Come on!" Adrian quoted their favorite line in *The Nutty Professor* and Camille busted out laughing. "What else you got to say?"

"Girl, you are crazy! You'd better get on out of there and get to church."

As they concluded their conversation, they agreed that their friendship had taken a hiatus because they were at different seasons in their lives. They both offered all-encompassing apologies, agreed to let bygones be bygones, and promised to talk again soon.

As she pressed the off button on the receiver, Adrian knew that she wouldn't dare call Camille that evening and burden her, especially not now that she was engaged. Camille had better things on her mind. Besides, how could she even begin to explain all of this to Camille? What could Adrian say? *Daryll and I are just not getting along. I simply don't like him anymore. We don't see eye-to-eye.* None of those statements gave proper weight to what Adrian felt, perhaps because what she felt was indescribable. She got married for better or for worse—not THE worst. Barring an affair, things could not possibly be any worse between her and Daryll.

Adrian headed toward the kitchen to combine Daryll's pancakes with her bacon and eggs for breakfast. Her food slipped down tastelessly as she chewed most earnestly on her thoughts.

"Are you ready yet?" Daryll called between plays on his video game.

"Give me a minute," Adrian said as she gulped down the last bite of bacon and hurried back to her bedroom closet. She selected a simple, black, A-line linen dress and a pair of black sandals with 3-inch heels. A perfect match for her mood. After dusting on powder, gliding on lip gloss, and massaging oil into her kinky mane, Adrian snapped on her earrings and pronounced herself as ready as she wanted to be.

Adrian laughed at herself for a brief moment, thinking of how her mother would not approve of her going to church on Sunday morning with bare legs.

Daryll stood as Adrian stepped into the living room.

"You look good, baby," he smiled warmly at her, "and natural. Not every woman can get up, throw on anything, and look as good as you."

When Adrian didn't respond, he sing-songed, "What?"

Adrian set her eyes squarely on his and wished for once that she had laser vision like a superhero so she could beam that smirk out of his eyes.

"What?" He was clueless.

She sighed. "I'm ready to go."

Daryll shook his head as he saved his game. "I don't know what's wrong with you, Adrian, but I think you're right about *you* needing that counseling."

In the car, Daryll tried to initiate a conversation. "What's up with Camille these days?"

"Nothing worth talking about."

They rode to church with the radio blasting gospel hymns about love and joy. Adrian sneaked a few glances at Daryll as he whistled along with the tunes. She wished he would quit that stupid whistling. *Doesn't he know how unhappy I am?* Adrian huffed slightly and rotated her face back toward the window. *He knows. He just doesn't care.*

By all appearances, Adrian and Daryll were doing just fine. The church always kept an eye on its newlyweds. For the first year, any time they were late to the service, there was a giddy whisper amongst the elders. All that giggling was warranted back then. No such luck now.

Daryll's father, Reverend Jacobsen, by far the wealthiest man in the pulpit, preached a sermon about trust. He recited Proverbs 3:5 (KJV), "Trust in the Lord, with all thine heart; and lean not unto thine own understanding." The message was obviously intended to encourage the congregation to give to Mt. Calvary's perpetual building fund. No use. At the end of the service, the look on the deacons' faces showed that the building fund hadn't taken up anymore than usual.

The after-church fellowship buzz brought mothers and sisters over to greet "Little Daryll" and Adrian. They remarked on how good they looked together.

Mother Jackson talked to them for a good five minutes about how much she missed the late Deacon Jackson. "Oh, I miss him so sometimes. But I know he's gone on to be with the Lord."

Daryll turned into Mr. Sensitive, hugging Mother Jackson and then holding both of her hands. "He was a fine man."

"Oh, thank you, Little Daryll," Mother Jackson nodded as she found comfort in Daryll's kind eyes, words, and gestures. Then she looked at Adrian and winked. "You got yourself one fine man, too, Adrian."

Adrian's smile wavered.

Daryll and Adrian joined his parents for the Sunday meal at the senior Jacobsens' home. For as much as Adrian disliked her in-laws, she had to admit that they followed all the rules of design. They didn't have family pictures in their dining room, they didn't hang art above eye level, and there was no television within view from the front entrance. Juanita Jacobsen's dining room was tasteful, with a classic cherry wood table with china buffet and hutch, and sideboard with mirror. Everything in the room was heirloom quality.

They sat at the table for six and Daryll's father blessed the food. The platters and serving dishes were passed around the circle and Juanita beamed with pride as their plates filled with the best of her cooking. Daryll loved going to his mother's home on Sunday because it was the only time all week that he could be assured of getting a home-cooked meal.

"The people don't believe that God is able," Daryll Sr. sighed later as he helped himself to a serving of his wife's Parmesan and garlic mashed potatoes.

"Hmph," Mrs. Jacobsen pursed her lips hard. "Black folks are stingy, that's all."

"Maybe if we made a model of the building, that might help people envision the plan," Adrian suggested.

"That'll only cost more money," Mrs. Jacobsen said, rejecting the idea.

"It takes money to make money," Adrian said under her breath, not wanting to cross Juanita in her own home. If Adrian learned nothing else growing up under Marsha Miller, she had learned to be respectful of her elders.

Mr. Jacobsen chewed quickly, maneuvering his food over to one side of his mouth. "That's a good idea, Adrian. I'll bring it up at the next deacons' board meeting. We need to make the vision plain."

Juanita Jacobsen hated it when her husband listened to Adrian. She hated it when *anybody* listened to Adrian—most of all her son. What he saw in this dark-skinned, big-booty, nappy-headed ghetto girl she would never understand.

The doorbell rang unnecessarily as Victoria, Daryll's sister, announced her entrance. "Hellooooo! Hellooooo!"

Mrs. Jacobsen nearly broke her neck trying to get up from the table to greet her only daughter. "Victoria's here!"

Victoria wrapped scarves of perfume around the room as she graced them all with her kisses and her presence. She wore a short, form-fitting, tailored fuchsia two piece pantsuit. Problem was, the tailoring had taken place fifteen pounds prior. Those buttons at her midsection screamed for mercy as each slit showed a speck of her light brown skin. Her black extensions wrapped around her forehead and chin in a tapered bob that could be made to swing if she stepped hard enough. Heavy makeup and silver accessories completed her outfit. All of her Sunday best, but no Sunday church service.

Victoria kissed the air alongside both of her mother's cheeks so as not to ruin her lipstick. She tried to do the same to Mr. Jacobsen, but he shooed her on out of the way. "Get on out of here with that stuff, girl."

After receiving Mrs. Jacobsen's compliments on her hair and outfit, Victoria finally took a seat across from Daryll and fixed herself a plate. Then she said, in her best Zsa Zsa Gabor imitation, "Sorry I'm late, my dears. When Neiman's calls, one must answer!"

Daryll kicked Adrian's foot under the table. Adrian elbowed him back. As much as they were at odds with each other, Adrian and Daryll were united when it came to their opinions about Victoria.

"Victoria, did you ever call my friend Carlton?" Daryll asked as Victoria double-checked her appearance in her compact.

Her lips tensed and she quickly clamped the compact together and threw it into her drawstring Gucci bag. "No, I haven't had the opportunity yet."

"Who's Carlton?" Mrs. Jacobsen gave a sprightly inquiry. "Is he single?"

"No, he's married. He's a financial planner and I think that Victoria should visit him before she runs through the rest of her money," Daryll said, directing his commentary to the Senior Jacobsen.

"Your brother's right," he agreed, pointing a spoon at his daughter. "You should be set for the rest of your life, but if you keep shopping at Neiman's every time the doors open, you'll be in the poorhouse before you know it."

It was straight from the poorhouse she had come. After splitting the $7 million dollar Texas Lotto jackpot with two other coworkers, Victoria quit her job as an administrative assistant and took to living a lifestlye of the newly rich. She took the lump sum payout, which left her with around $1.2 million after taxes. That was four years, a Mercedes-Benz, and two husbands ago. Victoria was down to her last hundred thousand dollars and she had very little to show for it other than the Louis Vuitton carrying cases for the cocker spaniel puppies that she got rid of after they urinated twice on the carpet.

"I gave money to the church building fund, didn't I? You certainly didn't have a problem with *that*," Victoria barked, absent her Gabor accent.

"To be perfectly honest, I'd rather have *you* at church than your *money*," her father said sincerely.

Victoria asked, "Is it possible for us to eat without discussing *my* money for once?"

Suddenly, rap music flooded the living room as Michael, the baby of the family, opened his bedroom door, approached the buffet-style table, and commenced making himself a plate without so much as a hello to anyone in the room. His hair was freshly braided in cornrows, with clear beads dangling just below the neckline. He might not have a job and he might not be a productive member of society, but the boy was well dressed in deep blue denim jeans and a shirt bearing the image of the late Tupac Shakur. Judging by the clarity of the screen print, Daryll figured that either it hadn't been washed yet, or someone had paid for Michael to have it sent to the cleaners. He also wore top-of-the-line athletic shoes and bling-bling on his wrists and fingers.

They watched Michael pile his plate high with meat, potatoes, and greens and then return to the blaring chaos speechlessly, like he was not even part of the family.

"*That's* who you need to be worried about," Victoria tipped her head toward her baby brother's bedroom, shifting the spotlight to the winner-take-all underachiever in the family.

"I done told your momma," Mr. Jacobsen passed the buck.

"When are you all going to kick him out of here?" Daryll asked matter-of-factly. Michael was an able-bodied twenty-four-year-old man who should have been on his own, as far as Daryll was concerned. "And where did he get money for all of those new clothes?"

"Those are his new school clothes," was Juanita's reply. "He's going back to start working on his GED."

Adrian's hand flew to her throat as she almost choked on mashed potatoes.

Daryll blurted out, "You don't need new school clothes to do work on a GED!" If Daryll hadn't been so incensed, he might have laughed.

"You baby that boy too much. Always have," Mr. Jacobsen added to Daryll's two cents. When he saw that he was getting nowhere with his wife, Mr. Jacobsen directed his comments toward Adrian. "Every time I try to put my foot down, Juanita comes right in the middle of us. I told her a long time ago that she was creating a monster."

Mrs. Jacobsen put on her I'm-not-to-blame face where she raised her eyebrows, tilted her head from side to side with every other word, but refused to look anyone in the eye. "We can't judge Michael by his past. Everyone deserves a second chance."

"He's had fifty chances, Momma." Daryll let every muscle in his face relax into a condescending frown.

"What you want me to do—put him out on the streets?" she hissed.

"Yes. If that's what it takes," Daryll said.

Adrian tried to inject a bit of optimism. "Maybe if he had the opportunity to stand on his own two feet he'd do well."

Mrs. Jacobsen pinned a napkin with the blunt side of her knife. "Adrian, *when* and *if* you ever carry a child under your heart for nine months, *then* you might understand. I'm the only person at this table who has given birth. I don't expect *any* of you to comprehend a *mother's* love."

For fear that she would say something irrevocably disrespectful, Adrian kept her mouth shut. Adrian took one good look around the table and decided that it wouldn't bother her one bit to kiss her in-laws good-bye once and for always, even if it meant that she would never inherit that dining room set.

On the way back from dinner, Adrian slipped off her shoes and laid her head back on the headrest. How was it that, at church, they'd appeared nothing less than pleasant toward each other? Daryll always opened the doors, looked up the verses in the Bible so they could both follow along, and gave all impressions of a happy marriage. Adrian wondered if he was happy— *really* happy. Maybe he was, considering his parents' marriage.

Tears of despair forced Adrian to look out the window again and hope to goodness that she wouldn't have to explain to Daryll why she was sniffing while he drove merrily along, whistling to the sounds of Wynton Marsalis. If she started talking to him now, he might sleep on the couch again. But if she kept it inside, like she was doing now, what good would that do? She wondered all the more why God wasn't answering her prayers.

Once at home, Daryll announced that he was tired and immediately undressed for a nap on the couch.

"What else is new?" Adrian asked rhetorically. With nothing left to do but read and write, Adrian headed toward their bedroom. She caught back up on her Bible-in-a-year program and then pulled out her spiritual journal. As hopeless as it all seemed, there was still a tiny bit of faith left. She'd seen people healed from cancer and, at the old church, people testified all the time about how God could pull a miracle out of nowhere. Well, she was nowhere and she needed a miracle.

> *Lord,*
>
> *I'm running out of time and patience and most of all, love. I know that Daryll and I haven't always put You first, but if You want us to stay married, You have to show me something because I can't take it anymore. He ignores me, he won't listen to me, he talks to everyone else but me, and he won't even have a child with me. I don't believe that it's Your will for me to spend the rest of my life being trapped in a decision that I made before I knew how bad things could get. Show me! Show me! Show me! I don't know what to do. I am desperate for Your direction.*
>
> *Your daughter,*
> *Adrian*

CHAPTER 5

Sunday was Men's Day. After their weekend of rededication, the brothers of the church took it upon themselves to perform duties traditionally reserved for women. For that, the congregation smiled and encouraged them with applause and amens. Sonia started off applauding them, but halfway through the service she had a change of heart. *Why should we applaud them for doing the things we do every Sunday?*

That kind of undeserved fanfare was right up her husband's alley, she thought. Like the time she had to attend a conference in Atlanta and Clarice was out of town with her church, so Kennard stayed home with the twins all weekend. It was an ordeal from the moment she informed him of his impending responsibility.

"So *I* got to keep the kids?" he'd asked, pointing at himself with a look of utter shock upon his face.

Sonia folded her arms across her chest and clarified. "You *keep* other people's kids. Kelsi and Kamron are *your* kids. You're not *keeping* them; you're being their father."

"I got a lotta stuff to do this weekend." He shook his head and plopped down on the couch.

"Stuff like what?"

He rattled off his agenda, holding out a finger for each item. "I've got to get the oil changed in my car, get my clothes out the cleaners, and go to the mall and return those shoes I told you about." Then he looked up at Sonia like she was actually going to sympathize with those three little pointless fingers.

"And?"

"What am I supposed to do with the kids while I'm out?"

She lifted both hands toward the ceiling. "Take them with you! They allow kids in gas stations and dry cleaners and malls!"

"Man, I'm gonna call my sister," he got up and walked toward the phone.

"Kennard, your sister doesn't have custody of her *own* kids. Why would you trust her with ours?" Sonia asked him.

Oddly enough, he listened.

Sonia laid everything out for him: clothes, shoes, toothbrushes, directions. Kelsi's hair was braided, so he didn't have to fool with bows or anything girly. By this time, the twins were almost four years old. If push came to shove, Sonia had no doubt that Kelsi would tell her father what he was supposed to be doing.

Despite the fact that Kennard called Sonia several times and asked if she could return home sooner than planned (which she did not), they survived the weekend. He spent all that next week telling her about the adventures of being with the twins. Sonia thanked and praised him profusely for doing the things that she did every day. She stroked his ego in a way that he never stroked hers. That was back when she was still feelin' the love.

Now, she would have told Kennard to get over himself the same way she wanted to tell the brethren that they didn't deserve a cookie for taking care of everyday business.

When church was over, Sonia stopped for a bite to eat and then went to Gospel Temple so that she could relieve Clarice of the children when church conluded. As usual, Pastor Williams was taking the podium well after one o'clock. After a quick glance around the sanctuary to spot her mother and her children, Sonia took a seat near the back and opened her

Bible to follow her former pastor as he preached from Deuteronomy, chapter one.

The centerpiece of the church was a large cross, set directly above the choir stand where the seam of the ceiling met the back wall. Four vents, oddly placed as they were, lined the wall beneath the cross. Just below the cross, choir members sat with unfastened robes, as the pre-spring heat had come into play after their part in the morning's worship and praise. A few rows ahead of her, Sonia could still see the word "Treymon" etched into the back of a wooden pew. Mother Bass almost beat Treymon to death in full view of the youth group when she discovered what he'd done to that pew.

Sonia followed along with Pastor Williams as he announced, "The title of this message is: You've Been There Long Enough."

Something within Sonia jumped. *Long enough. Long enough.* Pastor Williams proceeded to tell them about the directions the Lord gave Moses. They had been at the camp long enough, far longer than they were supposed to be there. And now it was time to make a move. *Make a move.* Sonia really don't know what else Pastor Williams had to say. She was stuck back at verse six where they were given the directive.

"Somebody in this very room needs to make a move today," Pastor Williams spoke with extended arms as the entire church rose at the conclusion of his sermon. "You've been in a bad situation for a long time and you don't know what to do. You've been wandering around for what seems like forty years, dealing with the same problems over and over and over again. Give it to the Lord and make a move."

A stream of tears etched its way down Sonia's face as she wrestled with that message. The Riley marriage was going nowhere and it was making Sonia miserable. Gina hit the spot when she said she missed Sonia's joy. But what kind of *move* was she supposed to make? How could she make a move that might restore her joy when that same move would go against God's Word? Doesn't God hate divorce? Furthermore, how could she find joy in a decision that would leave her children without a father in their home? Wouldn't that be selfish of her?

Then again, she had to consider Kennard. Was he doing more harm than good by showing their kids that a father doesn't spend time with his children? That a father is supposed to be in the streets and with his friends more than with his family? When it was all said and done, would Sonia look back over her life and shake her head with regrets that she had allowed such a poor father figure for her children, producing yet another dysfunctional generation?

Pastor Williams changed the course of the message a bit and called for sinners who wanted to make a move. "Go ahead and step into the aisle. Jesus is ready to meet you at the altar."

His second call was for plain old prayer, and Sonia, along with four or five others, leapt at that chance. When it was her turn to step forward, Pastor Williams smiled as he dabbed oil on her forehead. Back in the day, Sonia used to hate the way they slathered that oil on, with no regard for makeup or the bangs perfectly gelled across the forehead. None of that mattered now. Sonia was desperate. Pastor Williams asked, "How have you been, Little Sister Gibson?"

She barely mouthed, "I need prayer for my marriage."

"God is able," he said, his kind expression was unwavering. She bowed and he wrapped his hands around her forehead. Unlike with the woman before her, Pastor Williams leaned in and whispered the prayer into Sonia's ear. "Lord God, my sister is standing in the need of prayer for her marriage and her family, Lord. You created marriage, You created the family, and we come now pleading the Blood of Jesus over this marriage,

Lord. You know what has happened, You know the pain that this sister is feeling right now. Mmmm, my God, my God. We bind the works of the enemy in her home, Lord. Come in and transform, Lord God. Move out the old and bring in the new. Restore this marriage and this family in such a way that both she and her husband will know that it was You. It's in the mighty name of Jesus we pray. Amen."

"Amen."

The usher handed Sonia a tissue and led her back to her seat. "Give it to Jesus," she whispered in Sonia's ear. "He can work it out." Sonia couldn't talk, she couldn't move. She couldn't do anything but cry for the rest of the service. Pastor Williams had prayed for the Riley marriage to be restored, but Sonia wasn't quite sure that she even wanted her marriage anymore.

There wasn't much to her marriage to begin with. They met, dated, and married without much spiritual discourse. They stuck to the things that are important to the typical twenty-some-things: employment, attractiveness, ambition.

It started off sweet enough at the post office, but in retrospect, Sonia and Kennard were Clarice and Buddy all over again. Sonia didn't know how to pick a good man anymore than she knew how to pick a bale of cotton. The only point of reference she had for marriage was her parents' marriage, and there weren't enough dots there to connect to come up with any kind of decent picture.

Kennard's job on the assembly line at the General Motors plant brought in decent earnings, despite the occasional layoffs. Like her father, Kennard brought his check home so that Sonia and the kids could have nice things. It seemed that this was Kennard's entire definition of what it meant to be a husband and a father. He didn't beat Sonia, he wasn't gambling all their money away, and so far as she knew, he wasn't cheating on her. In short, Sonia got what she thought she wanted in a man.

"Baby, you all right?" Sonia's mother asked after church dismissed. Clarice had watched her daughter sob throughout the service.

For a sliver of a second, Sonia thought about telling Clarice. "It's...Kennard and I are having a rough time."

"Well, you know I say all the time, God is a miracle worker! If He parted the Red Sea, He can take care of me."

"I know," Sonia sighed in agreement. There was no use in having this conversation with her mother. Clarice seemed to live in this perfect little world in her mind.

"Your daddy and I have been married almost forty years. I know it gets tough sometimes, but you got to hang in there. Go to the Lord in prayer. If you take one step, He'll take two! There's no secret what God can do!"

If I hear one more cliché from this woman today! Sonia knew that everything Clarice said was true, but she wasn't trying to hear clichés right now.

Kennard was asleep when they got back, so Sonia told the kids to be quiet upstairs. She gave Kamron explicit directions, "No stomping, no jumping, no running!"

"Yes, ma'am," he nodded and hopped up the stairs two at a time. Sometimes things just went in one ear and out the other with him. Sonia thought about fussing at him, but figured it was futile. *Besides, why should we have to accommodate somebody who doesn't come home until well after two in the morning? My kids shouldn't have to stop being children in our home. If anything, our home should be the place they feel most at ease.*

Sonia approached their master bedroom as though Kennard did not exist. Years ago, she had tried to turn this room into a love nest. Sheers hanging from the canopy, pillar candles on the nightstands, dimming lights overhead. Now, their bedroom was strictly functional. Kennard's treadmill in one corner and the ironing board in another. Both were collapsible, but why bother?

Despite the fact that Kennard lay sleeping in bed, Sonia turned on the TV, slammed the drawer when she put her Bible in the nightstand, turned on the lights in the closet, bedroom, and bathroom while she changed clothes, and proceeded to hum a little tune. If Kennard was going to act like he didn't have a family, then she had every right to act like there was no big hundred-and-eighty-pound man lying in her bed trying to recover from a night of hanging with the homies.

Finally, she heard him sigh and call out, "Turn that off!"

"Turn *what* off?"

"The TV, the lights, everything!" He dug his face deeper into the pillow.

"It's not my fault that you have a hangover. That's a *personal* problem."

"I don't have a hangover; I was 'sleep!" His clear speech convinced Sonia that Kennard was, at least, sober. "I've got a long week ahead of me!" She'd heard about the new line of cars that they would be making at his plant. It was sad that she had to learn about these things on the news.

A tiny knock at the door brought a temporary truce. "What?" Sonia called out.

"Can me and Kelsi play Hungry-Hungry-Hippo?"

"No!" Kennard answered. "That thing is too loud. Wait 'til later."

Sonia overrode Kennard's orders. "Yes, you *can* play Hungry-Hungry-Hippo. Go right ahead, baby."

Satisfied with Sonia's answer, Kamron's shadow disappeared from beneath the door.

Kennard sat up now and faced his wife. "How you just gonna tell my son he can play Hungry-Hungry-Hippo when *I* told him he couldn't?"

"*We* are not going to walk on *eggshells* all day because *you* don't know how to come home and get in the bed at a decent hour," Sonia said as she wagged her head on over to the next topic. "If you don't want your kids making noise in the house, why don't you take them somewhere and *do* something with 'em?"

"Y'all just got back from church. They've already done something for the day."

"*You* weren't there." Sonia stood at the foot of their bed in panties and a bra with both hands on her curvy hips.

"I'm already saved," he said.

Her stern face crumpled in laughter. "Mmmm," was all she could say as she shook her head and reached into her chest of drawers for a pair of jeans.

"Don't put those on just yet," Kennard eyed his wife's body now. He made a sweeping hand motion for her to join him in bed, like she imagined gangsters must do to their women. Okay, maybe that silent, primitive, thuggish kind of sexual advance used to turn her on ten years ago. Matter of fact, it might have worked *that* day under different circumstances. But Sonia was not about to hop her butt into that bed and subject herself to ten minutes of vacant sex.

She could have said a whole lot of things, but Sonia decided not to waste her breath and settled on, "Please."

He rolled back on his stomach and said, "Al right," with a hint of warning. "If I can't get it from *you*...."

"What?" In an instant, Sonia was at the bedside towering over him.

"I ain't *got* to beg," he declared.

Sonia pulled the covers off him like a magician whisking a tablecloth from beneath a table set for four. Slowly, he sat up to take repossession of the comforter and sheets, but she pulled the whole mass of cotton onto the floor and stood on top of it. "I know you did not just threaten me with the prospect of another woman?"

"I ain't sayin' nothin'." He pulled two pillows over his body.

Sonia climbed onto their bed and pulled those pillows away.

"Quit playing, Sonia," he winced.

"I am not playin' with you," Sonia said, her index finger bouncing with every word.

"I ain't playin' with you, either," Kennard lay there with his backside sticking up in the air. It occurred to her that he had that cliché all too ready on his lips. He wasn't just saying that to make *her* think. He said it because he had *been* thinking about it already.

There Sonia stood, steaming, looking at the man she'd married. The father of her children just told her that he had considered throwing it all away for sex? True, Sonia had her own reasons for wanting to call it quits but they had to do with maturing priorities, family values, legacy. Things of substance, not *sex*. Furthermore, Sonia hadn't considered moving on to someone else. She'd just as soon be single than go through all the changes again. Not Kennard, though. Here he was, already on to the next person, as though the kids and Sonia meant nothing to him.

That hurt. Physically. It felt like a part of her heart seeped out of her chest. *I could go temporarily insane right now. Just long enough to slash a few tires, bust out a windshield, drop a Play Station 2 entertainment center, with CDs, from a second-story window.* Well, she wasn't that distraught, but if she stood there and thought about it long enough, she could have worked herself up to it.

She grabbed the pillows and the covers and threw them on top of him, like that was really going to do something. The fitted sheet wrapped around her elbow and she flung it off of her like "get back." She must have looked like a mad woman trying to hurt somebody with a heap of cotton. On top of all that, Sonia felt stupid. For all her education, all the things she had done right, all the rules she had followed, and all the mercy and understanding she had dished out, there she was acting out her frustrations on some of her linens.

Kennard pulled the heap of cotton over his head and kept lying there like they weren't in the middle of a heated discussion. Sonia froze there as she stood beside him. She entertained several evil thoughts that she didn't even know could have existed in her right about then. One of them was that it might actually be nice if he went out and got drunk and didn't make it home one night. Maybe he could just run into a tree and kill himself, and then this whole nightmare would be over. True, her kids wouldn't have a father, but they were young enough that Sonia could plug wonderful, loving memories of Kennard into their heads, God rest his soul.

The other thought was just as devious. If he *did* go ahead and cheat on her, Sonia could get walking papers, guilt-free. Pass GO and collect her $200. Then, when people asked why they divorced, she would at least have a biblical reason, not this seemingly shallow business of "we grew apart." Yes, an affair— without STDs— would suit her just fine. Though Kennard had never given her reason to doubt his faithfulness before, she wouldn't put it past him.

Wait a minute! Wait a minute! What am I thinking? I want my husband dead or in bed with another woman? That wasn't Sonia. She didn't want him dead, she didn't want him to cheat, and she really didn't want a divorce. She just didn't want *him*. All these thoughts, all this stress, and he lay there like a bump on a log. She could rant and scream and holler, but that wouldn't change anything. *This is childish and I'm tired of it.*

It takes only a moment to make a decision. Sometimes the consequences last a lifetime, but the decision is made at some precise, marked millisecond in time. As Sonia stood there for all those minutes watching Kennard breathe calmly, in and out, she realized that there was absolutely, positively nothing else she could say or do to change her husband. For all the bickering and complaining and maneuvering she'd done on behalf of herself, their kids, and their family, Kennard had not changed. Sonia's efforts to change him fit the definition of insanity: doing the same thing over and over again but expecting different results.

There would be no more drama, no more ultimatums, no more words. Breathlessly, Sonia announced, "I'm tired of fighting with you."

He poked his head out long enough to spurt, "That's the best thing I've heard all day." He withdrew into his pocket of warmth.

Sonia's heart beat faster with its newfound certainty. "I've still got the number for that counselor I told you about last year." Sonia didn't have the number, really. She only wanted to give him the chance to say no to counseling so that, for the record, she could say that she'd tried everything humanly possible to reconcile this marriage.

Sonia took another deep breath and pushed her culpability right out through her lungs. "Like I said, I'm not going to argue with you anymore." Softly, she stepped out of the room.

Sonia was tired.

The rest of the day proceeded like it always did. Sonia cooked dinner, she and the kids did their thing upstairs while Kennard did his downstairs. Sonia talked to Gina later that evening and made a conscious effort to talk about something other than Kennard. Gina remarked that Sonia seemed "a little better" today, and she was right. As crazy as it may sound, there was a certain peace that came with the decision to cease bickering. Beyond that, Sonia wasn't sure what to do. She only knew that this new resolve brought a hush and a comfort to her spirit.

That night, as she went through her calendar and got her thoughts ready for the work-week, she came across her church bulletin and glanced through the *Vitamins for Life* section. One said, "Read one chapter of the book of Proverbs each day."

Hmph. Sonia reached over and pulled her Bible from the nightstand. For as many times as she had read chapters in Proverbs, she hadn't noticed that there are thirty-one chapters; one for every day of the month. As Sonia flipped through the Word, she uttered a prayer of repentance. It had been a long time since she had even approached her Bible outside of church. With the twins and work and home, there just weren't enough hours in the day.

There was also the issue of her frustration. She had prayed about her marriage and asked God to change things. She had asked God for specific things like helping Kennard to grow up and showing him how to be a good husband and father. Nothing had happened. If anything, he had gotten worse.

She was past that now. This wasn't about Kennard or the kids or her raggedy marriage. This was about Sonia and the preservation of her sanity. At that point, she didn't know exactly what to do, but she *did* know what she was *not* going to do: keep the status quo. It was one of those situations in life where you can be sure of only one thing at a time.

After reading the first chapter of Proverbs, Sonia reached into her briefcase and grabbed a highlighter. The second part of verse 3 needed some yellow because, according to this introduction, the Proverbs could help her arrive at *"what is right and just and fair."* Whether that meant counseling, separation, divorce, reconciliation, death of a carmaker—Sonia really didn't care. She wanted only what was right and just and fair. She lifted her hands toward the sky, closed her eyes, and flushed her will completely out of her heart.

Lord, I'm tired. You're the only One who knows what is right and just and fair. I'm at peace with Your will, whatever it is. Work it out. All I ask is that You show me what I need to do to make it happen.

It was out of Sonia's hands.

CHAPTER 6

Four weeks and counting since Sonia had relinquished control of her marriage to God. For the most part she was on track with her study of Proverbs. She was on the last week's worth of chapters, yet she didn't feel any closer to a solution than before that line-in-the-sand decision. The whole thing had become a game to Kennard. "Two can play this, you know," he had said to his wife one morning as she gathered her things for work.

"I'm not playing with you," Sonia responded in monotone. To lay all the cards on the table, she had been so busy handling things in her new position since the promotion at work that their cease-fire at home was actually beneficial, professionally speaking.

The information technology department called a meeting of senior staff in the conference room, announcing a humongous project that would merge local, state, and national data so that they could analyze accounts with greater ease and report more efficiently. So long as Sonia had access to a network computer, she really didn't care what they did.

"We're pulling in an IT team from San Antonio to help integrate our programs. The project should take six to eight weeks," the resident technology guru, Steven McAllister, informed them enthusiastically. Steven tried several times to simplify the computer jargon for the crowd of management experts who stood there giving him the get-on-with-it-already look. He finally closed the speech by telling them that they should be prepared to walk through the systems and procedures as though training a new employee.

One week later, the IT team from San Antonio descended upon the office. Steven set them up with makeshift headquarters in some of the vacant spaces, including one in Sonia's old cubicle. There was a lot of office buzz surrounding the IT folks; it gave people something to discuss over coffee. In a few days, the San Antonio IT team had a nickname: SAIT, pronounced "say-it." It became as common as any other acronym they had floating around the office.

Sonia had been so busy trying to streamline her procedures and review and update the training manual that she hadn't really paid much attention to all the new activity. Maybe, for senior staff in other departments, it wasn't such a big deal. They were comfortable in their positions. Sonia, on the other hand, was relatively new to her position and didn't want to come out looking like the least competent senior employee in the building. Sonia didn't want to be *the one* who held up the project and she surely didn't want to be *the black one* or *the woman* who didn't know what she was doing.

The unexpected knock on her door signaled that her time had come. For the next several days, she'd have to do her bit in the project and explain things to whoever was on the other side of that door.

Sonia put on her best professional face and said, "It's open."

The doorknob turned and, gingerly, one of the SAIT guys entered her office. The first thing she noticed was his massive body. No ifs, ands, or buts, the man was unmistakably fat. Sonia pried her eyes from his waistline and stood to greet him. "Hello. I'm Sonia Riley." She could take in the details now. He was at least five-foot-ten. His face was dark brown, almost reddish. The texture of his closely cropped hair revealed his

African-American and Native American heritage. He donned the IT staple pair of 60's round glasses, but on him they weren't simply old-fashioned. They were fashionable, actually, with a subtle tint. Too fashionable. Sonia had questions about his sexuality until he reached out to shake her hand and spoke.

"I'm Morris Dupree," he introduced himself with a firm handshake.

Okay, Sonia knew that it was impossible to speculate about a man's sexuality by his pitch or diction. It probably wasn't right to go there, either, but she did. Judging by his masculine timbre and the certain rugged strength in his handshake, Morris was a metrosexual. Stylish and straight. The black slacks and solid blue Polo shirt were pressed "to a T," as her grandmomma would say, and though his stomach did a little overtime, he still tucked in that shirt and threw on a belt, as if to say to the world, "I *meant* to be this size."

"Morris," Sonia proposed a first-name address, "how are things going?"

"Fine. Just getting things in order. As I understand it, I'm housed in your old cubicle. I came across *this* in one of the drawers," he said, handing her a computer-generated sketch of Sonia and her children at a local pizza parlor. She couldn't have paid more than fifty cents for that thing, but it was awful cute.

"Thank you," Sonia sang as she took the picture from Morris.

"Twins?" Morris took a few steps back toward the door.

"Yeah. Six years old."

With a smile, he asked, "You must be a very busy woman, huh?"

"Most definitely."

"I feel ya," he said with a touch of Ebonics, enough to let her know that she was in good company. "I've got two boys—five and eight. I get them every other weekend. Takes me two days to rest up before I see them, and two days to recover after they leave."

"Kids can be a handful," she agreed. "Thanks," Sonia said, gesturing to the picture he returned.

"No problem."

Sonia passed him a dismissive smile and he left her office as quickly as he had come. She counted it a blessing that it wasn't her turn to explain everything to SAIT just yet. The more time she had with the manuals, the more she could prepare herself.

Sonia found it hard to steer her thoughts back to business that afternoon. She wondered if Kennard would be so fatherly as to spend every other weekend with their kids if they split up. *Who am I kidding? That would be like pulling teeth.* She knew her husband. If he asked for any type of visitation, it would only be in an attempt to lower his child support payments. Beyond that, Sonia couldn't imagine Kennard actually spending forty-eight consecutive hours with their children regularly. They would end up at his sister's house watching R-rated movies and eating cold beans out of the can. Eventually, they would put two and two together and get to a point where they didn't care to see their father anymore. That's how it had happened with Sonia.

Some folks would say that her parents did the right thing to stay together, but Sonia would disagree. Perhaps there was a time when her parents used to love each other, but there was no way to tell when that love left. Maybe it was gradual, like hands slipping loose in a crowd. However it happened, by the time Sonia was in middle school, the only time they did anything together was on holidays, before sundown, before Buddy slipped into the streets. What their actions said to Sonia was that all the Christmases, all the Thanksgivings, all the family portraits they took, were lies. She looked back at those pictures now and wondered when the smiles went from authentic to counterfeit.

Sonia placed the kids' picture in her top drawer and grabbed her keys from her purse. It was quittin' time and startin' time all at once. She needed to stop by the grocery store and pick up some eggs, return the kids' books to the library, and get Kamron another writing tablet.

She decided on a beef-and-noodle casserole with cornbread for dinner that night. Once the kids had had their fill of playing outside in the backyard, they washed up and helped Sonia cook dinner. She handled the casserole, and they made the cornbread. Between buttering the pan, cracking the eggs, and mixing the batter, those two were self-proclaimed chefs. When it was all finished, Sonia pulled dishes from the cabinets and asked them to set the table as she had taught them.

Kelsi took a quick inventory and asked, "Where's the stuff for Daddy?"

"I don't know if Daddy is coming home tonight," Sonia answered coolly.

"I want to make a place for him," Kelsi beamed with hope.

"Yeah," Kamron concurred, removing a fourth set of silverware from the drawer.

Sonia wondered where on earth her children got all this hope. It was as though they hadn't lived with the man for the previous six years. They personified the definition of love in 1 Corinthians, chapter 13, always hoping, always trusting, and always believing for the best.

Sonia went to the master bedroom and called her husband's cell. "Kennard?"

"Yeah." Music and conversation made it hard to hear. He was obviously at somebody's happy hour. Sonia covered one ear with a finger. "Listen, the kids helped me cook dinner tonight and they've set the table for you and everything. Do you think you'll be home in a little while?"

"No. Probably not. I'm waiting for Victor to show up."

"We've got enough for Victor, too. Really, it would mean a lot to them if you came home."

"Would it mean a lot to *you*?" he asked.

Sonia would have answered "yes" in a heartbeat if it meant that he would come home and grace Kelsi and Kamron with his funky presence. Yet, there was something about the way he said it. He was fishing for her feelings perhaps, but there were none to catch.

"I'm not asking for *me*; I'm asking for *them*."

"Whatever."

"Don't you care about your children? Don't you care about how they feel?" she pleaded on their behalf.

"I care about the kids, but *you* don't care about how *I* feel."

"That's not true, Kennard. I *do* care. I simply don't want to argue anymore."

He rambled on, "You and the kids just act like I'm not even there. Come in laughing, playing, acting like I'm invisible or something. You don't even speak when I come in the room."

"Can we have this conversation in person?" Sonia requested. It was nice to know that Kennard had feelings, after all.

"I don't want to talk right now."

Sonia sighed and placed a hand on her forehead, reminding herself that the purpose of the call was to see if the man would come home and eat the food his children had helped to prepare. "What about dinner with the children tonight?"

"Sometimes the children have to suffer because of the parents."

The Momma Bear in Sonia came out swinging. "You're crazy! You know that? Children suffer when *one* of the parents is an idiot." Click!

Sonia could go from zero to sixty when it came to her kids. The difficulty, however, was coming back down to zero and explaining things to the children in such a way that removed the sting from the truth.

Swiftly, Sonia walked back to the kitchen. Perhaps if she moved fast enough, the kids might forget the conversation they'd had earlier. Fat chance. The fourth place setting was there on the table. Kamron suggested that they wait on Kennard, but Sonia overrode that motion with all kinds of gibberish about them needing to clean their rooms, take baths, and other things that didn't really have to take place for another hour or so.

"Let's go ahead and pray, okay?"

Throughout the meal, Sonia praised their cooking dramatically. "This is delicious! It's the best cornbread I *ever* tasted!" The talk of "Daddy" appeared to be over until they got into bed a few hours later. Kennard entered through the front door just as Sonia was preparing to read the bedtime story.

"Ooh, Mommy, let Daddy read the story to us!" Kamron begged.

"No, honey, Daddy just got home. He's had a long day at work. Let's let him rest."

Kelsi looked at Sonia defiantly, with her lips puckered and eyebrows drawn tight. She threw the corner of the comforter across her body and hopped out of bed. "I'm going to ask Daddy to read to us."

"No, you are not."

"How come you don't want Daddy to read to us?" she asked, arms folded across her chest and chin tucked in tight to her neck.

Whose child is this? "Kelsi Danielle Riley, get your behind back in the bed!"

She stood there for another second, challenging with her body. Sonia gave her "The Look" and Kelsi reluctantly crawled back into bed.

Sonia finished eyeing Kelsi's attitude down as she searched for any book on the bookcase near the foot of her bed. Her hands managed to land on a story about a man spending time with his son. She read two pages and called it quits just in time to keep herself from imploding or exploding. She was on the verge of both.

"Kids, Mommy is tired. I'll finish the story tomorrow night, okay?" Sonia asked.

"That's all right." Sadly, her son seemed to understand. "I don't like that book anyway, Momma."

"I like the book, Kamron," Sonia softly disagreed. "It's a beautiful story. I just don't feel like reading it tonight."

Kelsi kept her mouth shut, but the anger was still engraved in her face as she pulled the covers to her chin. Sonia wondered if her daughter would ever understand that this slight pain she'd dealt was nothing compared to what Kelsi would have felt if she had gone down those stairs and been rejected by the first man in her life. That kind of pain doesn't stop when you get back into bed. It wakes up with you, grows up with you, follows you into every relationship thereafter.

Sonia kissed Kamron and Kelsi on the cheek and left them to sleep. She went back to their bathroom, cleaned out the bathtub, and straightened up the children's rugs and towels. Five minutes later, Sonia passed by their room again for one last check-in. Her heart broke as she heard Kelsi's soft whimper. Sonia peeped through the crack and saw Kamron standing over his sister, rubbing her back. "Don't cry, Kelsi," he comforted his sister. "It's okay."

Sonia leaned back on the wall across from their doorway and thought, tears matching Kelsi's. She wanted to go into that room and say something, but what? She couldn't make their daddy act right, and without that power, Sonia was fast becoming the villain.

"It's okay," Kamron repeated.

And then came the straw that broke the camel's back. If Sonia had heard that sound once, she'd heard it a million times—the sound of a Microsoft x-Box booting up. Sonia knew that she was not supposed to act out in anger. She had to stop herself for a hot minute—she really did. Sonia paced that upstairs hallway several times as she whispered in prayer, "Lord Jesus, I need Your help. What do I do, Lord, what? My baby is in there crying, and my other baby is in there rubbing her back. I feel helpless, Father." Sonia did *not* feel like crying anymore.

That night, Sonia had never been clearer about what needed to happen. Divorce might be bad. Coming from a broken home might be bad. But there might be nothing worse than coming from a counterfeit family where elephants loom in the living rooms, skeletons scratch in the closets, and one can hardly walk for the mounds of dirt amassed under the rugs. Sonia wanted more for herself and her kids. Above all, she had spent enough time with God over the past month to know that it wasn't His will for her to spend the next fifty years with a man who stroked the knobs on a video game more than he stroked his wife.

Sonia waited in that hallway until Kamron climbed back into his bed and Kelsi's heaving stopped. In a matter of minutes, they were both asleep. Sonia wanted them to be asleep.

Somebody was going to have to vacate the premises. Immediately. Sonia didn't know who it was going to be or where that person would be going, but she did know that something had to give. This feeling wasn't just a notion. It was more a certainty. A peace.

Sonia went back downstairs, walked past Kennard, and went straight into their bedroom where she lay facedown on the bed and prayed again. *Lord, I thank You for the wisdom to know when enough is enough. I believe that You have a plan for me, a plan for my children, and a plan for what to do about me and Kennard. I don't know the whole plan, but I need space, Lord. Space to live and learn and hear from You. I know that I can't move any further with us living under the same roof. If I'm the problem, show me. If he's the problem, show him. Whatever, however, Lord, do Your thing.*

Then Sonia sat up and pulled paper and a pencil from the nightstand. She did what every woman in this situation must do: the math. Figuring in her raise from the promotion, Sonia was still several hundred dollars short of making ends smile at each other. No room for surprises or extras. It would have been nice to think that she could count on Kennard to help with the expenses associated with the children, but his words came and slapped her into reality real quick. *Sometimes the children have to suffer because of the parents.*

Sonia began thinking of ways to cut back. The kids could take their lunch to school. She could get a cheaper cell phone plan and take the railway to work a few times a week to save on gas. No more housekeeper. Stop making the IRA and ESA contributions for the time being. She could, eventually, take Kennard off her health insurance and change her W-4 withholding. There was money in savings to supplement her income for a couple of months. Push come to shove, she could ask Clarice to keep the kids while Sonia worked a part-time job evenings and weekends.

After reducing the budget to the bare minimum, she was still short. It occurred to Sonia then that she could not stay "separated" indefinitely. At some point, finances would force her to either reconcile or regulate Kennard's financial contributions through a divorce agreement because, if she didn't, there would be no money for Kelsi and Kamron to go to college and she, personally, would be burned out by the time she hit forty—assuming that she would make it to that age without cracking up.

This single mom business was no joke. Women are always talking about how they would leave if their husband did this or that or how stupid so-and-so must be for staying. Well, Sonia would tell anybody: separating from your husband ain't easy. It's hard. It's scary. It's a situation where nobody really wins. There is just an exchange—one set of problems for another. You hope and pray that when the total is displayed, you'll get some change back instead of owing.

Sonia put the pencil and paper back in the drawer and drew a cleansing breath. It had to be done. "Kennard, I need to speak with you," she called to him.

"Wait a minute," he whined as though her voice had caused him to miss five hundred points.

"I need to speak to you now." Her voice was steady.

"I'll be there in a minute."

Sonia wasn't sure whether or not she should get dressed for bed because she had no idea where she'd be spending the night at that point. Then again, Sonia thought about the children. It was enough trauma for her and Kennard to be separated. She didn't want to pull the rug completely out from under the children by taking away their home, too. *No, I'm not leaving. Kennard is leaving.* Now Sonia had to figure out how to kick a man out of his own home.

When he had finally finished his game, Kennard dragged himself to their bedroom. "What is it?" he asked as he removed his shirt and walked past her to their bathroom. He turned on the water in the sink, causing Sonia to yell.

"Kennard, I've been thinking. We need to separate."

"What?" he turned off the faucet.

"We're not fooling anybody—least of all our children. I'm not happy, you're not happy, and this is not what God had in mind when He created marriage. We need some time apart," she summarized.

"Here we go with God again," he rolled his eyes and turned the water back on again.

"Don't change the subject." Sonia entered the bathroom suite. She needed him to see that she meant business. She rested one hand on the counter and continued. "Why are you willing to hold on to something that's not there?"

"This is life, Sonia! Do you think everything's supposed to be all perfect?" He bobbed his head for emphasis.

"No, but I do think that you...no, let me take that back. I have allowed you to think it's okay to act like you did before we had kids. I'm sorry that I let you fall under the impression that I was Superwoman. You know what I found out, though? I'm not. I need your help. I need you to help me with this house and these kids and this marriage. But right now you are either unwilling or unable to do so."

He finished his brushing, spat out the remains, dried his mouth with a towel, and turned to Sonia. Kennard stood right next to her, pointed his index finger, and said, "You knew what

I was like when you married me." Kennard left her standing there to swallow his words.

Sonia had to give him that one. She followed him to their bed. "We are *grown* now. We are married, we have kids and obligations to each other and to the children. Somehow, you missed all that."

He piped up an octave and sidestepped her point. "My daddy was hardly ever home when I was growin' up—he worked all the time. We saw him when we saw him. Look at me now, though. I got a job, I got my own car, my own house."

Then Kennard went into his spiel about how hard he worked, how he had learned to fend for himself as a child, yada, yada, yada. And it occurred to Sonia that they were going in circles and neither of them was hearing the other. When he was at a stopping point, Sonia jumped in. "I've heard your side and you've heard mine for the past several years. Nothing has changed. The only thing I need to say at this point is that I would like to stay here in the house with the kids. I would hate for them to lose their home on top of everything else."

He laughed so hard he started coughing. "Oh snap! You think I'm going to leave *my* house 'cause *you're* crazy? Please."

"Not for me, Kennard."

"Naw, you got me messed up. If *I* leave, *everybody* leaves. That's all there is to it. You're not getting this house."

Sonia knew how to push her husband's buttons. "Well, get your check stubs together 'cause I'll be requesting a temporary child support order."

"Oh, it's like that now, huh?" Kennard's smirk disappeared.

"Yeah, it's like that. How else is it supposed to be?"

"You the one got the new raise on your job—yeah, I heard Kamron talking about it the other day. Can't you pay your own way?"

"That's irrelevant. I don't care if I make a million dollars a week, you're still paying child support." Sonia really didn't know how a conversation about temporary separation got all the way this far. They were talking about things that she never wanted to discuss and it saddened her.

"A lot of strong black women just say 'thanks for my child' and go on," he taunted her.

"Don't act a fool, Kennard. Just leave," she sighed.

"You want me to leave?"

"Yes."

"You want me to leave?"

"Yes. I want you to leave," Sonia repeated clearly.

"You brought this on yourself. Remember this. Remember this moment."

"I'm sure I always will."

They didn't say another word to each other. Apparently Kennard didn't take her seriously. He packed only one pair of underwear. Sonia went back upstairs to the living area and waited. As she listened to her husband pack his belongings, she held her quivering stomach and rocked herself on the sofa. When he finally left, she could only cry.

Sonia kindly packed the rest of Kennard's clothes for him the next morning. His scent was in every party shirt, every low-hanging pair of jeans, every stupid pair of socks. Even his work clothes smelled of the man she had once loved. Through the blur of emotion and tears, Sonia stuffed four 30-gallon garbage bags full of Kennard's belongings and loaded them into her car. After she dropped the kids off at the daycare, she stopped by Kennard's place of employment and helped him out by putting the rest of his clothes into the backseat of his car.

CHAPTER 7

Irma let herself in and started cleaning the Riley home with a special song on her heart that morning. Sonia kept the place organized. All Irma ever had to do was the actual cleaning; the mopping, scrubbing tubs, dusting the furniture, and sanitizing counters. The kids' room was a special treat. Irma often encountered the children's artwork. She'd watched their growth as Sonia marked off the inches on the measuring giraffe inside their closet. It wouldn't be long before they'd need separate bedrooms.

Irma didn't have any children of her own; hence no grandchildren. It wasn't like her to get all in her clients' business, but she did find herself stopping every once in a while to admire the twins' school pictures. She prayed for them as though they were part of her own family.

If she'd had a daughter, Irma would have wanted one like Sonia. Respectful, poised, confident. Irma also liked Kennard. He reminded her of her own husband. Kennard worked hard, as evidenced by the soiled work pants in the hamper. Here lately, though, Irma had become concerned for the family. Sonia had not mentioned any visitors, but their guest bedroom had obviously been used by Kennard on more than one occasion. His facial hair was absent from the master bathroom, his toothbrush was in the wrong holder. Irma had even moved a pillow and a blanket from the couch a few times. All of this was bad news. As much as Irma wanted to dismiss the signs, she couldn't.

When she returned to her own home, Irma found her husband sitting in his usual chair watching The Weather Channel. "Hello, Harvey," she said as she kissed his forehead.

He didn't look up from the television. It took him another minute or so to respond to her entrance, and Irma was okay with that. "Hey, baby. How was your day?"

"Fine. Fine," she sighed.

Harvey understood his wife well enough to discount the words and listen to the sigh; a trick that had taken him decades to master. "What happened?"

Like clockwork, Irma rushed back into their quaint living room and took a seat on their covered couch. She had been meaning to replace some of that old furniture, but the likelihood of finding a couch that didn't clash with her husband's favorite recliner was nil. "I went to the Riley's home today and I saw some things I didn't like. I think...no, I *know* they're having some marital trouble."

"They've got the twins, right? The ones whose pictures you put up on the refrigerator?" Harvey asked, with a sincere crease in his brow.

"Yes," Irma answered.

Harvey read his wife's body language. Irma sat on the edge of the couch wringing her dry hands. There was worry in the corners of her mouth. Harvey often wished that his wife would give up this line of work. They didn't need the money; they hadn't needed it for a long time. Once he got that big promotion at Bryer-Blue Technical back in '79, money ceased to be an issue, especially since they never had children. Then again, that was why she still cleaned, Harvey knew. The mother in her couldn't rest unless she had someone to fuss and pray over. He had succeeded in getting Irma to cut it down to just a few homes which she cleaned every other week.

"Well, Teacake, you can't make folks stay together," Harvey said, unfurling his own lips and raised his graying eyebrows. Aside from wearing a wig, he no longer had to transform himself for the role of Santa at their community's annual children's Christmas party. Harvey had the stomach, the chunky cheeks, the bubbly voice, and the ready smile to play the part convincingly.

"I know I can't make folks stay together," Irma conceded. "I just wish there was something I could do. Young couples today are breaking up left and right."

"More than fifty percent will end in divorce," Harvey repeated a quote he'd heard on television.

"Lord, what is the world coming to?" Irma looked toward the ceiling.

"You can't save the world, Teacake."

"I just hate to see families torn apart like this. We've been through some hard times. I mean *real* hard times. But we made it through," Irma looked into her husband's eyes, knowing full well that she was preaching to the choir. He had been with her through three miscarriages, the violent death of her brother, and an addiction to painkillers. She had been with him through prostate cancer, the loss of his mother after a lengthy battle with diabetes, a mid-life crisis, and a failed attempt at a business enterprise. Not to mention the day-to-day issues that arise just as a result of living.

Harvey agreed with her. "We have been through a lot, Irma. But not everybody has the kind of faith you've got, nor do they have a husband as handsome as I am." He stroked his chin between his thumb and forefinger.

"Harvey, please," Irma tried to hide her smile.

Irma prodded Harvey for a minute more, asking him if he'd be willing to talk to Kennard. "You think you can talk some sense into him?"

"How do you know it's *his* fault?" Harvey stood up for men everywhere. "I can't just walk up to a man and start in on him. For all you know, *she* could be kicking his behind every night."

Irma dismissed his second attempt at humor. "No, baby. I'm pretty sure it's nothing like that. When I walk into their home, I don't feel violence. It's more strife...friction."

"Well, maybe you can start by talking to her. And don't forget—we can always pray for them," Harvey added. In his experience with Irma and with the Lord, things happened when he and his wife prayed.

"Yes," Irma looked up at her husband. "Prayer *does* change things."

That night, the Parkers brought the Rileys before the Lord together and asked for His guidance in how to best help this younger couple stay together through thick and thin. They sealed the prayer with an amen and a kiss before climbing into bed.

The Senior Swimmers met on Tuesday and Thursday mornings for fellowship and fitness. Irma was always the first one there because she liked to warm up her joints in the hot tub before hitting the pool. Now that the New Year's resolutioners had come and gone, the group had whittled itself back down to its three faithful founding members: Irma, Beverly Moore, and Rose Weldon. The three had been friends for many years. Every so often, Deborah Cole, a friend of theirs from their Watch-Your-Weight days, dropped by and caught up with them, but not today.

Their instructor, Jenny Swanson, was a 30-something aerobic instructor who had initiated the class shortly after her own mother was diagnosed with rheumatoid arthritis. In all honesty, the program was barely carrying itself financially, but Jenny decided that as long as Irma, Beverly, and Rose kept coming, she'd continue to lead their 30-minute class before her hour-long kickboxing session.

Irma donned her one-piece swimsuit, swim cap, and swim shoes, then readily submerged herself in the hot tub. The bubbles soothed and relaxed her as she stretched her legs beneath the water's surface. Slowly, she bobbed her knees up and down to warm them for the morning's workout. Jenny, Beverly, and Rose strolled into the pool room at 8:30 on the dot, and Irma greeted them all with brief hugs. Rose's face was perfectly round, a trademark of her grandmother that Rose gladly accepted because with that roundness she also received smooth skin. At sixty-two years old, people had to search the perimeter of Rose's face for hints about her age. Were it not for the sag of skin beneath her chin and the graying at her temples between touch-ups, Rose could have passed for a much younger woman. When Theodore stepped out with his sharply dressed wife, he was often accused of robbing the cradle.

Beverly's swimsuit, a red and white polka-dot one piece she bought back in the 80's, was a testament to her character. It did nothing for her shape because her pronounced midsection was the overriding feature on her body. However, Beverly pranced in there, stomach first, like a woman on a Hollywood runway. It was *her* swimsuit and she was proud to fit into something she'd worn since she was in her late thirties.

One by one, they entered the main pool and age became simply a number as Jenny led them through a half-hour of running, moving, and resistance with foam noodles. To the outsider, it looked like a piece of cake. This was one case where looks were deceiving. The Senior Swimmers were both pooped and pumped at the end of their workout.

"Thank you, Jenny," Rose said breathlessly as she stepped from the pool.

"You're welcome, Miss Rose," Jenny answered, twisting her long blonde hair into a rope to express the water.

"Baby, how's your momma?" Beverly asked, releasing her gray nest of hair from her swim cap. In all her years, Beverly had never really mastered her hair.

"She's fine, Miss Beverly. I spoke to her just this morning."

"Well, you tell her we're still praying for her," Irma said.

"I sure will, Miss Irma. I appreciate that, and I'm sure my mother does, too," Jenny smiled back.

The Senior Swimmers waved good-bye to Jenny as she rushed off to change for her next class. By this time, the hot tub was calling the Seniors Swimmers' names and each of them reveled in the warmth of the water. They sat there for a moment and soaked up the heat before catching up with each other.

Irma's thoughts flew to the Riley household. She didn't make it a habit of telling her clients' business, but these women had been friends for more than thirty years. Irma and Rose grew up in and still worshipped at the same church, and Beverly used to be married to Theodore's brother. Rose and Beverly had remained friends after the divorce, some thirty years ago. Naturally, their friendships folded into one another over the years.

Irma immediately shared her concerns about the Rileys. "I just don't know what to do."

"What do you think the problem is?" Rose raised her head.

"I don't know for sure. I just know they have slept in different bedrooms," Irma surmised.

"I remember when Theodore and I used to do that." Rose couldn't help but chuckle, "I used to get so mad at him!"

"I remember those days, too," Beverly chimed in. "They'll make it through, though. At least he *is* still sleepin' in the house."

"I just hate to see folks goin' through this."

"Well, you know they've got to go *through* it in order to learn each other," said Rose. "You can't expect two folks to live together and not have their ups and downs and differences. You can't expect everything to be peachy all the time. The sooner people learn that, the better off they'll be."

"*I* know that and *you* know that and *Beverly* knows that, but I don't think the young lady I'm working for knows that," Irma's eyes narrowed as she pondered the difficulty.

"You can't tell young folks nothin' these days," Beverly voiced her concerns as she read Irma's mind. "They already know everything. This generation of young folks is used to having everything so quickly. They ain't tryin' to work hard at nothin'. They don't believe in sowing first, tending to that seed, and reapin' later. They want to sow a seed, put it in a microwave, come back in a few minutes, and reap. It's no big surprise to me that they can't stay married. It's just another illustration of who they are."

By this time, Rose and Irma were busy looking Beverly upside the head.

"What?" Beverly sat up.

"Ain't that the pot callin' the kettle black?" Irma teased.

"I would've listened if someone had told me not to get divorced," Beverly sang on a high note.

"Really, now? We all tried to tell you to at least *talk* to J.D. after he lost all that money gambling," Rose reminded her. "You upped and left that man on the first train smokin'. Sent him the divorce papers in the mail."

"Hmph," Beverly had to laugh at herself. "I know. I was just lookin' for a way out. I was sick of him, he was sick of me, and that gambling was the last straw. Now I *loved* my second husband, Malcolm—God rest his soul—but I have to tell you: if I knew then what I know now, I would have stuck it out with my *first* husband 'cause ain't no such thing as a perfect man. Took me thirty-two years of marriage to two different husbands to figure that out."

"Took me the first twenty years of my marriage and a separation," Rose added.

"Took me fifteen years," Irma echoed.

They sat in that hot tub, letting those truths marinate for a moment. Beverly thought of how truly sorry J.D. had been about losing their little piece of savings in a horse race and how, after all she'd put into their relationship, some other woman reaped what Beverly had sown in those three years. J.D. was good people. Beverly had always known that. If she hadn't left, he might never have had the impetus to get himself together. She never regretted leaving J.D., but she did regret the lack of closure, so much so that even Malcolm told her that she needed to get some counseling.

Rose thought of how close she and Theodore had come to divorce after his affair. To her, infidelity is inexcusable. There were no ifs, ands, or buts about the situation. Try as he might to explain the how and the why, none of it ever made sense. It was only a matter of deciding whether or not to forgive Theodore and move on. When she sat down and took inventory of their relationship, of all they had invested, of all the good she knew about her husband, Rose had made a decision to forgive him. With the help of the Lord, their marriage had come out stronger than before. No, it wasn't that simple, but after so many years, Rose had made a conscious decision not replay the whole thing over and over in her mind. Instead, she put on her spiritual armor and covered her family all the more in prayer. Theodore was never unfaithful again, and Rose gave *that* credit to *God's* faithfulness. The affair happened very early in their marriage. It hurt like nothing else she had experienced at the time. Now, when the memory popped into her head (which wasn't often), she could see only a twenty-something-year-old boy making silly, stupid mistakes.

"So," Irma broke the silence, "what do you think I should do?"

"About what?" Beverly tried to remember where they'd left off.

"About the couple that I work for. They're at a crossroad right now."

"Talk to her, I guess," Rose offered. "Do you think she'll listen?"

"She might. She usually calls me in the evening after I clean their home. I'll try then. Y'all put the Rileys on your prayer list, okay?"

"Will do."

CHAPTER 8

Adrian fixed both lunches out of habit; ham and cheese sandwiches, potato chips, and a bottle of water. She sat Daryll's sack on the edge of the counter where she knew he'd look for it. She had a fleeting thought: why not write him an encouraging note? *For what?* she answered the thought. *He would not do the same for me.* And with that, she dismissed the notion.

On to work, now. She needed to close out several purchase orders before the end of the month, which would involve getting in touch with vendors who'd failed to provide all the required information on their invoices. In the office lot, Adrian parked, turned off the radio, and hopped out of her hybrid Honda Civic. With each step toward the building, she distanced herself further from the reality of her troublesome marriage and into an atmosphere where she was respected, cherished, and appreciated.

Adrian opened the door to this other world, blew out a cleansing breath, and slid thoughts of Daryll into the back pocket of her slacks. "Hey, Miss Adrian," Priscilla, the receptionist, greeted her.

Adrian felt all the muscles in her face hoisting up her lips as she made her face do what her heart could not: smile. "Hey, Priscilla! How was your weekend?"

"Oh, it was great! How about yours?"

"Not long enough!" Adrian twittered right along with her. That was an honest answer, at least. She walked past the lobby area and turned right down the second corridor toward her corner of City Hall and braced herself for another barrage of "good mornings." First, there was Cynthia from the public relations office. Another hello from Bob, an intern. Finally, as Adrian approached the entrance to her office, Guadalupe gave her a vigorous smile and said, "Hola, Senora!"

"Hola! Comó estás?"

Adrian entered her office, shut the glass door behind her, and flung herself down behind the chair. Thankfully, one of the worst parts of her business day was over. Though Adrian genuinely liked the people she worked with, it was hard to come in, day in and day out, and put on this smiley face when her spirit was crying. Still, there was work to be done. She'd have to separate how she felt from what she had to do. She went into professional autopilot.

After a morning of crunching numbers and pushing papers, Adrian and several other senior employees met her boss in his office for an unusual 1:30 conference. Mr. Rodriguez sat at his desk with his lips rolled between his teeth; his moustache touched the spike of hair just beneath his bottom lip. Mr. Rodriguez's thick brown fingers enclosed the circle on the table that he'd made with his hands and body. He had bad news, Adrian already knew. She braced herself for what the numbers had shown. It didn't take a genius to figure out that the city's expenditures far exceeded revenues. Adrian braced herself for a mandate to cut down on office supplies and donuts.

Sure of what she was about to hear, Adrian sat across from Mr. Rodriguez and shot him a confident smile. She pulled out her legal pad and clicked her pen into ready position.

Once all of the managers had been gathered, Mr. Rodriguez got straight to the point. "I'm afraid I've got a bit of bad news. We're going to have to put a freeze on hiring. And some of the junior staff members from less essential departments will be let go."

Let go? "I'm sorry?" Adrian asked for clarification.

"Well, the projections have come in, and it appears that we're going to be a lot worse off than we thought. We're going to have to implement a hiring freeze," he sucked his lips back. "And there's a good possibility that we'll have to temporarily lay off some of our non-essential staff as well. The rest of us will have to double up on our work."

"Will I be losing anyone?" Adrian asked. Honestly, she had no problem seeing lazy folks go out the door, but she and the other senior analysts had many hard-working employees under them. In particular, Adrian supervised a group of two men and one woman who had families to support. How could she possibly choose which ones left or stayed?

"No. Accounting is running on a near-skeletal staff already," Mr. Rodriguez recognized. "You're safe.

"Anyway, the city manager's spokesperson plans to announce the impending layoffs in a press conference this afternoon, and I wanted to give you all the courtesy of hearing the news before the rest of the general public does."

Adrian and the others dragged themselves back to work, each of them pulling their associates aside and delivering the bad news only moments before the local news stations interrupted their regularly scheduled programs with the announcement. Of course, the media had to pick some of the most ill-spoken people in the community to make comments. Adrian just prayed they wouldn't be black.

"I think it's a shame when folks lose their jobs."

"No job is really safe anymore."

"They ain't firing the trash man, is they?"

It didn't take five minutes before Daryll called Adrian. "Baby?" he asked, anxiety apparent by his lack of breath.

"Yeah."

"My mom just called me and told me what she heard on the news. Is everything okay?"

"I'm fine," Adrian said. Bad news always traveled quickly on Juanita's lips.

"So, do you know anything yet?"

"It's so nice to hear your voice, Daryll. You haven't called me midday in I don't know how many months," Adrian strung him along. She could hear his hand hitting his forehead flatly and imagined how he must be agonizing now over whether or not his precious currency-cosmos had become unaligned.

"Adrian, I need to know. Are you going to lose your job?"

"What difference does it make, Daryll? Is that all I am to you—a paycheck?"

"You know that's not true."

"Well, why does it takes a multimillion-dollar city deficit for you to call me? Why can't you just call to say 'I Love You?'"

"Okay, Adrian, I love you."

"No, you don't."

"Yes, I do," he whimpered.

"It's all about the money with you, Daryll. This is why we're gonna end up in divorce court!"

"Stop being ridiculous, Adrian. We're not getting a divorce." Just that quickly, he'd dismissed her.

"Well...." Adrian grew angrier by the millisecond and wanted more than anything to see Daryll fly off the handle because, for once, the money—the world indeed—was out of his control, "I've been fired! So you can just count my check out!"

She hung up the smoking gun and sat there fuming. Tears sprang forward. Adrian swiveled her chair toward the back corner and angrily swiped the evidence away. She wanted to be angry, but it didn't last long before pain seeped in. Once upon a time, Daryll would have called to say "I Love You." Even Guadalupe's live-in boyfriend of five years had the sense enough to say little things like that. How is it that two people who are living together and have no plans to make a permanent commitment could have it better than two people united in holy matrimony?

Instinctively, both hands flew beneath her chin and she folded them as though praying. She thought of how she needed to call Daryll back and let him know that she hadn't been fired—that God had spared her from the ax. She knew that she should be praying for those who would soon be unemployed. And deep down inside she knew that, ultimately, God's way of uniting a man and woman was better than anything the world had to offer.

Alas, there was Daryll. He had called to see if she could still bring home the bacon. A suggestion came. *It's just not right. It's not fair.* And Adrian agreed.

Well, she could show Daryll *not fair*. And she was just about ready to withdraw the one thing that seemed to mean the most to him: money. She picked up the phone again and called the payroll department. "I'd like to stop my direct deposit immediately." Since it was after the 15th, it was too late the stop the next check. But Adrian could seize the next one, and that was exactly what she intended to do.

Upon leaving City Hall at the end of the day, she went straight down the street to Main Bank and opened up an individual checking account. She already had her own spending money in an individual account, but *this* would be one that Daryll knew nothing about. *A little bit of money laundering never hurt anybody,* she thought.

Adrian didn't dare pop in her gospel CDs on the way home. She felt more like classical music—no words, just instruments to serenade the way home without threat of conviction.

Adrian stopped and got herself something to eat on the way home. A 2-piece fish and chicken meal with baked beans, mashed potatoes, and a roll. As she sat down to eat, Daryll rushed through the front door and found Adrian seated calmly at the table. "Adrian, I brought home the newspaper."

"For what?"

"So you can start the job search. Here." He held up the employment section of the classifieds. Adrian glanced up at the paper and took another bite of her chicken. Daryll continued, "Here, baby. I know you're upset, but take this. It'll make you feel better." He poked her arm now with the rolled up paper.

Oh, I'm baby *now?*

Adrian hadn't quite decided what she was going to do about that big bold-faced lie she'd told Daryll earlier. She should have known that he would jump into action and come up with a plan to maintain their financial well-being. If she didn't do or say something soon, Daryll would probably have interviews set up for her.

"I just need some time." *There. That's not a lie.* Adrian never said what she needed time *for.* Just time.

"We don't *have* time, Adrian. It's a dog-eat-dog world. I can't call the phone company and say, 'Oh, we need *time.*' What you don't understand is that we don't have *time. Time* keeps on ticking!" There was a whiff of Southern Baptist preacher passing close by, and evidently Daryll caught it. "I can't call the investment company and say, 'Oh, could you go ahead and yield some interest even though I didn't invest this *time.* Time is of the essence and right now you need to spend it trying to find a job, and a better paying one if at all possible." Daryll was nearing a temper tantrum now. Adrian actually marveled at how much energy he could muster up when it came to money.

When she finally tired of his badgering, Adrian licked her fingers and told Daryll, "I don't need you to find a job for me. I'm perfectly capable of getting one myself."

"All right," Daryll slapped the newspaper down on the table in front of her. "You need to get something quick because we can't afford to get off track."

The phone rang and Adrian pushed herself back from the table to answer. "Hello."

"Hey! Haven't heard from you in a while." Adrian's mother's voice had changed with the years. "How are you?"

"I'm making it."

"Well, aren't we all," Marsha agreed. "What you and Daryll up to this evening?"

"Nothing."

"I heard about the thing with the city. Are you gonna get laid off or fired or what not?"

"Probably not." No need in lying to her mother, too.

"That's good. Well, you might have to think about working part time so you won't turn into a burden on your husband. That's when they start cheating, you know."

Adrian pulled the phone receiver from her ear and took a deep breath. It never ceased to amaze Adrian the things her mother could say. Just as quickly as that off-the-wall comment came, Marsha changed the subject, "Listen, we're all going over to your Uncle Maynard's tonight. It's his birthday today, you know. He hasn't been doing so hot with his diabetes lately. So we're gonna go on over and have some cake and ice cream to celebrate his birthday."

"Momma, do you really think Uncle Maynard needs cake and ice cream at a time like this?" Adrian asked.

Marsha laughed at her daughter's observation. "Girl, you know you right! That's the last thing he needs! He probably won't do nothing but blow out the candles—but this ain't about cake and ice cream. You never know when it'll be your last birthday, so I called around today and told the family to drop by, you know?"

Adrian knew what was coming next.

"So, you think you could just stop by the store and pick up a cake and some ice cream?" Just thinking about the words, the request was simple enough. But this was not a question, it came out like an if-then statement: if you don't go get the cake and ice cream, then you'll ruin what may be your Uncle Maynard's last birthday party.

Were it not for the tone, Adrian might have jumped at the chance to share her blessings. But this whole you-owe-us thing, that was something else. "Well, have you asked any other family members? They might be willing to help out, too."

"Chile, please. You know Maynard's kids ain't got two cents to rub together. And Alvia n'em *just* got that oldest boy out of jail. Now they got to turn around and get a lawyer."

"What about Nikki?"

"Well, I really hadn't thought of asking your sister. You know, she's been having a hard enough time with the kids. Really, Adrian, you the only one can do it so far as I know. But if you don't feel like it, don't worry about it."

Adrian decided that this battle wasn't worth fighting. She *was* going over there, and it would be no trouble—financial or otherwise—to stop and pick up cake and ice cream. "I'll be there around seven thirty."

"All right, Adrian. Don't be too late. Folks got to get up and go to work in the mornin'. Bye."

On Uncle Maynard's porch step, Adrian took the receipt for the cake, ice cream, and plasticware from the sack and stuffed it away in her front pocket before ringing the doorbell. With her Aunt Alvia's sons around, Adrian didn't want to take the chance of having her Visa check card number recorded and used in one of their criminal escapades.

"Hello, baby!" Adrian's mother met her at the door, but her eyes quickly swooped down her daughter's body to count the bags Adrian carried in her hands. "Let me take those from you, baby."

Adrian handed her mother the guilt offering and smoothed out her pants, taking the single step down into Uncle Maynard's sunken living room. It was the kind of house made for entertaining with its open concept of all living space except the one bathroom and three bedrooms. Absolutely nothing else was hidden, which inadvertently put every guest in the spotlight if only for a moment or two.

"Hey!" they shouted out to Adrian the way she imagined old drinking buddies welcomed each other at a bar. Half-hearted, preoccupied hellos.

"Hey, y'all," Adrian said, trying her best not to sound too educated. In fact, she gave the word 'y'all' two syllables for effect. Tonight, Adrian wanted to fit in; to let her hair down and forget about all the trouble she had going at home. Just be Adrian, Marsha's baby girl, for a little while.

Since they needed another hand at the Spades table in the kitchen, Adrian jumped in as Nikki's partner. As usual, Nikki was dressed to the nines in faux Gucci, a pair of 6-inch heels, and a swooped-up hairdo topped with a bouncy synthetic pony tail. Her makeup was applied with precision, right down to the black eyeliner she still used as lip liner. Adrian used to live with Nikki. This was a 90-minute makeup job, minimum.

Adrian played herself down, wearing an athletic outfit with a pair of Nikes.

They'd only begun making their first bids when the great inquiry began. Tosha, a cousin, first complimented Adrian on her silver chain with a butterfly pendant. "Ooh, girl, where did you get that?"

Rather than say "Nordstroms," Adrian diverted, "Ooh, girl, I got this a long time ago." Tosha, pleased that Adrian's necklace was not new, relented.

Adrian hmphed and said to her sister, "I've got one and a possible."

"Dang, that's all you got?" Nikki scrunched up her nose at her older sister.

"That's it."

"Girl, you about as much help as lips on a chicken. We'd better go board."

Tosha scribbled down the number four on the back of a wrinkled envelope and the game began. Adrian and Nikki were up 40 points before the fourth person at the table, their aunt Cassandra, took her stab at Adrian. "Yeah, I heard the city is laying off. What's gonna happen to you?"

"I'm believing God that everything is going to be fine," Adrian shrugged as she slapped down the king of hearts and swept up their book all in the same motion.

"Well, it just goes to show you—it don't matter how much education you got or how much money you make, you can be back in Groverton in the twinkling of an eye." She winked at Adrian and Adrian tried her best to smile back.

"Hmph," Nikki threw in her favorite line, "girl, you know what they say: it don't matter to the white man what kind of degree you got—you still just an educated *Negro*," then she tossed a glance at Adrian.

Adrian literally bit her tongue, clamping her top teeth tight and working hard to keep her face from saying what her mouth shouldn't. Adrian blinked slowly as she led the next play with the ace of diamonds.

"Sleepy?" Tosha asked.

"I'm just a little tired," Adrian opened her mouth a little and thought of yawning. The real yawn followed and soon everyone at the table was yawning.

"Girl, you've got to stop that!" Cassandra laughed.

Nikki eyed her sister for a moment, fishing for a hint of unhappiness. She could sleep better at night knowing that Adrian was having trouble. "What you so tired for?"

"That fine man of yours been working you overtime?" Tosha teased.

Adrian just smiled. *Working my nerves.*

Tosha winked. "If I had a sexy yellow brother like that, I'd be tired all the time, too, girl. Tired, dehydrated, foot ache...."

"*Foot* ache?" Nikki stopped and laid her cards on the table facedown.

Tosha winked at Nikki and purred, "I'll have to draw an illustration for you sometime."

"She ain't had no dern foot ache from sleepin' with no man," Cassandra laughed, throwing out the high joker and collecting the last book.

Tosha added, "All I'm saying to Adrian is, I ain't mad atcha."

"Well, if it was all *that,* she wouldn't be here playing cards with three other women on a Friday night," Nikki pried. She never could stomach the Adrian-Advantage, and Adrian was not one to go down without a fight.

"Daryll is hanging with some of his friends tonight. We decided to come up for air." Adrian kept her eyes on her cards and reveled in her cousin's and aunt's reactions. Their predictable whooping and high-fives followed, and Nikki gave a sly smirk of her own.

"How's your foot feeling?" Cassandra asked.

This time, Nikki had to laugh, too. Adrian tried to her best to join in.

Uncle Maynard's birthday party was a bust. It did little to distract Adrian from her hardship. In fact, she felt worse now that she had semi-lied to her family about the state of her marriage. What if she'd stayed in Groverton? Would she be happier now? What if she'd held on to that same scatty feeling she had for her old high school love? She might be better off.

This moping was starting to get on Adrian's nerves. She hated feeling so helpless—like there was nothing she could do to stop the destruction of their marriage. At this point she didn't know if she *wanted* to save the marriage. Was it worth it to spend her time and energy in efforts to revive it? Maybe she should just quit while she was ahead. Maybe it was God's will that she never had any children with Daryll because He knew all along that the relationship wouldn't work out. If she left now, she could wash her hands clean of this marriage and move on with her life.

Then came guilt as Adrian wondered if she was the only Christian woman who had ever loathed her husband.

CHAPTER 9

So far so good with the fake job hunting. A week had gone by since Adrian's alleged layoff, and Daryll was still convinced that she was one more unemployed sister. Every morning, Adrian got up and helped Daryll get out of the house on time. Then she rushed off to work after him. The flex-hours allowed her to work through lunch to make up for her tardiness, and since she always beat Daryll home, she was able to dress herself down before he came walking through the door.

Her plan was all good and dandy until Saturday morning when Daryll asked her if she was going to clean up.

"No," Adrian replied with a whip of her neck.

"I know you don't think I'm paying for a housekeeper while you're sitting at home every day," he almost laughed.

Dang! She hadn't thought this out too well. "Well, if we don't use Miss Irma, she might get another client and we'll...we'll lose our spot."

"So be it." Adrian just knew Daryll was smirking behind that newspaper. "We're gonna have to cut back."

She didn't have a leg to stand on. The best Adrian could do was stick her tongue out. *Cleaning? Cleaning!* "You mowing the grass today?"

"It's raining."

Adrian wanted to scream!

So there she was on a rainy Saturday morning tilted, like a scale from the weight of this steaming hot bucket of a cleaning concoction that she guessed up and hoped would work before she passed out from the fumes. Daryll conveniently slipped off to the Internet to research stocks. Adrian went mad; half talking to herself and half talking to her Father. She got louder and louder with each counter wiped, knick-knack dusted, and floor mopped.

"All he cares about is money, Lord." She spelled it out for Him, "M-O-N-E-Y." *Spray the furniture polish.* "How can he love money and You and me all at the same time? I don't think we're equally yoked, Lord. What kind of man doesn't want to have kids with his own wife?" *Too much.* "Sometimes I wish we'd never met."

Adrian ran two more buckets of hot water and solution before it was all said and done. That was hard, menacing work. Nothing near the labor of love Daryll was hoping for. Daryll came into the utility room just as she put the last of the dishrags into the washer.

"Smells good in here, babe," he announced, like somebody on a household cleaner commercial. "Real good."

Adrian looked at him and gave him a less than sincere smile.

"What?" Daryll smiled at her warmly. "Come here, baby. Let me give you a kiss."

"Is *this* what I have to do to get a kiss?" Adrian rested her weight on one leg and crossed her arms. Wild wisps of hair poked out from beneath her head scarf, beads of sweat glistened on her forehead, and her nails were scuffed from scrubbing the tubs. Was this his idea of a kissable woman?

Daryll stood clueless. "All I want to do is kiss my wife," and with that, Daryll crossed the three feet of tile separating them in the kitchen, placed one hand beneath his wife's chin, and covered her lips with his own soft, broad lips. He kissed her a few times before she reciprocated. Her arms went limp at her sides. Adrian had almost forgotten how good her husband's kisses always made her feel. In fact, she almost forgot that she was angry with him for making her clean up to begin with.

Almost.

She jerked her head back, breaking the seal of their kiss. "Like I said—is this what it takes to get affection from you?"

"You can get a whole lot more than a kiss from me if you want it," he propositioned as he worked his kisses down to her neck.

Good Lawd—it's been, what, almost a week? Adrian's resolve was slipping fast as her husband pushed all the right buttons. Her earlobe, her chin, her shoulders. She had a fleeting thought of savoring the moment—reach up and kiss him, tell him that she loved him, but his touches were too good for talk. Instead, she closed her eyes and let the pleasure carry her away.

Later, Daryll collapsed on top of Adrian, their breath mixing in space between them. "Why did you do that?" he panted.

"What?" Adrian asked, as if she didn't already know.

"I was *trying* to make love to you but you turned it into a wham-bam thing," he said as he rolled off Adrian and landed at her side.

"Why do I have to clean up for you to have the desire to make love to me?" Adrian asked, baiting Daryll.

"It's not like that's the only thing that attracts me to you, Adrian, but since you asked—yes, I do like it when you show that you appreciate what I'm providing for you by taking care of it. Yes, that turns me on."

"That's sick." Adrian raised herself off the floor and went to rinse in the shower. Daryll followed her now.

"How is it sick?"

"Because I'm not your maid, Daryll," Adrian said to him over the sound of the splattering water.

"It's not about being a maid. It's about a man wanting his wife to treat him like a king and treat their home like a castle. That's all it is." He made it sound so simple.

"Well, maybe if the king treated his woman like a queen, there wouldn't be a problem. Besides, if this really were a castle, we'd have servants." Adrian crushed his analogy.

"Why are you being so difficult? Am I asking for something unreasonable?" Daryll stepped into the stream now, leaving Adrian in the cold.

She shoved him over. "You wanna talk unreasonable? Unreasonable is when a man and a woman have ample finances to bring a child into the world, but for some unreasonable reason, the man doesn't want to have a child with the woman he claims to love. Now *that's* unreasonable."

"It isn't unreasonable," Daryll defended himself.

"If your reason is that we don't have enough money, when clearly we do, then it *is* unreasonable, Daryll." Adrian wanted to beat it on his eardrum. "I'm beginning to think that you've got some *other* problem. Maybe you're like your momma—you don't want dark skin in the family tree. "

"That's ridiculous, Adrian," Daryll shook his head. "We don't need to be having this conversation, especially not now that you don't have a job. It's politically incorrect, but nobody will hire you while you're pregnant knowing that you're going to have to take off in a few months. And it wouldn't be in your best interest to get pregnant before you get some kind of seniority going for you."

"Daryll, you make enough and we've got enough money saved up for me to stay home until the child is in kindergarten, if we wanted me to. Money is not the issue!"

"Adrian, why you wanna go and mess up a good thing?" Daryll thrust his face closer to the showerhead and let the water pelt his face.

Adrian grabbed his chin, forced him to look at her and asked, "You think this thing we've got now is good, Daryll?"

"Yes, it's *very* good. And as soon as you get back to work, it'll be even better."

"I'm not talking about money, Daryll! I'm talking about *us!* Children! A *family!*"

"Just worry about getting a job right now. Can you do that?"

Adrian sighed as she stepped out of the shower and grabbed a drying towel. It took everything within her not to flush that toilet.

The annual Homecoming Sunday at church filled the sanctuary with people who hadn't visited Pleasant Hills in a while. The pews were adorned with flowers, the choir was in full bloom, and the church bulletin was a booklet instead of a brochure. Over the years, Homecoming Sunday had become quite an event, with former members making weekend travel plans to attend this service in hopes of being reunited with old friends. The congregation doubled in size to about two hundred churchgoers who donned their very best church attire for the special gathering.

All of this commotion put Adrian on autopilot again, smiling at seasoned women who remembered Little Daryll's mischievous days in Sunday school. They pinched his cheeks and kissed Adrian, oblivious to her pain.

"Oh, you two look so good together!"

"She's taking good care of you, I see!"

"No babies yet?" one woman asked.

When Adrian didn't answer, Daryll wrapped one arm around Adrian's shoulders, hugged her tightly, tilted his head in so that his cheek touched Adrian's crown ever so slightly, and replied, "No, ma'am. We're happy with each other."

Adrian elbowed Daryll in his side when the woman looked away. She warned him between clenched teeth, "Don't sit up here and lie in church!"

Daryll performed his best ventriloquist act to date, "Do *not* make a scene in front of all these people, Adrian."

"Don't *make* me make a scene, Little Daryll."

During the sermon, Daryll scooted closer to Adrian as he turned his King James Bible to Ephesians 4:1-3. *"I therefore, the prisoner of the Lord, beseech you that ye walk worthy of the vocation wherewith ye are called, With all lowliness and meekness, with longsuffering, forbearing one another in love; Endeavouring to keep the unity of the Spirit in the bond of peace."*

Adrian wrestled her attentions to the Word of God and followed Daryll's left index finger across the page. She analyzed the scriptures with an attitude. Prisoner was the perfect word for the situation. *I am definitely a prisoner for the Lord, because if I wasn't saved, I would have been long gone from this marriage.* The qualities of lowliness and meekness were not quite Adrian's forte. She had, however, been suffering for some time, and there was no peace to preserve. Collectively, none of it made sense. Adrian wished she was at home instead of in church with the Jacobsens.

She kept her eyes on the Word but her attention drifted. She noticed that the three diamonds set within Daryll's platinum wedding band sparkled as brightly as the day they'd exchanged vows. It had been a beautiful wedding. Everything done according to the book—Daryll's mother made sure of that. Juanita Jacobsen was not about to be shown up in front of the congregation of Pleasant Hills Baptist Church. No, if it meant that the Jacobsens paid for both the wedding and the honeymoon, the senior Mrs. Jacobsen was not going to have fried chicken and mashed potatoes served at the reception.

"This wedding is going to have some *class*," she'd announced during the Sunday dinner following their official engagement.

When he saw that Adrian's good home training was under fire, Mr. Jacobsen spoke on Adrian's behalf. "Who said it *wouldn't* be classy?"

"I'm just saying...this wedding needs to be nice," Juanita puffed out her cheeks in an expression all her own. It had hurt Juanita to lose her son to this simple girl. Daryll always did have a thing for those hoodrats, as his mother called them, and Juanita never had a problem with him sewing his wild oats on the other side of the tracks. After all that money they'd spent to make sure he got a good education, he didn't have the sense to marry better than Adrian. At least somebody whose parents had enough money to throw a decent wedding, for heaven's sake.

Adrian now looked over at her mother-in-law as Juanita sat on the front pew with her royal purple suit with oversized cubic zirconium accents lining the lapel. Her hair was pulled up into a French roll, showing off a neckline, bone structure, and skin that could have advertised plastic surgery. Adrian had to give it to Juanita; she was nearing sixty but didn't look anywhere near her age. Whether it was good genes or good maintenance,

Adrian couldn't take anything away from her mother-in-law's outer beauty.

It was the stuff inside that made her so ugly.

Pastor Clark got all into the message that morning, urging them to "hold on" because help was on the way. Adrian managed to snatch a few nuggets of encouragement from the sermon. Pastor Clark also reminded her that there were lots of people who had it worse off than she did. Somebody was sleeping under a bridge. Somebody else was lying in a hospital bed. Somebody else didn't wake up. Adrian knew all of that to be true, and she was indeed grateful for the things God had done for her. Gratitude was one of the things that kept her in the marriage.

In the middle of all this, she did feel ashamed. How many women out there wish they had a man who worked, had an education, wasn't cheating, wasn't beating on them, didn't have a criminal record, went to church, knew how to lay it down in the bedroom, and had the desire to provide for them financially? Adrian felt the pang of a million women bopping her upside the head for feeling the way she did.

Maybe those other million women had men who weren't in a position to give them all that Daryll could. Some men didn't have good male role models but they're doing the best they can with what they know. Some men didn't have the educational opportunities that Daryll had so they're not in the best of financial positions nor do they know how to become financially secure. Some men are hustling just to make ends meet, and those are the men that the other million women might have. So far as Adrian was concerned, that was just fine. Those men can't give what they don't have. But to *have* and *refuse* to give—that's worse than not having it in the first place. Now *that's* the kind of man Daryll was. And if those million women knew all *that* about her husband, maybe they wouldn't be so quick to jump in Adrian's pumps.

As Pastor Clark prayed the standard benediction, Adrian prayed her own prayer: *I will hold on, Father. But I am numb.*

The best thing about Homecoming Sunday was the fact that the hospitality department served dinner, which meant they didn't have to go to the Jacobsen home after service. The fellowship hall was lined with fold-up tables and chairs. Adrian piled her plate higher than usual with chicken, Sister Frankford's greens, Juanita Jacobsen's cabbage, and some of her own hot-water cornbread. She and Daryll took a seat at the table with his parents, but it quickly filled with other members, to Adrian's relief. They chatted about the Wal-Mart coming to town, the new subdivision, regentrification. It wouldn't be long, they said, before developers began offering outrageous sums of money for some of the homes in Groverton.

"They ought to clear it all out," Juanita barked. "I mean, make it flat as a prairie."

Brother Hall, an active member on the hospitality committee, countered Juanita. "My aunt lives in Groverton and she doesn't mind moving. She just wants a little more time."

Juanita, who did not appreciate being contradicted by a mere usher, gave one of her favorite maxims, "Well, the people in hell want a drink of water, but they can't have one."

Adrian fought to keep her facial expression in check, "Sister Jacobsen, I think the people in Groverton just want what's fair for their properties."

Juanita seemed to remember, suddenly, that Adrian was from Groverton. "Mmm," she heaved.

Adrian suggested, "Well, since so many in the congregation have ties to Groverton, we should put some pressure on Senator

Wheaton to get involved in these buyouts. Maybe we can get a petition going around the church to...."

"We will not!" Juanita protested, slamming her hand flat against the table, causing the silverware on the table to hop. Silence consumed her immediate vicinity and Juanita took a sip of water to compose herself. She straightened her back and said softly, "Let the Lord handle it."

"Okay," Adrian relented.

Daryll quickly changed the subject to football. Though the season was months away, every man at the table put in his two cents about trading players, long-term injuries, and a bunch of other mess that none of them should have been worried about, so far as Adrian was concerned.

All the way home, Adrian wondered why Daryll insisted on dancing around this beef that his mother obviously had with his wife. True, he never let it get out of control, but every once in a while, like today, he walked a tightrope.

Adrian set the empty cornbread pan in the sink. They both changed clothes and then Daryll went to the living room to watch basketball.

"We've grown apart. We have literally grown apart," Adrian whispered to herself as she curled her knees up to her chest and pulled the shapeless, lifeless pillow in closer. She marveled at her body's ability to make emotional pain tangible. Adrian could actually feel the weight of her heart in her chest.

She thought about storming into the living room, ripping the television out of the armoire, and letting it fall right on the floor. Or maybe she could start on another one of her yelling and screaming jaunts—anything to get something out of Daryll. Anger felt better than pain. But the truth of the matter was, Adrian was past being angry. There was nothing left to be angry about. Really, very little left to cry about. Daryll wanted things one way and she wanted things another. No amount of demolishing or arguing or crying could change that.

Adrian gathered her thoughts and tried to express them in her journal. Try as she might, the only thing she could find to write was:

Dear God,

I can't take it anymore. I have to leave. I'm sorry.

Adrian

CHAPTER 10

Irma needed to get to bed early in preparation for her cleaning week. She and Harvey had prayed special prayers for the Rileys all weekend and Irma was ready to get into Sonia's home and do some serious speaking into the atmosphere. It should have come as no surprise to her that there would be adversity.

"Hello?" Irma answered her telephone. It was late on Sunday—much later than anyone would normally call the Parker household.

"Miss Irma, it's Sonia Riley. I hope I didn't wake you."

"No, Sonia, I'm still up," Irma assured Sonia.

"I've been meaning to call you. I...I'm really sorry, but I...we've had some changes around here and...." Sonia paused and sighed before spilling the truth. "Mr. Riley and I have separated and I'm really not in a financial position to continue to pay for housekeeping right now."

Irma's heart fell to her stomach. "Oh, Sonia. I'm so sorry, baby. What...," Irma didn't want to pry, so she didn't finish the question. It might be better not to know all of the details. "Well, I understand how things can be rough in a marriage sometimes. Have you all tried to talk things out?"

"Yes, ma'am, we have tried." There was a slight crack in Sonia's voice.

Miss Irma prayed for the right words. "Sonia, God knows I don't want to get all in your business. I just want you to know that my husband and I have been praying for you and Kennard. I mean really, really praying. I know that God will answer."

"I've been praying, too, Miss Irma. I think that maybe this separation *is* the answer."

Miss Irma was not a minister, neither did she claim to know the answers to everything. But when God put things on her heart, He didn't make mistakes. She had to act on her conviction. "Sonia, do you think it might help to talk to other women who have been through the ups and downs of marriage? Some of my friends and I have been thinking about starting a group to help younger couples make it through."

Sonia wondered what these women could tell her that she hadn't already considered. It was simple: Kennard still acted like a bachelor. What could Miss Irma and her friends possibly do to make Kennard mature? "I don't know, Miss Irma. There's really not much to be said or done, at this point."

"Sonia," Miss Irma said with all the Power vested in her, "you may not realize it, but whatever you're going through, there's another woman who has been through it. I don't know what all God has in store for you, but I do know that you owe it to yourself to leave no stone unturned before you throw in the towel on your marriage."

Just when she thought she had exhausted every avenue of compromise, Sonia was faced with another pesky prospect. One more thing to try and fail. But at least she'd be able to say that she *did* give it her all. If nothing else, she might learn how to pick a better man the next time around. "When...when does your group meet?" she sighed.

Irma didn't have a date. In fact, she didn't even have commitments from the women she hoped would be a part of the group. "What works best for you?"

"My mom keeps the kids on Friday nights. Is that a good night for you all?"

Irma spoke in faith. "I'm pretty sure it'll be fine. I'll call you later this week with a time and location."

"Yes, ma'am."

"All right, baby. Thanks for calling. You sure you don't want me to drop by and run a few loads of laundry for you on Friday? I don't mind," Irma offered.

"Oh, no, Miss Irma. I wouldn't dream of it," Sonia rejected the suggestion.

"Well, you just let me know if you need anything."

"Yes, ma'am. And thank you, Miss Irma."

"You're welcome, Sonia."

By Tuesday, Irma had her thoughts all prayed up and lined up for her big proposal to the other Senior Swimmers. Rose would be open. Beverly would be a challenge. Irma and Beverly had had their fair share of run-ins over the years; the kinds that close family and friends tend to have in due time. Nothing that either of them could even remember with great specificity because they were both experienced forgivers.

"I think it's a great idea, Irma." Rose was delighted to be on this topic again.

"Mentor whom about what?" Beverly asked without lifting her head. The water felt too good to move.

"You *know*. Young women. Young wives. We've talked about this before, remember?"

"I distinctly remember saying no," Beverly recalled to the best of her ability.

Rose remembered differently. "You didn't say no. What you said was that you didn't think young folks would be open to the idea."

"That's right. I said no," Beverly repeated.

Irma gave Beverly a do-we-have-to-beg-you stare. Beverly always said no to everything initially. For as much as Irma disliked having to go the long route to persuade Beverly to do things, Irma did actually admire Beverly's ability to say no. It was a skill that Irma herself had not quite mastered yet.

Beverly sensed the two sets of eyes fixed on her. "What?" she sat up abruptly.

"You have a lot to offer, Bev," Rose lectured, "and you can't take it to heaven with you. Might as well pass it on."

Pleased to have a ready partner, Irma added, "We've learned a lot in life, Beverly, and we owe it to the next generation to share our wisdom. I've been looking at this in the Word. I re-read Titus 2, verse 4, last night. It says that the older women can *'train the younger women to love their husbands and children.'* That means we're not born knowing how to be a wife or a mother—it comes through training. The Bible is very clear about who's supposed to be doing the training. The responsibility is on *us.*"

"They've got a responsibility to listen!" Beverly bugged her eyes out. "Let me tell you— at New Bethel, we tried to start fellowshippin' with the young women. They didn't ever want to meet on the weekends because they're too busy partyin' with their worldly friends. Then they don't want to meet at the church. All they want to do is get together and show off their two-story houses. Take you on a tour and everything! They ain't tryin' to pray. They want to make it into some kind of social event. I don't know if I'm willing to fool with that mess."

"Sonia is willing to meet on Friday evenings," Irma advised. "It's her only time away from the kids, but she's willing to sacrifice that time in order to meet with us."

Beverly slid her eyes across the two other women and then laid her head backward on the rim of the hot tub. "Hmmm. She's one in a million."

"Just think about it, Beverly. The Rileys have split up."

"Hush!" Beverly jerked her head up.

"That's how it goes sometimes when we get to praying," Rose encouraged Irma. "Sometimes things get worse before they get better."

Irma and Rose shut their mouths and let Beverly think. The news of the Riley split caused Beverly to replay some of the details of her own divorce. Hasty. Premature. That wasn't the case for every divorced woman, she knew, but Beverly hoped that no other woman would—in the words of a Natalie Cole song—take "a fool's way out." The thought of reliving her own mistakes didn't exactly excite Beverly. Still, there were families at stake. Children, in this case. It was then that she realized how selfish it would be to withhold her life's lessons. There was both pain and deliverance in her experience.

"So, Bev, what do you say?" Rose asked.

Out of habit, Beverly replied, "Let me think about it some more."

Rose and Irma took that as a yes.

Irma rushed home and went straight to the phone where her message light blinked the number one. Irma pressed the play button and listened. "Hi, Miss Irma, it's Adrian Jacobsen. I'm sorry to call you at such late notice, but we're having a little...trouble right now and I...Daryll...um, we're going to have to stop using your services for the time being. If you'd call me back and give me your address, I'll send you a check for the rest of the month since I really didn't give you much notice. Okay, bye."

Irma put both hands on her cheeks, "Lord, another one?" Irma had been cleaning the Jacobsen home for only a year. Someone from Daryll's father's church referred Irma to them. From her first meeting with Adrian, she had liked the couple. Adrian had walked Irma through the house, pointing out a few of the problem areas and assuring Irma that she would see to it that the cleaning load wasn't too heavy. Irma had just smiled and taken in Adrian's vibrant energy, thinking of how the young woman's bushy hair was the perfect match for her personality.

Halfway through their time together, Daryll had come home. Adrian introduced the two, and Daryll went back to their bedroom, leaving the women to continue. There had been an unmistakable fire between the two, and Irma smiled at their love.

As they finished up the tour of the house, they had taken a seat in the living room and Irma asked about the original inhabitants. They got to talking and Irma realized that she knew of Adrian's family and the Jacobsens. "What a small world," Irma had remarked.

When they started discussing payment, Irma noticed that Adrian lowered her voice a bit. When Adrian made a few comments about Daryll's reluctance to have a housekeeper, Irma decided she'd better speak up. "Adrian, honey, I don't mean to be all in your business, but if you and your husband aren't in agreement about this, maybe you shouldn't be hiring me."

Adrian had seemed almost shocked at the idea that she should agree with her husband about things first. Irma kept that same sweet smile plastered on her face as Adrian's expression went from shocked to dismayed to considerate. Adrian figured Irma was just concerned about who held the purse strings. Adrian assured her, "I will be the one paying you, Miss Irma."

"Oh, it's not about the money," Irma shook her head. "I know how things can be between newlyweds. You're just getting to know each other. I don't want to be in the middle of any conflict."

Adrian simply threw out a halfhearted, "I'll be sure to double-check with him."

Adrian's voice message said that they were having "trouble." What kind of trouble? If it was financial trouble, the last thing Adrian needed was to be transferring more money from the Jacobsen household to the Parkers. She called Adrian right away.

"Adrian, this is Irma. Is everything okay?"

"Yes, Miss Irma, we're fine. Daryll and I have had some... disagreements and I... guess I'll have to make some changes around here for a while."

Irma wasn't one to say, "I told you so," she kept it to herself, almost laughing at Adrian for not having listened. She was actually surprised that it had taken Daryll this long to put his foot down. No matter how progressive men and women are, there is always a need for agreement. "Well, you have to do what's best for your family."

"We don't have a family," Adrian blurted out. "It's just me and Daryll."

"You two are a family. You know, my husband and I never had children. Just because you don't have kids doesn't mean you're not a family," Irma encouraged Adrian.

"But I *want* kids—Daryll doesn't," Adrian confided in Irma. There was nothing to lose.

"Well, it's all about agreement," Irma brought up that word again.

"I can't agree with someone who is irrational," Adrian sighed.

"Adrian, I've got an idea for you. My friends and I are starting a mentoring group for young wives like yourself who are having trouble in their marriages. We're going to meet on Friday at my house. Would you like to join us?"

"Misery loves company," Adrian muttered. She was beyond propriety at that point. "I guess it can't hurt to come."

"Great! My address is 1200 Melody Lane, in the Oakley Hills area of Dallas."

As Irma ended the conversation with Adrian, she suddenly felt the heaviness of what was about to happen. She, along with Beverly and Rose, was about to embark on a mission to save marriages. All at once, she was afraid of this task; it was overwhelming. She had no game plan, she had no format, and Lord knows she had no formal training in counseling or mentoring. What if she let these families down?

Then Irma closed her eyes and replayed all that the Lord had confirmed—the sweet whisperings in her spirit, the visions, the way in which He had arranged for Irma and her friends to be ready to mentor at just the time that Sonia and Adrian needed them most. Irma opened her eyes and spoke the words, "By the power of Christ that lives within me, I am ready. I call the Riley and Jacobsen families healed in the name of Jesus. I call the Riley and Jacobsen marriages whole in the name of Jesus. Lord, You said that the prayers of the righteous avail much, and I am standing on Your Word. This job is too big for me, but I know what You have shown me and told me, and I'm standing in the gap for these families and I claim the victory right now, in Jesus' name."

Then Irma praised the Lord in advance for what He was about to do and how His purposes would prevail.

But everybody knows that the enemy does not go down without a good fight.

CHAPTER 11

On Monday morning, Sonia opened her eyes and wondered exactly when she had fallen asleep. Seemed like only moments ago the clock had read 3:52 A.M., but she must have stayed up another hour or so just thinking about when and how to tell the children their daddy was gone. Sonia knew she was doing the right thing, yet there was a certain embarrassment about the whole situation. Sonia hadn't even returned Gina's call Sunday as she had planned to do after church. Sonia wasn't ready to disclose the precise state of her marriage to anyone.

The weekend had come and gone, with its time to recoup from those sleepless nights. Now it was Monday, time to resume her life, and Sonia felt as though her body weight had doubled overnight. Maybe she could call in sick to work. She *was* sick—emotionally—but this was not time for a pity party. She would have to get herself and the kids up and ready for another weekday.

Perhaps the hardest thing about a life-changing event is the fact that the sun still rises every morning just like the day before. People still carry on like nothing has changed. No matter how sad life gets, no matter how much loss a person has suffered, the trash man still comes on schedule and life really does go on.

On to work, now.

When Morris walked into Sonia's office for the second time in two weeks, she was ready for him. They were holed up in tight quarters for two days straight, hammering out all of the procedures. Sonia talked and demonstrated, he took notes and asked questions. It was the best assignment she could have had; it took her mind off things at home and exhausted every minute at the office. SAIT was no joke.

At 4:59 on the second day, just as Sonia finished answering Morris's final question, he shut down his laptop and shook his head. "I've gotta give it to you, Sonia, you know your stuff."

Sonia let her head hit the headrest on the back of her executive chair in satisfaction. Then she rocked her head toward him and said, "I've only been in this position for about a month."

Morris relaxed a bit with Sonia. "Are you serious?"

"Yes," she nodded with the little bit of energy she had left.

"That's amazing," he nodded. "In two days, we knocked out about four days' worth of work. You've got it together, my sister."

Sonia laughed to herself and hummed a sliding note. How she wished that statement were true. "Thank you, Morris. You're not too bad yourself. It's been nice working with you."

"Same here. Hey—maybe we could do lunch one day," he asked. "Steven is cool and all, but I'd like to get some *real* barbecue from the hood, if you know what I mean."

"Yeah, Steven is fun...."

"No, Sonia, he took us to this barbecue place and when we got there, they had all these high-antioxidant beans and leaner-ized ribs and low-sufractosis barbecue sauce." Sonia laughed as Morris animated his nonsense words. "I had to walk across the street to 7-11 and get me a king-size Snicker's just to get my taste buds back on track."

When Sonia caught her breath again, she told Morris that she'd take him out for lunch one day to some nice, unhealthy restaurant where there wasn't so much as a diet Coke on the menu. They didn't set a date, but he said he'd stop by and let her know when he was available to go. "You know where I am," Sonia left it open.

On the way home from work, Sonia thought about what a productive two days it had been. Being new to her position had probably been a benefit since she had only recently learned the rules and procedures. Thankfully, the new system would be up and running soon, and Sonia wouldn't have to unlearn the old one.

She was too exhausted to cook that night. Mickey D's would have to do, and the kids were all the happier for it. At the drive-thru, she ordered a salad for herself and two kids' meals for the twins. Kamron leaned forward and asked, "You gonna order something for Daddy?"

Snap back into reality.

"He's not eating with us tonight," Sonia replied in her best don't-ask-no-more-questions tone.

Kamron sat back in his booster seat. Kelsi either didn't get it or she didn't *want* to get it. "Where has Daddy been, Mommy? And where is he going to eat?"

"He's with Mr. Victor," Sonia assumed.

Kamron complained, "He *always* eats with Mr. Victor."

"I know, sweetheart. And I think that Daddy will be eating with Mr. Victor a lot because right now Daddy is staying at Mr. Victor's apartment."

Sonia hadn't meant for it to happen that way, but that's how it all went down. She told them at window #1.

"That'll be nine seventy-four," the young girl said as Sonia stretched out her hand and gave her a ten dollar bill. She returned Sonia's change and directed her to the next window.

"When is he going to come back?" Kelsi wanted to know.

Your guess is as good as mine! "Mommy and Daddy have to talk about that. We'll let you know."

"Are y'all getting a thivorce?" Kamron asked.

In a calm, even pitch, Sonia asked, "Where did you hear that word?"

"At school. Jayce Armstrong said it's when your daddy moves out because he doesn't love your mommy anymore, right?" her son asked with fear in his eyes.

The driver behind Sonia honked his horn slightly. Time for window #2; a timely reprieve. Sonia loaded the passengers' seat with sacks and a drink tray and pulled back into traffic, fully aware that she hadn't answered Kamron's question.

"Here. Take your fries." Sonia single-handedly distributed the kids' meal sacks.

"We can eat in the car?" Kelsi asked in amazement.

"Yes. Go ahead and eat your fries in the car."

"Thanks, Momma!"

With the children's attention temporarily diverted, Sonia could concentrate on the thumping in her chest. She realized how close she had come to connecting the dots for her children. *No, your daddy's never home; therefore, Mommy asked him not to come home anymore.* That would be too much information. And as Sonia listened to them laugh and talk with mouths full of french fries in her car, which had always been a no-no, she wondered how many more of these no-no's she would rescind in an effort to keep her children's attention off the fact that Mommy and Daddy weren't together anymore. Maybe she could get a puppy to distract them.

Kennard didn't like dogs; at least not the kind of dog Sonia wanted. "If we get a dog, we're getting a pit bull," he had declared clear across the first floor. He sat in his favorite chair, his body leaning left and then right as he dodged bullets on the video game screen while Sonia got dinner under way in the kitchen. "I ain't gettin' no punk dog."

"There is no way on earth we're getting a pit bull, Kennard. They're way too aggressive." Sonia searched the freezer for the oven pizza and frozen strawberry lemonade—a favorite of the children.

"It's all in how you raise a dog, Sonia. If you treat them right, they won't turn on you. Victor knows somebody with some pit puppies for sale right now."

"Please. If we get one from Victor, it'll *really* be crazy," Sonia said as she laughed at the idea.

"Tell you what," Kennard proposed, "I take full responsibility for anything that happens."

"Like that's going to help *after-the-fact.*"

"Sonia, any animal with teeth can bite!" Kennard sat up in agitation at that point.

"NO. I'm not having a pit bull at *my* house with *my* children. Matter of fact, I don't want a pit bull with me—*ever!* That's out, Kennard." Sonia had slammed her hand on the counter emphatically.

"You don't have to stay here," he snapped.

Sonia declared, "I *won't* be staying here if you bring a pit bull into this house."

"Dang, Sonia, you would think with all your *degrees* you'd have more sense!" He shook his head and added, "Ain't no fool like an educated fool."

"Who you callin' a fool?" she slammed the pizza box on the counter.

"If the shoe fits," he smirked.

"Negro, pulleaze! It takes a bigger fool to get a full scholarship to college and then lose it 'cause he's too busy partying to go to class!" Sonia hit below the belt with that one.

"Hey, at least I've got an excuse—I didn't finish college," Kennard defended himself.

"That's not my fault."

Kennard turned off his video game, grabbed his keys, and left.

That was then. Before Sonia decided to put a stop to the madness, before their period of silence. Before she was separated and maybe on the way to divorce. Sonia kept saying "maybe" to herself because...she wasn't ready to call it quits. She was in marital limbo, if there is such a thing. Her at the house with the kids, Kennard at his friend's house doing whatever it is that men do when they get together. Come to think of it, things really hadn't changed all that much for her because, to some degree, she had always been a single parent.

In all of her deep thought, God guided her on home. Sonia had no recollection of stop lights, signaling, turning. "Bless the name of the Most High," Sonia said with a sigh as she pulled into the driveway, thinking of God's goodness and how, even on a little ride home from work, He always watches over His children. Once inside, Sonia ate her salad, the kids finished their meals, and the evening routine began: playing outdoors, homework, baths, laying out clothes for the next day, reading.

When the kids were in bed and ready to doze off, Sonia read them their nightly story and the children chimed in whenever possible. Sonia knew it wouldn't be long before they asked when their father would be home. She didn't have an answer other than, "*When* and *if* he starts acting right," but, of course, she couldn't say that.

When Kelsi asked the question, Sonia answered honestly, "I don't know, sweetheart."

"Is he in heaven already?" Kamron asked.

Sonia frowned. "No, Kamron, he's not in heaven." *He may not ever be in heaven, sweetie.* "Why did you ask me that?"

"This girl at school named Abbie, she had a picture of her grandmother and she said that her grandmother is gone away for a while and the next time Abbie gets to see her will be in heaven."

"No, Kamron," Sonia assured him, "your daddy is not in heaven. He is still alive here on this earth."

"Can we call him?" Kelsi asked from her bed.

Sonia had to think about that one for a second. Did she want to get into the habit of *them* calling *him* rather than vice versa? He ought to care enough about his own kids to call them. That was expecting too much, Sonia knew. He'd never made it a point to speak to them before they went to sleep while living at home and there was no reason to believe that things would be different now. Sonia just didn't want to see her kids chasing their daddy down the way Sonia chased Buddy when she was younger, all to no avail. There is no rejection like a father's rejection.

"Can we call him, Momma?" Kelsi repeated.

Sonia realized then that allowing her children to have contact with their father wasn't about right or wrong. It was about setting them up for disappointment and heartache. Most women want their children to have a relationship with their father, but not at the expense of their tender little hearts. Sonia would rather have people say that she was ignorant for keeping her kids away from their father than watch her two children spend the night on the couch with their backpacks strapped to their arms, waiting for their father to arrive.

Sonia answered Kelsi's question. "It's really late right now, sweetheart. Maybe tomorrow, okay?"

To Sonia's surprise, Kelsi didn't press the issue. "Okay. Tomorrow."

"Tomorrow," Kamron reiterated.

"Good night," Sonia said as she blew them kisses.

It was time for Sonia and God now. She needed direction regarding the children. *Was I wrong for putting the call off until tomorrow? Are we supposed to hunt him down to say good night?* In the two days that he had been out of the house, neither of them had made an attempt to communicate. *Is it time to file papers, Lord?*

Loneliness crawled between the sheets with Sonia that night. Even as she opened her Bible to read, Sonia felt it wrap around her and wondered how long that feeling would stay. "You'll get through it, Sonia," she said out loud to herself. If she broke down, there would be no one to hold her up.

She was on the last chapter of Proverbs. Imagine her disappointment as she read this chapter consisting mostly of a description of a godly wife which, to Sonia, read like she was nothing more than a glorified servant to her husband. The woman does all this work in the background—getting up early and making sure things are well for her children and helpers, she's always busy watching over the affairs of her household, she works vigorously. *Yada, yada, yada.* Sonia had no doubt that this woman was noble and virtuous. Sonia figured that she could be noble and virtuous, too, if she had a noble husband.

*Wonder what her husband does all day? Probably chillin'
with the concubines.* Sonia reread the chapter—not to learn
more about this description of a godly woman—to figure out
more about the man she was married to. And that's when verse
twelve spoke to her. *"She brings him good, not harm, all the
days of her life."*

"I would *bring* him good if he *acted* good," Sonia spoke
back to her Bible as she slammed it shut and slid it back into
the nightstand.

Sonia fussed and showered and showered and fussed while
thinking about this chapter. *Please! He's a grown man. I don't
see nobody trying to build* me *up! I don't see nobody bringing*
me *no good!*

And yet for all her arguing, Sonia knew that God wasn't
going to change his mind about things. He had spoken to her
in His Word. *"She brings him good, not harm, all the days of
her life."*

Sonia Gibson-Riley was not trying to hear that.

CHAPTER 12

Irma walked through her home touching and praying, touching and praying. In the days leading up to their meeting, she had been fasting and asking God to guide her and her seasoned friends in mentoring the younger Christian women. Now it was time for all of that fasting and praying to pay off. She and Rose had talked through some ideas about how the meeting should go, but they both knew that the Holy Spirit would ultimately direct the agenda. Beverly was coming, too, despite her initial reluctance.

Irma double-checked her home as she waited for her guests to arrive. Irma's khaki skirt swished as she scurried from corner to corner making sure that everything was in its place. The doilies she crocheted sat perfectly beneath the candy jar, candles, and figurines on the coffee table and end tables. She was not concerned that her guests would think less of her if her house was not perfect. Her greatest concern was for simplicity. She wanted no distractions, no conversation pieces, nothing but sincere order as a symbol of their solemnity.

She hummed *Something About the Name of Jesus* in the final moments before Beverly and Rose arrived. They'd decided to meet fifteen minutes ahead of time in order to pray together before the mentees arrived.

When they both arrived, Beverly prayed, "Lord, open their hearts to Your will. Quicken their spirits to receive from You."

"Father, let the words of our mouths and the meditation of our hearts be acceptable in Your sight, O God," Rose pleaded.

Irma added, "Father, let Your Holy Spirit fall fresh on us this evening. Mmmm, we come against the enemy tonight and cast down everything that's not like You, Lord Jesus. We bind every evil scheme that the enemy has in mind for these young women and these young families, mmmmm."

"Yes, Lord," Beverly and Rose agreed.

"In the precious name of Jesus we pray, amen."

Rose and Beverly echoed, "Amen."

With knees popping, and muscles talking, the three women rose to standing positions and lifted hands toward the sky to praise God, in advance, for what He was about to do.

The doorbell rang, and they all greeted Sonia with hugs and holy kisses. Sonia was almost overwhelmed by their warmth and she wondered how long she'd last in this meeting before she fell apart in these women's arms. Even as Irma introduced Sonia to Beverly and Rose, Sonia felt her breath tightening, her eyes watering. So far, she had been holding up very well since she'd kicked Kennard out. She had not skipped a beat so far as anyone could see. She had even managed to convince herself that she was as solid as a rock in her own strength. But somehow, being in Irma's house and coming face-to-face with someone who knew the magnitude of her situation was tremendously emotional.

Adrian pulled into the driveway and parked. This prayer group was probably a bad idea. Then again, so was the idea of marrying Daryll and she had gone through with *that*. One bad turn deserves another.

Adrian wasn't even living at her home anymore. Her new address was the Holiday Inn on Main. Room 326. Moving to a hotel (courtesy of their joint account) had been a very liberating step for Adrian. To add to her liberty, she didn't plan on going to church on Sunday. Let Daryll show up without his wife and that would throw Juanita Jacobsen into damage-control mode. Adrian could almost hear her mother-in-law lying now, "I talked to her just this morning. She's not feeling well." That was the Jacobsens for you. Maybe if Adrian could just divorce her in-laws, she might be able to work things out with Daryll. Alas, that wasn't possible. When you marry someone, you marry their whole family. Adrian reasoned that sometimes it may be necessary to throw out the baby with the bath water.

Adrian opened her car door and followed her feet to Irma's doorstep. Potted plants decorated the porch and Adrian couldn't help but smile at the white screen door and windows. She wondered if they even made those anymore. Irma opened the door and gave Adrian a huge smile, pulling her across the threshold and making her the object of sisterly affection. Adrian received their greetings, but she felt like this was an intervention or a hidden-camera show where she would be ambushed.

Upon seeing the other young woman, Adrian was convinced that this was indeed a pathetic case of bad judgment. To Adrian, Sonia looked no more than 30 years old. She wore a fitted, button-down blouse, a pair of jeans, and high-heeled sandals. Adrian felt pretty sure that she and this younger woman were in the same boat: the bad-marriage canoe, rowing upstream, getting nowhere fast.

"Adrian, this is Sonia," Irma introduced them.

Sonia was the first to offer her hand, "Hi, Adrian."

"Hello," Adrian replied as they shook hands. She felt like asking, "What are you in for?" But there was something about the mood in the room that wouldn't allow for jokes just then.

Instinctively, Adrian sat down next to Sonia and waited for the lecture from Irma and company. She already knew what they were going to say: listen to your husband, be submissive, roll yourself out like a doormat in the name of Jesus, and sooner or later everything will get better.

Beverly got a whiff of Adrian's attitude even before Irma and Rose picked up on it. It was written in Adrian's take-it-or-leave-it kinky hair and her deliberately wrinkled retro skirt, earth-toned shawl, and sandals with strings that criss-crossed to the middle of her calves. This girl had her own mind, she went against the grain, she liked to speak now and apologize later. Beverly held back a grin, imagining that God Almighty must have been laughing at that very moment. He'd sent Beverly nothing less than a replica of herself, circa 1965.

"Well, we're all here," Irma announced, "so let's go ahead and open in prayer."

The women stood in a circle around the coffee table, clasped hands, and listened as Irma prayed again. Sonia had no choice but to allow the tears to fall from her eyes all the way to the floor. She couldn't catch them with the palm of her hand, and she realized that they would all see her pain and her shame when the prayer was over. Not that it mattered now. She was beyond embarrassment. It reminded her of the hours leading up to the birth of her children. At the height of labor, she was in so much anguish that she would have allowed live cameras in the delivery room if that had meant that the pain would end.

Adrian didn't close her eyes for the prayer. She saw the wet dots hit the floor at Sonia's feet and wondered what horrid thing Sonia's husband must have done to make her cry like this. Adrian grew angrier with each tear that fell from Sonia's eyes to the floor. She made up her mind that she would pull Sonia aside after the meeting and give her a good put-your-big-girl-panties-on talk. *She has no business crying like that over a man, even if it is her 'ole sorry, no-good husband.*

"Amen."

Irma pulled a box of Kleenex from beneath the cabinet coffee table. She gave Sonia a few sheets and set the box on the table for the rest of the night. Adrian looked at the box for a second and wished it wasn't there. She couldn't stand it when people started all this crying over things they couldn't control. It reminded her of funerals, where emotion charged through the pews, people fell out with grief and shrieked uncontrollably. Funerals were too much for her to handle, and maybe this was, too. She zipped the butterfly charm back and forth on her necklace.

"Beverly, Rose, and I will start off by telling you a little about ourselves and why we're here tonight, and we'd like for you to do the same. And then Rose is going to lead us in a discussion. Beverly will lead us in looking at what the Word says about the issues that we bring up tonight." Irma nodded with each new sentence, soliciting the same from everyone in the room.

"Beverly, why don't you go first?"

Beverly nodded. "Okay, well, I'm Beverly Moore. I've been divorced and widowed, so I guess you could say I've been through a lot. My first husband, J.D., is Rose's husband's brother. We were married for a few years and I just got tired of it. We were both tired of each other, I guess. I married again when I was 31. My second husband, Malcolm, and I have one son, who's a football coach at Texas University. He and his wife have two kids, Madison and Erik, my grandbabies. Malcolm died six years ago. Since then, it's just me and the Lord, and that's fine with me.

"I've been saved since I was a child, but I can't say that I really began to know the Lord until I was in my mid-thirties. That's when I *really* got to know Him. I wish I'd known Him sooner, but..." Beverly shrugged. "I'm thankful that it happened and I'm here tonight because I want to share my experience and help someone else."

Rose introduced herself next, sharing some of her wisdom after thirty-seven years of marriage. "It took me many years to discover the essence of marriage, and I'm still learning. There's lots of trial and error, and I'm here tonight because I'm a living witness to the fact that prayer changes things. It changes hearts and it changes circumstances. Don't let anybody tell you otherwise. Prayer works on husbands, kids, jobs, *everything, and everybody.*"

Adrian was not in the praying mood. She abruptly excused herself to go to the restroom and the meeting came to a pause. Once inside the small bathroom, Adrian took a long look in the mirror and had a bit of a self-talk. *I am not here because I want to save my marriage. I am here because I felt guilty about cancelling my housekeeping appointment at the last minute.* Against her will, Adrian's eyebrow twitched. She put one hand over the traitor-eye and then, to keep the other eye from twitching, Adrian covered it, too. As Adrian stood with her hands in the universal crying position, the tears seemed to arrive on cue. *Lord, what am I going to do?*

Adrian threw her head back and forced the encroaching tears to retreat behind her calm exterior. She grabbed a few squares of toilet tissue and used them to erase all traces of this mini-meltdown. *You'll get through this, girl.* Adrian pulled herself together, splashed a smile on her face, and returned to the circle so the meeting could continue.

Since Irma knew everyone in the room, she provided the link between old and young by taking her turn next. "I've been married to my husband, Harvey, for forty-two years. We have no children." Irma paused. "That was a major problem in our marriage, especially considering all the pressure that the church and society used to put on couples to have kids. But we're still together. Harvey and I have been through a lot together, but God is faithful. Marriage is a tough, full-time job. But it has its rewards."

Adrian looked down at her watch. *Only twenty minutes had gone by?*

Sonia spoke next. "My name is Sonia Riley. I'm senior account manager for a transportation firm. My husband, Kennard, and I have been married for almost ten years. I have six-year-old twins, a boy and girl. I'm here tonight because nine years ago, I made a big mistake and I need the Lord to show me what to do about it. My husband is gone because I asked him to leave, and I don't want him back if he can't be the man I need him to be."

Adrian felt like standing up and cheering. This Sonia had a backbone after all.

Rose asked, "What do you mean by 'be the man you need him to be'?"

Anger rose in Sonia's voice. "I need him to be a *man*. Help me raise these kids, help me take care of the house—everything. I need some *help*."

"Hmmm." Rose nodded.

"How's your relationship with Christ?" Irma asked.

Sonia thought about the question for a second. Coming from anyone else, she might have been insulted. Her relationship with Christ was her own business, at least up until now. "It's...it's okay. I go to church, I pray. I've been reading the book of Proverbs."

"That's one of my favorite books," Beverly said with a reflective smile. Then she dropped her head as she asked Sonia, "What happened when you got to the last chapter?"

"I got a little angry," Sonia admitted and enjoyed a laugh with this woman she'd just met. Irma and Rose laughed, too.

Adrian couldn't laugh because she couldn't quite remember what the last chapter of Proverbs was about.

"We'll talk about that later," Beverly whispered and winked.

"Adrian?" Irma prodded.

She rattled off her introduction, telling them that she, too, was in accounting. Then she ran through the current state of affairs, telling them all about staying in a hotel and the circumstances that led her there. She ended with, "I guess I'll be filing for divorce soon." Then Adrian smugly sat back into the covers on Irma's couch, folded her arms and settled her eyes on that irksome box of tissues.

"Well, okay, then. I think we've put it all out on the table," Irma said.

"I think it's important for you both to know that the three of us have been exactly where you are, felt exactly what you're feeling," Rose took over her part of the meeting. "And what you're feeling is perfectly normal."

Adrian's defenses retreated as she absorbed the women's affirmation. *Normal?* "How can it be normal to almost hate the person you once loved? I can't even look at his face without getting angry. I'm getting mad now just thinking about him." Adrian had to catch her breath.

Rose asked, "What are you afraid of?"

Adrian sucked air through her teeth and tipped an eyebrow. "I'm not afraid of anything."

"The source of all anger is fear, so let me rephrase the question." Inwardly, Rose asked the Holy Spirit for the right words. This younger generation of girls didn't like to admit weaknesses. They were taught by Rose's very own generation to be every woman. "When you think about Daryll, what comes to mind?"

All eyes were on Adrian as she rambled off a list of descriptive phrases. "Selfishness, smart-aleck comments, laughing and carrying on with everyone else but me." Adrian snapped her eyes open and wondered why their stares were blank.

"Okay, it sounds to me like you've got a bad case of the 'my-husband-ain't-making-me-happy-no-mo' blues," Beverly diagnosed.

"He sure ain't," Adrian agreed, Ebonics and all.

"That ain't his job," Beverly dispensed the medicine. "That's *your* job."

"How is that *my* job? What's the whole point of getting married if the other person doesn't make you happy?" Adrian argued with this old-school logic.

"Amen," Sonia affirmed as she and Adrian slapped hands. The two younger women sat and waited, eyes bugged and lips poked, for a response to top *that* one.

Beverly gave them a sigh and shook her head. "I hate to be the one to tell you this, but if your happiness depends on somebody else, you are in for a long, sad life. Matter of fact, if your happiness depends on *you,* that's a problem, too. You have to find your joy in the Lord. He's the *only* constant source of joy there is."

After a moment of quiet, Sonia spoke. "I think that, at some level, I do understand what you're saying. But in my case, my husband *steals* my joy. If he would just be a *regular* person, I could live with that. I can be happy all by myself. But he's...he's...."

"Irregular?" Rose played on Sonia's words, a welcomed spray of humor.

"I'm about to be irregular myself, fooling with him," Sonia said as she laid back fully on Irma's couch. The weight of Sonia's life lessened as she opened up and gave away pieces of her burden to women who were ready and waiting to help her bear this adversity. "I do think that I'm better off without him. He's about to make me lose my mind."

Irma pointed to a picture of herself and Harvey that was mounted over the mantel. They were dressed in black—Harvey with his 3-piece suit and Irma with a simple V-neck knit shirt and white pearls. In print, they were the perfect couple, with the passing of time having etched a series of hills and valleys into their aging faces. They had been married almost twenty years when they had that picture taken, and just about everyone who saw it said that Irma and Harvey were starting to look like each other. "That's real love," they'd say.

Irma, however, had different thoughts tied to that picture. She thanked God for the memory, as she now realized the importance of the story behind the photograph. "The morning that Harvey and I had that picture taken, oooh, we'd had it out! I mean O-U-T out! I got up early and made breakfast. He got up right after me, complaining that I had left the lamp on in our bedroom and woke him up from a good sleep. I told him that he should have just turned it off. We got to arguing and fussing so 'til I didn't even want to take the picture with him by the time ten o'clock rolled around. I mean, he was downright ornery that morning and I had a bad headache. By the time we finished fussin' and cussin' that morning, I would have just as soon gone to an attorney as a photographer. We had the picture taken and I was thinking, *This may be the last one we ever take together.*

"Well, on the way home from the photographer, we had a car wreck. Wasn't nothin' serious, just a little one. But when that car hit us on Harvey's side, I thought for a moment that he was hurt. And I started thinking about what my life would be like if Harvey was gone. It scared both of us so 'til we apologized for everything we'd said to each other all that morning. Every time I look at that picture, I'm reminded that life is short.

"Sonia, be careful when you say that your life would be better off without your husband because you never know how quickly that could become your reality," Irma warned.

Sonia looked Irma square in the eyes. "I could live with that, Miss Irma. I really could."

"You say that now, but I don't think you mean it," Irma kindly, optimistically disagreed.

"I understand exactly how you feel," Rose stood up for Sonia. "There were times when I wished my husband would leave this planet—or at least get hurt so badly that he couldn't do anything but sit up and think about how much me and the kids meant. I know, it was crazy. But I will say this," Rose steered the conversation back on track, "you are not the first woman to want to take the easy way out. The fact that I preferred my husband's death to a divorce says that I still valued the institution of marriage. I'll bet it means something to both of you, too. If it didn't, you wouldn't be here tonight."

Rose pointed to Sonia and Adrian. "The covenant you made was an agreement between you, your husband, and the Lord. God is faithful. He'll do His part. You're trying to be faithful to your vows. No, you can't make your husband act right. He is a grown man and he has a will just like everybody else. The Lord never overrides a person's will. But you *can* work with the other partner—the Lord—to play a bigger role in your marriage."

Adrian spoke for both of them. "So, what are we supposed to do? Just pray until God shows up and changes things?"

"Well, yes and no," Irma predicted. "God has heard your cries. He has seen all that you've been through. He has watched your marriages spiral down, down, down."

Sonia felt the sting of tears and Adrian crossed her arms again to put up a barrier.

Rose picked up next. "God cares about you, He cares about your marriage, and He cares about this covenant. God himself created the spiritual institution of marriage, so He knows how to make it work. You can't solve a spiritual problem with a natural solution; you'll be forever struggling like a beetle on its back. So, I don't want you to think of it as you praying until God *decides* to get involved. He's *already* involved because marriage was *His* idea to begin with. When you decided to honor Him with the commitment of marriage, He became a part of that covenant. It's time to give Him His space."

Beverly could see that, while Sonia and Adrian wanted and needed to grasp hold of these words from Irma and Rose, it was time to hear these things from the Word of God; hence, the seamless progression to Beverly's vital role in the meeting. "Did you bring your Bibles?" Sonia and Adrian shook their heads no, and Irma handed them the extra Bibles she'd brought from her church's lost-Bible collection.

"We want to share some scriptures that you can take and use, okay?" Beverly sought Adrian's and Sonia's agreement, and when they both nodded she was ready to proceed.

"I marked off several verses that I know the Lord wants us to visit tonight," Beverly said as she fanned through her Bible, stopping at the first sticky note in Ephesians. Irma unwrapped and distributed note cards to everyone in the room. Pencils and pens came flying out of purses, reading glasses were unfolded and put in to place, and these women delved into the Word of God to find out what He had to say about the situation.

"Our first stop is Ephesians 6:12 (NIV)," Beverly said. "When you have it, say Amen." Four amens later, she read, *"Our struggle is not against flesh and blood, but against the rulers, against*

*the authorities, against the powers of this dark world and against
the spiritual forces of evil in heavenly realms."*

"Think about it for a second. Write it down on one of the
cards," Beverly instructed them. Everyone in the room obeyed,
and as the Spirit of love flowed through their hearts, He also
brought revelation to Sonia and Adrian. The revelation came as
a shock to Sonia, and no sooner than she got it, she said out
loud, "So, this isn't about me and Kennard."

Rose's heart leapt with joy at the quickness of the Holy
Spirit. "Sonia, this is about good and evil. This holy institution
created by God is under attack by the enemy."

This news was not welcomed by Adrian. "Why do I have to
fight? I mean, I just wanted to be married and live my life
happily ever after. Is that too much to ask?" This whole *war*
thing was way over Adrian's spiritual head. There were women
at her old church who called themselves prayer warriors, inter-
cessors, whatever. It was all too extreme for Adrian.

"Well," Irma dangled the carrot, "you don't have to fight.
You can just let the enemy come into your home and snatch your
marriage and rip up the covenant. Or you can stand up and fight
for the glory of the Lord to be revealed in your marriage. The
choice is yours."

"Do you want to divorce your husband?" Beverly asked
point-blank.

"No, I don't want a divorce—I don't think anyone ever
wants to divorce. It's just the last option," she stated.

"So you don't want to get divorced, but you don't want to stay
married," Rose summarized the impossibility of Adrian's desires.

"Right," Adrian agreed, as silly as it sounded.

Rose nodded in complete sincerity. "I have been there and felt that. You don't want to be reconciled with your husband. You just wish the whole thing had never happened. Right?"

"Right," Adrian agreed again, amazed at how well Rose related.

"You know what? You can pray for God to restore your desire to be married to your husband in accordance with the covenant you made. That may have to be square one for you," Rose offered.

Adrian had never heard of such a thing—praying for the *desire?*

Irma sensed that Sonia and Adrian were on overload now. It would be the job of the Holy Spirit to churn these thoughts through their hearts and minds, to make the scriptures come alive for them in the way that only He can do on an individual basis. Beverly and Rose were both in tune, and they agreed that it was time to let the Lord do His thing.

"Well, ladies, we all have a lot to pray and meditate about," Irma said. "Take the verses that we learned tonight and read them. Keep the cards with you so that you can put this Word in your heart and on your lips, and by that I mean say it out loud. Speak it into your lives, into your homes."

Rose closed them in prayer and, with a peaceful silence, the women left Irma's home in thought and meditation.

When they had all gone, Irma collapsed in prayer, crying into the throw pillows on her couch. She felt drained, empty. She had given all of herself to Sonia and Adrian. "Lord, I thank You that Your grace and righteousness are new every morning."

She fell asleep in a matter of minutes.

CHAPTER 13

The last thing on Adrian's mind after Friday night's meeting was returning Camille's phone call. However, after the fourth missed call, Adrian had no choice but to call her back. "Hey, Camille, what's up?"

Camille announced, "We're getting married Sunday, girl. I need you."

"Sunday? What happened to next month?" Adrian screamed.

"I'm pregnant and I don't want to go another day in this pregnancy or this relationship being out of line with God. Sheldon and I realize that we've messed things up enough already. We need the Lord's covering. So, Sunday is the big day."

Adrian couldn't believe her ears. *Pregnant? How could somebody who is sleeping with someone they're not married to end up with the answer to my prayer? It's not fair, Lord!* Adrian was fit to be tied. She was angry with the Lord, with Camille, and with whoever this Dr. What's-his-name was.

"How could you let yourself get pregnant, Camille? You're smarter than this! And what makes you think that you have to marry him because you're pregnant?" Adrian fussed.

"I was not trying to get pregnant, believe me. The last thing I thought I wanted was to be tied to some snotty-nosed, whining baby. But I guess you could say that my maternal instincts have kicked in. I have accepted the fact that I will be a mother soon.

"As far at the marriage goes, I know that I don't *have* to marry him. We've talked about it and we both *want* to get married. We love each other very much and we both feel that family is important. Why is this a problem?" Camille questioned.

You weren't worrying about God's blessing when you made the baby, now were you? Why start now? Adrian couldn't answer Camille's question, at least not truthfully anyway. Despite the fact that she loved Camille, Adrian had come to realize that there was always an element of competition in their friendship. Right now, Camille was winning. She had the baby on the way, and she had a man who probably loved her and treated her well. All Adrian had was a lonely hotel room, a shaky job, and a couple of old ladies who were praying for the Jacobsen marriage.

"You think you can get away from Daryll so you can help me tomorrow?" Camille begged.

Of course Adrian was available; she was separated. Kind of. "I don't know. I'll have to see, Camille. Are you sure this is a good idea?"

"Adrian, check your calendar. Today is *not* spoil-my-friend's-wedding day. It's what-can-I-do-to-help-my-friend day, okay?"

Camille managed to rent a hotel suite, order a cake, round up a preacher and a singer, and stuff Adrian into a yellow taffeta dress that made her look like a banana with brown fur on top. Less than forty-eight hours after Camille's announcement, Adrian was standing before the preacher alongside Camille and Shervon...or was it Sheridan? Whoever he was, Adrian didn't know him from the man on the moon and she suspected the same of his new bride.

"I now pronounce you man and wife," the preacher proclaimed. Sheldon and Camille faced each other and drew a long, sultry kiss that made one of Sheldon's older relatives holler out, "Wait until tonight!"

Adrian suppressed her feelings long enough to congratulate Camille with a genuine hug. She wouldn't wish a bad marriage on her worst enemy, let alone Camille. The quaint, quick ceremony was just enough to remind Adrian of her miserable marriage—all those flowers and the wedding cake with that silly plastic couple kissing on the top layer.

For all the conversation and merriment taking place around her, Adrian couldn't take her eyes off of Camille's midsection. Camille was a happily married, happily pregnant woman, and Adrian was not.

Adrian returned to her hotel room and flopped the top half of her body back onto the rigid bed. This was it. Adrian was convinced that she'd messed her life up royally and irreversibly by marrying Daryll. Now she was stuck in this passionless deal that she'd made before God and witnesses. *But how is that my fault? How could I have known that it was going to turn out like this?* Adrian's tears fell from the corners of her eyes down to the cliff of her ears and then on to the bedspread—a trail of turmoil. She looked up at the ceiling between overflows and noticed how blurry things got just before the tears overtook the lip of her eyelids and flowed on to their final destinations.

Adrian had been here and done this before, many times. Growing up without a father was a painful experience, though at the time the rest of the world seemed to feel that it wasn't such a bad thing. Seemed like only one in ten families in Groverton had a steady man residing with his children, assuming they were his. That was more like one in twenty, perhaps. Adrian, her sister, and her mother all had different last names.

The first time Adrian could remember crying—*really* crying—was in fifth grade when Kesha Bachman (from a one-in-twenty family) made the remark on the school bus, "*Dang,* girl! Ya'll got *three* last names in one house! Girl, your momma is mixin' your family up!" It was probably something she'd heard some grown-up say. The kids in their immediate vicinity laughed nervously, hoping that Kesha wouldn't do a last-name count on their own households. Adrian gave Kesha a good beat-down after they got off the bus, and when Kesha said that she was going to tell her daddy, Adrian froze. Everyone had said that Adrian won the fight, but Kesha had delivered the most crushing blow. Who would Adrian tell? Maybe her mother, when she got home from work at 11:00 P.M. By that time, Kesha's father would have kissed Kesha's head and tucked her in bed. Adrian had to disagree with the crowd. Kesha won that fight.

That was the first time Adrian had cried herself to sleep over a man. Since then there had been many others. Lewis the liar, Melvin the manipulator, and Donnell the darn-near-demon. Adrian had kissed a lot of frogs before finding her Prince Daryll, who used to make her laugh so hard that she almost peed on herself. Perhaps that was one of the worst things about this pothole in their marriage. Adrian missed her *friend* Daryll; hanging out, whispering to each other at church, giving each other wedgies in bed at night. Aside from the baby issue, the lack of companionship was what she missed most. If Daryll couldn't be her friend again, maybe they didn't *need* to be together anymore.

Adrian's cell phone vibrated in her pocket and she answered it without looking at the caller ID. "Hello."

"You coming to midweek service?" Daryll asked. His voice was full of feigned concern. He was doing damage control, trying to preserve his family's church reputation.

"Hello, Daryll, it's nice to hear from you. Oh, me? I'm just fine," Adrian said patronizingly.

Daryll released the breath he'd been holding and played her game. "Hello, Adrian, it is nice to speak to you. Will you be attending church?"

"I'm not sure...."

"Forsake not the assembling of yourselves," Daryll quoted scripture.

"I was just about to say that I'm not sure *where* I'll be attending service, but rest assured that I will be in the house of the Lord. Amen?"

"You know I'm talking about *our* church? The church where we are active, *tithe-paying* members?" For a second, he sounded like a preacher, a charismatic man of the cloth. Daryll and his father had similar speech patterns when they voiced righteous indignation.

"Like I said, I don't know if I'll be there or not. But since you called, I will make an effort," Adrian answered, her voice bouncing higher at the end of each sentence.

Since the scripture didn't work, Daryll tried a different route. "So, you gonna make us another statistic? Another *broken* black family?" He waited for her response. "Adrian. Adrian!"

"This is hard for me, too!"

Time for strategy three: money. "It's going to be even harder when I call and close that credit card. I don't know what you think you're doing, Adrian, but I will not let you bring this family to financial ruin on account of this...thing you're doing. See how far you get without moola!"

Adrian stood up and walked to the sliding glass mirrored doors to watch herself argue with Daryll. It added a degree of attitude—not that she needed anymore of it. "You aren't the only one with finances, you know?"

"I'm the only one with a *job*."

"Are you threatening me?" she sucked in her stomach, leaned back, and put a hand on her hip for her own visual effect. "I've got money in places you don't even know about."

"We've worked too hard to build our status...."

"What about our love, Daryll? What about our family?"

"Adrian," Daryll took a moment to collect his thoughts. "I love you, okay? I show that by providing for you, making sure that you have the things you need, being faithful to you, and setting things up to ensure that if something happens to me, you won't ever have to struggle. That's my role and I've accepted it. Why can't you accept yours?"

Adrian let the phone slack a bit next to her ear as she took her right hand and stuffed it under her left elbow, kicking her weight to one side. "And what exactly is my role, as you see it?"

"To be my helper, to support me in supporting you." He said it like his definition of a wife was written in the Encyclopedia Brittanica.

Adrian softened a bit and walked back to the bed, leaving a good chunk of her attitude back at the mirror. She wasn't excited about Daryll's definition, but she had to admit: this was the longest civil conversation they'd had in a long time. Too bad she had to leave the house in order to get it.

"Why do you *really* want me to come to church, Daryll?" Adrian asked. She would have gone back home in a heartbeat if he had answered correctly.

"To keep us strong."

Anck! Wrong answer.

"We're *not* strong, Daryll."

"We could at least *look* strong."

Double Anck!

146

"I'm not into appearances, Daryll. That's what's wrong with people today—everyone acting like their marriage is perfect when what we really need to do is be honest and open up with someone about what we're going through so they can help us."

The thought was horrendous to Daryll. Tell somebody else his business? He'd seen first-hand how a person's sensitive information could quickly become the topic of gossip, mayhem, and blackmail. He was, after all, Juanita Jacobsen's child. "I think we can handle this in-house."

"How can we fix this *in-house* when the problem is *in the house?*" Adrian asked. "Stop being so proud, Daryll. Admit it: we have a problem and we need help!"

"Adrian, just come home. Or at least come to church. Everybody was asking about you Sunday and I really don't want to have to cover for you again." He said it like she was skipping school.

Adrian's Sunday had been crazy, with her and Camille running around like ants in an anthill, preparing for the last-minute wedding. She imagined that Juanita and Daryll must have verbally scrambled to quell the questions.

"I don't know if I'll be there."

"So, do you want me to go ahead and tell the truth; tell my parents and the church members that we're...I guess, separated?" Daryll tightened the screws.

Why did he have to say it like that? As much as Adrian wanted to keep things real, she was not ready to admit to their separation. It was too soon. Too soon to give it a name. Too soon to announce that they had called it quits. "I'll be there."

They held the phone for another ten seconds, both waiting for the other one to speak, realizing how close they had actually come to reclassifying their relationship. Daryll ended their conversation with, "I look forward to seeing you. Good night."

"Good night." Adrian pushed the end button on her phone and found herself in the exact same position as before—feet flat on the floor, top half of her body on the bed, looking up at the ceiling. The stream of tears started again, but this was a different set of tears, flowing from a completely different well in her soul. Before, her tears had come from the pool of her past and all of its painful memories. These new tears came from the present and, maybe, from the future. If she could get the present right, this well could bring tears of joy in the future. Maybe if the winds changed or the tide changed. *Change. Change.*

Adrian suddenly remembered what Miss Rose had said, "Prayer changes things." Things definitely needed to change between her and Daryll. Adrian laughed as she thought of all the television shows she'd seen and all of the little anecdotes she'd read here and there about how to make marriage work. All the experts said that most people's problems were simply a matter of communication; that if they just made time to go out on a date, pencil each other in on their calendars, have these civil little sit-down meetings of their minds, things would work out. Adrian and Daryll were beyond talking it out, working it out, increasing communication. There was no middle ground—there's no such thing as having half a child, no such thing as being a half-husband or a half-wife. Bottom line: things had to *change* or it was over.

Adrian imagined herself single—back in the game, dating, trying to land Mr. Right. Again. Wondering if this new Mr. Right would turn out to be Mr. Wrong in three years, wondering if her new husband(s) would bail on her and her children over and over again, the same way Adrian's daddy bailed so many years ago. Was it worth having kids if it meant that they'd simply repeat the pattern? She wondered who would break the cycle—her children? Her grandchildren? Herself?

Adrian spoke to the ceiling and hoped that her words would reach heaven. "God, You know. *You know.* I don't even know what to say. Whatever You have to do, just do it. I give myself and this marriage to You." She remembered the rest of what she was supposed to be praying. "Lord, while I'm at it, I ask that You would restore the desire for my husband and my marriage. In Jesus' name, Amen."

Adrian stayed there, with her eyes closed, and came very close to falling sleep. With the calmness came a whisper that she needed to pull out those scriptures that she and the other women had discussed on Friday night. Beverly's suggestion was that they read verses ten through nineteen of Ephesians, chapter six. Adrian obeyed and cried, obeyed and cried.

She cried for the loss of herself more than anything else. She was supposed to be Adrian the independent, Adrian who don't-take-no-mess. *Adrian—the prayer warrior? Adrian—the scripture-quoter?* Adrian never wanted to be *this* holy, but it looked as though she was going to *have* to be holy if she planned on staying married; remaining in an unhappy union was not an option. The change *had* to come. She read the verses out loud again, speaking them with authority this time. She lay back on the bed, mentally and emotionally exhausted. *The breastplate, the belt, the sword....*

CHAPTER 14

Daryll waited for Adrian in the parking lot so that they could walk into the sanctuary arm-in-arm. One look at Adrian and he knew that she wasn't playing fair—wearing that dress that always made him salivate. She was hitting below the belt.

Wednesday night at Mt. Calvary Baptist Church was reserved for either the seriously sanctified or the seriously scandalous; folks who wanted a midweek fill-up or whose lives were so lifeless that they came on Wednesdays to be first in line for rumors and hearsay. There were indeed those who had come just to see if Adrian would show up like Juanita promised, the same as she would have done for them if the shoe was on the other foot.

Adrian had barely stepped from her car when she heard Daryll's distinctive steps, strong and confident. He walked like he owned the path in front of him. She had always liked that sense of assurance about her husband. Now she wondered if she had mistaken assurance for arrogance.

"Hello," he spoke.

"Hi," Adrian answered while looking down to snap her purse closed. She took off in front of him, walking briskly toward the church building. Daryll kept pace and waved to other church members, calling their attention to the fact that he and Adrian were most assuredly entering the church together.

Inside the vestibule, Adrian took a detour to the restroom and Daryll waited for her. "Oh, she's in the restroom," he answered when a few members asked about Adrian. He even announced to Mother Newberry (head of the gossip board),

"Mother, sometimes I wonder why God made it take so long for you women to get ready. I've been waiting on Adrian for a good two minutes now." Mother Newberry nodded, took note of it. He half expected her to pull out a walkie-talkie and make an announcement over the gossip lines.

Adrian heard all of this from inside the two-stall restroom. As she dabbed lip gloss on her heart-shaped lips, she prayed and reminded herself that she was not there for Juanita or Mother Newberry or Daryll or even herself. She was there because of her commitment to the Lord, and she hoped more than anything that He would meet her that evening with a sound word from the preacher. She took a deep breath and opened her eyes, staring back at herself in the mirror. She hadn't meant to wear Daryll's favorite dress tonight, but she had. A simple, red, cotton number that puffed around her breasts, tightened at her waist and flung out at her hips, giving her more of a silhouette than she could have financed at a plastic surgeon's office. Adrian puckered her lips and smiled at herself. *I guess I am especially cute tonight.* She took a deep breath and opened her eyes, staring back at herself in the mirror.

Daryll kept his fingertips on Adrian's elbow as they proceeded down the main aisle and then took their usual seats down the pew from his mother. Juanita tipped forward, eyed the two of them for a moment, and then faced forward again, smoothing out the battery-powered blinking handkerchief on her lap. Daryll breathed a sigh of relief and Adrian decided not to pay this whole thing any attention. *I'm here for the Lord's purpose.*

She had spoken only one word to Daryll the entire evening— a simple greeting. Her only other words were those of praise as the choir sang *He'll Work It Out.* That was exactly the word that Adrian needed to hear, and she could hardly contain herself as the leader repeated the message in the simplest terms possible: *All on your job, He'll work it out. All in your home, He'll work it out.* Without thinking, without pretense, Adrian stood to her feet, raised her hands toward heaven, and cried out, "Yes, Lord! Yes, Lord! Work it out, Jesus!"

Daryll sprang to his feet, clapping to the beat. He didn't know what to say or do, so he hollered out, "Sang, choir! Sang!" He would have done a James Brown move if he thought it would take the attention off of his wife, who's cries sounded almost like a wounded animal. Daryll saw Adrian's sadness for the first time, along with the entire congregation. Suddenly, his wife was the one who was acting crazy at church, making a spectacle of herself and disrupting the entire service, putting everyone on edge and showin' out, as Juanita called it.

Juanita eyed her husband and motioned for him to take the pulpit so that the choir would end the song. Daryll Jacobsen Sr. ignored his wife, closing his eyes and swaying with the flow of the Spirit. Juanita got the organist's attention and stiffly crossed her fingers in the center of her chest. He succumbed to Juanita Jacobsen's request and slowed the music to a close. The leader took his musical cue and sang the final line, "I turned it over to the Lord, and He worked it out." The choir followed with, "Oh, yes!"

Adrian rocked herself back and forth, back and forth, during the service, dabbing at tears, crying, and tapping her foot. Seemed like she was having trouble keeping still since the choir sang that song. No sooner than she could wipe a tear, another one came to take its place. It reminded Daryll of the time that he cut his hand on a rusty can and had to get stitches. He'd wiped and wiped at the blood, but the wound wouldn't stop bleeding long enough to even gauge its depth. Daryll was as helpless then as he was now, with his wife's soul gashed open before everyone. Daryll didn't open his Bible during the sermon. He simply sat with one arm around Adrian, trying to perform two tasks at once; comforting Adrian and minimizing her movements at the same time.

When the service was over, Daryll whisked Adrian from the building and straight to her car. Adrian, still speechless, heard him say good-bye but didn't have the words to respond. Her spirit moaned, her soul groaned: *He'll work it out.* Back at the hotel, Adrian sang the song over and over again. *He'll work it out.* Though her heart ached and she had no evidence to support this idea that God was going to move in the Jacobsen marriage, Adrian simply leaned on His promise. It was all she could do.

She had just begun to undress when she heard a knock at her door. Quickly, she slipped the dress back over her head and looked through the peephole. On the other side was the last person she wanted or expected to see: Juanita Jacobsen with her bling-bling handkerchief and Bible in hand looking like she was ready to cast a demon out of her daughter-in-law.

She must have followed me here! Adrian unlocked the deadbolt and opened the door a few inches. "Yes?"

The words barely made it through Juanita's clenched lips, "We need to talk."

"Mrs. Jacobsen, I cannot talk to you right now...."

"But you can listen!" Juanita shook her white Bible in the air, the handkerchief streaming from her wrist. "I will not let you make a fool of this family. I don't know what's going on between you and my son, and I really don't care. I've got bigger fish to fry. Your father-in-law is about to be promoted to assistant pastor since Rev. Dewbo is moving back to his hometown in Mississippi. I will not have *you* up in the church making this family look unstable. You *have* to come to church 'cause of Daryll Jr., but you *don't* have to carry on the way you did tonight! Mt. Calvary ain't no holy-rollin' church like you went to back in Groverton.

"So, now, what's it gonna take to get you to *act* like you've got some class? I know you ain't workin'. You need some money?"

By this time, just about all the holiness had rolled right out of Adrian and she was ready to say some words she'd been holding back for the entire time she'd known Daryll. She remembered the first time Daryll had introduced her to Juanita and the cruel comments about Adrian's butt being big enough as "two booties" (message relayed courtesy of Daryll's sister, Victoria). Her first Christmas after getting married, Juanita had given Adrian a hat with a veil because she said Adrian was "blaspheming" by coming to the house of the Lord with nappy hair.

Like a pitcher preparing to let it rip, Adrian wound her mind around with those stories and tried letting the momentum carry through in words that she had never been bold enough to say before tonight. "You know what, Sister Jacobsen? No, I'm not going to give you the privilege of the word sister. *Juanita* is what I'm calling you tonight. I have always been respectful to you, I have always given you my other cheek, and all you've ever done is strike me over and over again. I know you don't like me because I grew up poor, I'm too black, I wear my hair the way God made it, and I'm just not the woman you want me to be."

Adrian's voice thickened with emotion. In the wake of her spiritual breakthrough, Adrian's harsh exterior was melting fast. She meant to tell Juanita off one good time, but the tender spot in Adrian's heart was still malleable from her worship and meditation, making her yelling sound more like whimpering and, quite frankly, puzzling Juanita.

Adrian ended their conversation without warning, closing the door in just enough time to keep from crying in front of Juanita Jacobsen. It was one of those times when Adrian wanted to beat her chest and say, "Toughen up, girl! Stop that stupid crying! Get your behind back out there and cuss her out!"

Adrian, instead, made the conscious decision to pick up on her victory song right where she'd left off. *He'll work it out. He'll work it out.* She didn't know what had just happened— like peace had rushed back in with this song. *He'll work it out. He'll work it out.* Adrian showered and put on her nightclothes, still humming.

Daryll's name and number illuminated the phone and Adrian just looked at it the first time. She was sure that Daryll wanted to talk about his mother, so she ignored his call. She waited a little while and then called him. *Might as well get it over with.*

"Hi, Adrian."

"Hello."

He sighed a weary sigh. "What happened between you and my momma?"

"Nothing. I just told her that I was tired of her mess."

"She seems to think that you need to see a psychiatrist."

Adrian laughed. "I just had a moment."

"Mmmm," Daryll's deep voice strummed through the phone and, for the first time, Adrian actually missed him. "I don't know what happened between you and my mother, but I do know that she's pretty upset. I guess I'll leave her alone for a few days. Let her cool off. She'll get over it. She always does."

Adrian wasn't so sure. "She never got over you marrying me."

"Don't sweat that. It's not really about you, Adrian. There's nobody good enough for me, according to my mother. You could have been the Queen of England and she wouldn't have found you fit," he laughed. Adrian wondered why it had taken him so long to give her this tidbit of information, this confirmation. Really, she was too tired to process the data.

"What have you been up to?" Daryll asked, sounding like he wanted to keep his wife on the phone.

Adrian thought for a second and then admitted, "Just working."

"Working?" he asked. "You found a new job?"

Adrian closed her eyes and confessed, "Daryll, I never lost my job. I just told you that to get under your skin."

Daryll gasped slightly but apparently didn't want to waste this precious time arguing. "Well, you definitely got under my skin."

"I'm sorry," she apologized. "I just got so angry. Listen, I'm tired right now."

"Can we talk tomorrow?" he asked.

"Yeah. Tomorrow."

Adrian put the phone back on the charger just in case Daryll decided to call back later. Already, she could feel the desire to talk to Daryll seeping back into her heart. She might have thanked God for this inkling of hope except that she couldn't shake the circumstances. He only called her because of this thing with his mother. She spoke out loud, something she always did when she was past sleepy. "Why do I have to move out of our house and stay in a hotel in order for him to listen to me?"

One final trip to the bathroom and Adrian would be on her way to a deep sleep. On her way back to the bed, she noticed something she hadn't before—something out of place. An envelope, under the door. "I didn't tell them I was checking out." Adrian finished her business and snatched the envelope off the floor. It was too thick to be a summary of stay. No return address, definitely not a commercial envelope; just something you'd get at the dollar store. Adrian opened it and fanned through the heap of hundred-dollar bills inside. "What on earth?"

Finally, she came to the simple, square, purple piece of paper from a desk cube.

Be sensible, be reasonable. Don't make a fool of us anymore. Stay away for as long as you need to pull yourself together! —Juanita

"No, she didn't!"

Adrian took the money out and counted it. Thirteen hundred dollars to show up at church, suppress her praise, and pretend that everything was fine between her and Daryll for the sake of the precious Jacobsen reputation. "She is crazy!"

So much for a good night's sleep. Adrian pulled out her notes from her meeting with the women's group and lost herself in the scriptures. At the end of the night, she wrote the Lord a note of thanks.

Father,

You are awesome. I felt You today, strong and clear. I want to know You more through all of this, no matter exactly how You decide to work it out.

Yours,
Adrian

CHAPTER 15

Sonia was too mentally exhausted *not* to go to church on Wednesday night. If she didn't get a boost of energy from the Lord, she would have to call in to work on Thursday. Maybe even Friday. After service, she and the kids ate in the fellowship hall as the congregation mingled, remarking on the minister's message and how quickly the twins were growing. Sonia was glad for the company and adult conversation.

The kids bounded into the car with their last burst of energy. They fussed about who would sit on each side, and Kamron came close to tears because he was having a hard time snapping his seat belt. Sonia smiled to herself, thinking that they probably wouldn't make it a mile before falling asleep. Sonia turned on the radio and listened to easy jazz, keeping the reality of home at bay for as long as possible. Upon reaching her street, she reached above her visor and pushed the garage door opener. That's when it punched her in the face. Kennard's Mustang was parked in the garage.

I know he is not in my house! Sonia pulled into her spot, lowered the garage door, and decided that it might be best to leave her zonked-out kids in the car for a few minutes while she went to see what business Kennard thought he had in the house. She rolled the windows down and stepped out quietly. On her way in, she touched the hood of his car. Cold.

Sonia swung open the door to her home like she was on the SWAT team. When she didn't see him in his usual spot—in front of the television playing video games—she called, "Kennard!"

No answer. "Kennard!" She had called his name so forcefully, she had to look back at her children and make sure that they were still asleep.

She found Kennard in their bedroom, laid out on their bed, asleep in a pair of boxers! She stomped over to him, "Kennard! Wake up!"

He grumbled, rolled over, and pulled the covers to his neck. She shook him again, determined not to stop until he explained his presence. "Kennard! Get up! Get up!"

"Dang," he hissed, "can't you see I'm asleep?"

"I see that you are asleep. Problem is, you're sleepin' in the *wrong* house in the *wrong* bed, Goldilocks!" Sonia yanked the covers off and stood back, crossing her arms and tapping her foot. Kennard needed to understand that his family was not a given; she would not allow him to walk back into their lives physically or emotionally without the understanding that things would have to be different. Hurt, angry, and confused, Sonia let out a final roar, "Get up out of my bed!"

"I ain't got nowhere to go," was his reply. He sat up on the edge of the bed now, hung his head down, and scratched the back of his neck. Sonia recognized this gesture from his past full of excuses. Kennard looked up at his wife and let his eyes plead the case for him.

Sonia gave him about as much sympathy as a front-desk government employee in a dead-end job. "That sounds like a personal problem to me."

"Victor's place is crazy. People coming and going, in and out all the time. I can't stay there anymore. I can't get a good night's rest before I go to work. That fool ain't got no food—I don't know how he's making it."

"Oh!" Sonia dramatized his epiphany by rolling her head over to one side. "*Now* all of a sudden you don't want to hang with the boys. *Now* you wanna have somebody cook your meals for you. *Now* you wanna come home to a *home*. I couldn't get you to stay home before, at least not without sitting up in front of the video game all day!"

Kennard shut her out. "Where are the kids?"

That was the last straw. "And *now* you wanna ask about the kids? Give me a break! You have *never* cared about our kids, Kennard! Don't try to use them now! When was the last time you took one of 'em to see a movie? To the park? Upstairs to tuck them into their own beds? Don't you *dare* ask about the kids tonight!"

"Whatever," Kennard waved her off. "I take care of my kids."

"Look, I don't know where you're going, but you've got to get out of here," Sonia ordered, "'cause if you think you can just waltz back up in here like you're the king and expect me and the kids to rearrange our lives and get hurt again...."

"Mommy?" Kelsi's voice froze Sonia's mouth. Sonia and Kennard turned to see both children standing in the doorway of the master bedroom. Sonia felt her stomach tighten as she wondered how long they had been standing there watching and listening.

"Y'all go on upstairs," Sonia could barely whisper.

Kelsi's heart quickened at the sight of her father, so much so that she couldn't even fathom her mother's soft command. Instinctively, she ran to her father and he, broken by his lack of sleep and order, embraced his daughter for the first time in months. The last time he had hugged her was at the insistence of Sonia when Kelsi gave him a Free Hug coupon she made at school for Valentine's Day. She'd made Kennard redeem it immediately, and Sonia supervised the hug, making sure that Kennard hugged her right.

Kamron was a bit more hesitant as he approached Kennard. Something in him knew that his momma wasn't happy and that his father had something to do with it. Nonetheless, he too was soon in his father's arms.

"Daddy," Kelsi whined, "I don't want you to leave. Please come home."

"Well," Kennard eyed Sonia as he spoke, "I wanted to come home, Kelsi, but your momma doesn't want me to."

No, he didn't just blame this all on me! Suddenly it was three-on-one. Kennard had one twin on either side, and six eyes were set on Sonia. But Sonia was quick on her feet; she had one for him. A great big smile came on her face as she made a proposal, "How about if Daddy stays here with you two. That would be great. He can get you guys up in the morning, take you to school, pick you up, get dinner together, make sure you get to bed—everything. How about that, guys?"

"Yeah!" Kelsi screamed.

Kamron wasn't so sure. "Where are you gonna be, Momma?"

"Momma will get a new place to stay. Y'all can visit me sometime."

Kamron scooted off the bed and let Kennard's arm drop to the side with a flopping, empty sound. He rushed to Sonia's hip and declared, "I'm comin' with you, Momma."

Kelsi sank deeper into her father's side. "I'm staying with Daddy."

The Rileys stood so decidedly, distinctively apart that someone could have taken a big black Sharpie marker and drawn a line down the middle. Kennard and Kelsi sitting on the bed, Sonia and Kamron standing near the door. Sonia didn't know what to do. If she gave in to Kennard's manipulation, the children would be happy, at least for the night. If she stood her ground, this would leave an indelible mark on her children. Somehow, this 100-pound ball had landed in her corner. If only the kids hadn't come in, she would have kicked him out with ease. But the thought of this impending scene with Kennard leaving while a heartbroken Kelsi cried herself to sleep changed everything. Everything.

Sonia simply left the room. That was all she could *think* to do under the circumstances. Kamron tried to follow after her, but Sonia pointed toward the staircase and he made the detour. Kelsi followed shortly thereafter.

In the guest room, Sonia slammed the door behind herself and paced from the window to the door. During her third trip back to the door, she caught a glimpse of herself in the dresser mirror. Though her hair had no reason to be out of place, it seemed to stand up on her head. One eye was tight, the other wildly open, her nose flared, her lips pulsed in and out. The woman in the mirror was flat-out frazzled; fried from one end to the other. Emotional electrocution. She pivoted back toward the bed and fell to her knees and tried to pray, but she could not find the words. In all her years, she had never been at a loss for words. Tonight, all she could do was let the Lord lift the lid off her mind and fill it with whatever He deemed necessary.

As she knelt there beside the guest bed replaying the scene that had just taken place in the master bedroom, she saw the door open ever so slightly. Sonia waited with her eyes barely opened but focused on the lighted triangle that formed between the door, its shadow, and the wall. God bless the child who dared to venture back downstairs that night. A second later, Sonia saw the tips of her husband's feet. Her heart stopped. Kennard obviously thought she was praying, and since she didn't know what to say to him nor was she in the mood to listen to him, she kept on acting like she was praying. He waited. Sonia waited. Finally, he stepped back and, instead of letting the door slam, he turned the knob, slowly pulled the door shut, and released the knob without a sound so as not to disturb his wife's talk with the Lord. Sonia released the air she didn't realize she'd been holding inside her chest.

After he'd left the room, Sonia tried to get her focus back on the Lord, but she kept wondering what it was that Kennard wanted to say. Well, whatever it was, the sight of Sonia praying had changed his mind.

Sonia made one quick trip back to their bedroom for a headscarf. Kennard's feet played peek-a-boo, and Sonia could barely think straight seeing those upturned size twelves sticking out from her covers. *Ooh! Help, Jesus! I can't stand him!* She'd said the prayer in frustration, originally, but it reminded her that she could actually get some help from heaven. Maybe she could find something in the Bible study that would help her through the night.

Sonia plucked her canvas tote from beside her bed and took it back with her to the guest bedroom. There, Sonia set her feeling aside long enough to pray and hear what the Lord had to say about relationships. She pushed thoughts of Kennard out of her mind long enough to meditate on scripture. If nothing else, the Word gave her a peace that allowed her to sleep that night.

Kennard felt Sonia standing over him bright and early the next morning. It took him a minute to focus and read the unmis takable message on her face: leave. He had hoped that her praying would change her mind and that she would let him stay until something could be arranged, whatever that something was.

Sonia watched him fidget; wiping his eyes, popping his neck, bending over and touching his toes. She waited until he was healed of all his morning ailments and then, just when he thought he had worn her down with his display, she calmly stated, "You need to leave."

"The kids don't want me to leave," he countered.

Sonia looked him all upside his head. "All they want is you to give them some of your time."

Kennard disagreed, "No, that's what *you* want—not them. I told you, when they get older, I'll start spending more time with them then, going to their soccer games, stuff like that. They're too young to hang with me right now."

"Why can't you adjust *your* lifestyle to *them,* Kennard?"

He started an instant replay of his fidgeting routine and Sonia knew that he was just trying to think up his next excuse. "You know what? You can do all this poppin' and yawnin' and stretchin' at Victor's house.

"And you know what else? Don't *ever* set my kids against me like you did last night. I will *not* be made into the bad cop. The only reason those two still adore you is because I have shielded them from your callousness with lie after lie—covering *your* behind. If I let the truth loose, if they really found how low they are on your agenda, it would break their hearts. But if you want to play dirty, I can go there with you. I can let them see the real you, and I can guarantee you all they'll *ever* want from you is money from now until they graduate from college. Are we clear?"

Kennard went through yet another round of stretching and popping. He hated it when Sonia stood over him and lectured him like a child. Granted, he might have been acting like one, but he couldn't remember which came first: Sonia treating him like a child or him fulfilling the prophesy.

"Well, we're gonna have to do something else. I pay bills here too, and I ain't movin' back to Victor's and I ain't movin' in with my mother or my sister. That's out."

"So what do you suggest we do—carry on as usual with me taking care of the kids and this home while you live like a single man doing what you want to do when you want to do it?"

He shrugged.

Maybe it was the result of her prayers, maybe it was in the way Kennard stopped his contortions and could do nothing but sit still. Either way, Sonia had a revelation: Kennard was just as lost as she about this whole marriage and family thing.

His eyes combed through the carpet looking for an answer, as though a resolution might lie in the cushioning beneath or maybe even in the home's foundation. Never had he imagined that it would take so much of him to be a father and a husband. Seemed like it would take *everything* to keep Sonia happy.

Sonia's hands dropped from her hips and hung helplessly at her sides. She trudged over to the foot of the bed and gave her husband another chance to understand her viewpoint. "I know that things are working for you, Kennard, but this relationship is not working for me. It's not fair to me or our kids or our future grandkids to set up this model for a marriage and a family. Your parents' marriage was jacked up, and my parents had a crazy marriage, too. Neither one of us knows what we're supposed to be doing. I just know that what we're doing now isn't right." And then she asked him a question that she hadn't asked him in all these years of fighting. "Is it working for you?"

Kennard lifted his brow and thought about it for a second. "I don't know. I don't know what it's supposed to be like, so I don't know if it's working or not. I know we've got food, shelter, and clothes."

"But do we have *love*, Kennard? Do you feel like I'm the person you want to grow old with? Are these the children that you want to come and visit you on Thanksgiving? Is this the home that you want to return to every day?"

"I guess we have two different ideas about family." He stuck out his lips and shook his head. Sonia prodded through silence. "I think that when you grow up and leave your parents' home, you close a chapter in your life and you go on. No looking back."

Sonia's face went sour. "Are you serious?"

He nodded, "Yeah, I mean, that's what I did. That's life."

"Well, I think that's okay if you're a...bird."

They couldn't help but laugh. Kennard rested his wrists on his knees and flopped his hands around as he spoke. "I think we both want different things, Sonia. I don't know that I could ever give you what you want or that you could ever give me what I want."

"What *do* you want?"

"I want to do what I want to do when I want to do it. I'm a grown man, and I shouldn't have to answer to anybody," he made his thoughts known.

"What about the marriage and the children you created? Do you feel that you should bear any responsibility whatsoever regarding your family?" Sonia asked.

Kennard reiterated, "I *am* responsible. I pay bills, I...."

Sonia stood up and threw her arms in the air. "Okay, we're back to square one. I'm going to work." She swished on out of the room and upstairs to get the kids ready. As she passed the upstairs guestroom, she had an idea. If she moved upstairs, she wouldn't have to see Kennard's face as often. This Plan B would have to work until something else came about. Kennard had called her bluff. He wasn't leaving the house, and he knew good and well that Sonia was not about to leave Kelsi and Kamron in their father's care.

Both kids inquired about their father and Sonia allowed them a few minutes to go down and say hello to Kennard before getting dressed. Their unconditional love for him was rather sickening, as far as Sonia was concerned. He coddled them and smiled at them as Sonia strained to listen from the kitchen. While she was busy packing the kids' lunches and making sure they didn't starve to death, he was in there all hugged up and having a good time. Mary and Martha.

He shooed the children out of the room so they could get ready for school. Happily, they bounded upstairs and proceeded to brush their teeth, wash their faces, and carry out the well-orchestrated regimen Sonia had established for them. Meanwhile, Sonia and Kennard dodged each other in their bedroom. Were it not for the morning news, the room would have been silent. Kennard was running late, but he did manage a good-bye as she left. Sonia grumbled a farewell back.

After dropping the kids off at daycare, she reveled in the routine of her new position at work. She would do mindless tasks today because her mind wasn't ready to tackle the things that would require her undivided attention. That was one of the things she liked best about her new job. There was mental flex-ibility. The first four hours of the day went by with little fanfare, and just as she prepared to go to lunch, she heard a gentle knock on the door.

Morris peeped into the small space between her door and the frame. "You up for a soulful lunch today?"

"Ooh, yes," Sonia said as she recalled her offer to escort Morris to a down-home lunch. She grabbed her purse and met him in the hallway. Within minutes, they were strapped into

Morris's BMW, a rental expenditure that would surely come across Sonia's desk at some point.

"Okay, did we *have* to rent you a BMW? What happened to economy class?" She fussed on behalf of the company's investors.

"It's in the budget, that's all I can tell you. Besides, I'm too big to be in an economy class car," he joked about himself and Sonia took note of his breadth again. He *would* look awfully funny all crumpled up in a tiny hatchback. At the parking lot's exit, Morris asked, "Which way?"

"To your right," Sonia motioned as she spoke.

They chatted freely about how things were going at work and about his upcoming weekend with his boys. Morris planned to fly out on Friday afternoon and come back late Sunday evening. "I'll be beat, I'm sure."

"My mom keeps my kids for me on Friday nights. I can't imagine my life without that time off at least once a week," she shared.

"So, what do you do on Fridays, then?"

"I rest!" she looked at him like he should have already known that answer. "It's the only time I get to really go somewhere and sit down."

"Well," he proceeded with caution, "don't you and your husband, you know, go out or do something together?"

"Not really," she spoke truthfully. No need in lying to the man.

"Mmmm," Morris murmured. "I ain't trying to be all in your business, but y'all need to go somewhere together. That's important."

Sonia laughed, "How you gonna tell me what's important. Aren't you divorced?"

"Yes," he confirmed, "which makes me an expert in what *not* to do."

Sonia took that as an invitation to ask, "So, is that what happened between you and your ex?"

"Basically, I stopped being her friend," Morris nodded and stared ahead in a mini-trance, apparently thinking about his regrets.

"Can't you all just work it out?" The hopeless romantic in Sonia woke from a long slumber. "I mean, obviously, you learned your lesson and you still care about her."

"I'd like to work it out, but she has moved on. She's involved with someone else and...I don't think I could ever get past...," he searched hard for appropriate words, "the thought of someone else being with my wife."

"That's completely chauvinistic, you know?"

"I know," he agreed, "but a man has his pride."

Sonia warned, "Pride goeth before a destruction."

"Proverbs sixteen and eighteen," Morris added.

"Hey now," Sonia rolled her neck, "my brother knows the Word?"

"I know the Word if I don't know anything else. My father is a preacher."

"Oh, we got a P.K. in the house," Sonia clapped her hands and stomped one foot, imitating the soulful sounds of a church in praise.

Morris unleashed a voice that could have come only from years and years of singing at his father's church. "I say the Lord's been good to meeee, all the time."

Sonia smiled and gave the brother his props as she pointed for him to turn left. "You can saaaang, Morris! I'm talkin' about throw down!"

He shrugged, smiled, and looked away from her. "I used to love to sing. I just haven't had much opportunity lately. Working, you know?"

"Sometimes, people work on the wrong things," she counseled him as though she had known him all her life.

"Look, you just need to work on going out with your husband on Friday nights so maybe you won't end up like me," he teased her.

"Point taken," she assured him, and then it was her turn to look away. *Point taken.*

The restaurant was one of those hole-in-the-wall joints where, inevitably, the food was better than any ritzy "atmosphere and experience" eatery. All they needed to experience was barbecue, and Alderman's was just the place. "Lawd, have mercy," Morris said as he rolled his eyes in baked bean bliss. "Sister, I'm about to hurt myself up in here."

"Don't hurt yourself." Sonia took note of how quickly he ate—a telltale sign of overeaters; something she herself had overcome shortly after giving birth to the twins. "Slow down. The food ain't going nowhere."

"My momma used to say that all the time," he recalled.

"Well, it is true. I put on quite a bit of weight after my kids were born, and it took me almost two years to take it off. I know my way around the food rules."

Morris listened with all his heart. For as much as he enjoyed being a big man with exceptional fashion sense, he would gladly trade in his Big&Tall credit card for one at The Gap. "How did you do it?"

"I started drinking more water, eating more fruits and vegetables. And I worked out like crazy for about a year. Exercise is invaluable when you're trying to lose weight. There's just no substitute."

He took another swig of sweet tea and shook his head. "I can do the water and the fruits, but that exercise is a deal-breaker. I can't get my big ole self on any of those machines. I tried to get on that...what's that thing—Lipton rider?"

"*Elliptical* rider," Sonia corrected him with a smile.

"Whatever."

Sonia couldn't help but laugh harder. "Lipton rider," she teased, and Sonia felt a flicker of electricity when Morris's eyes passed over hers.

"I don't care if it's the Nestea rider, I ain't gettin' on it," Morris joked, and Sonia found herself laughing harder than she had laughed with a man in a long time.

CHAPTER 16

Irma, Rose, Beverly, & Deborah

Deborah Cole joined her friends at poolside and inched into the water as they waited for Jenny. Rose was the first to hug her, Beverly second, and finally Irma. It had been at least a month since Deborah met with the group, but that was normal. Since Peter's heart attack, Deborah had been very busy taking care of her husband. She hardly had time for her church duties, let alone herself. Seeing Beverly, Rose, and Irma if only for a little while made Deborah think of better days gone by and hope for better days ahead, when she could again meet regularly and catch up with the group.

When they first met at a Watch-Your-Weight meeting more than fifteen years ago, Deborah was their group leader. Each week, she tried her best to follow the script as outlined in the leader's notes, but Deborah found it hard to talk about hope, motivation, and keeping the faith without mentioning her Lord and Savior, Jesus Christ. Evidently, someone got offended and reported her to the national office. Deborah was asked to relinquish her position as group leader, something she did with no regrets. She later told her newfound friends, "I've been fired for worse!"

From time to time, Rose and the girls stopped by the Cole household to pray for Peter's and Deborah's strength, and to drink tea (Deborah seemed to always be drinking tea). "Part of my English heritage, I suppose," she answered when Beverly questioned her once.

Beverly laughed. "Have you got truffles, too?"

"Not this time. But next time, I will," Deborah had responded as she mentally noted the promise. And she made good on it, too.

Jenny apologized for her lateness and plunged right into the pool so as not to waste anymore of her clients' time. In her thirty-something, rush-rush world, every one second lost felt like ten seconds lost. She had not yet learned that everything always works out for the best, and people who understand that concept don't sweat the little things, least of all the godly women in this class. They would gladly wait for her if it meant that she would arrive safely.

"Good morning, Jenny!" Rose welcomed her and they all encircled Jenny in a group hug. Jenny apologized for her tardiness and quickly got the workout underway.

"Ladies, let's get some movement going while we're having this talk, okay?" She started them off with an underwater jog. Watching the older women frolic around the pool was like watching carefree youths playing at the park, and Jenny was hopeful that one day she would have weathered friendships to enjoy.

Following the workout, the Senior Swimmers wrapped themselves in the warmth of the hot tub. They breathed easier now and relished something comparable to dessert after eating less desirable vegetables. "What's been going on, ladies?" Deborah asked, her arms stretched out and propped up on either side of her body.

Rose talked about her grandchildren, Beverly talked about her nieces, Irma talked about her in-laws, and Deborah filled them in on Peter, who was doing better. "I know the prayers of the righteous avail much," Deborah referenced James 5:16.

"Yes, they sure do," Irma agreed.

"And speaking of prayer, we're meeting with a couple of young clients of mine whose marriages have been under attack."

"Really?" Deborah perked up. "How's it going?"

"So far so good," Beverly was the first to speak, surprising Rose and Irma. "But I guess we'll see tomorrow when we get to talking about the scriptures I gave them to look up. We'll see how dedicated they are to getting in the Word."

"Oh, Bev, you always were a teacher and a prophetess," Deborah referenced one of the spiritual gifts given to women in the body of Christ that they had all studied in a Bible study at Beverly's church a few years before.

"And you were always a mercy-giver," Beverly cut her eyes at Deborah, and then they chuckled at each other. Those two always seemed to keep the see-saw balanced.

"I'll tell you what, Theodore and I could have used some help when we first got married. Sometimes I think we could use some help now," Rose laughed.

"You are so right!" Deborah interjected. "Well, I'll be praying that God will open the hearts of these women to receive what He has to give them through you three. I'm sure these families will be blessed because of your obedience."

Irma remembered how often she had leaned on her friends for encouragement during difficult times, and she hoped to be able to set up many more young women in similar, godly friendships. However, the upcoming meeting with Sonia and Adrian was a source of concern. She had been praying but had not yet received an agenda from the Lord other than to review last week's scriptures. Suddenly, a thought flashed into her mind. "Hey, Deborah, doesn't your church have a mentoring group for young women?"

"Yeah. It's the Titus2 Women's Ministry," she recalled.

"Other than the Bible, do they use any certain format or a certain book to guide them through the ministry?"

Deborah looked toward the ceiling in thought. "I think there's a whole line of Titus2 materials that they use. I can't think of the publisher, but I'm pretty sure you can get it at our church's bookstore."

"Oh, that would be great," Rose sighed. She, too, had been thinking about a course of study. "With Beverly's expert knowledge of the Word and some kind of book that we can all read during the week, I know we'll see God's hand move!"

Irma invited Deborah to come to the next meeting, but Deborah had to turn down the opportunity. "I've got too much on my plate already, but I can assure you that I stand in agreement with you for the ministry and for these families."

"I understand," Irma nodded, wishing that she had what it takes to so gracefully decline a proposal.

With that, they all prayed for Friday night's meeting.

On her way home, Irma stopped by the bookstore at First Baptist to pick up the Titus2 Ministry book on marriage restoration. The man behind the counter introduced himself as Bob and when Irma told him that she was looking for the Titus2 book on marriage, he asked her a series of questions that narrowed down the choices. "Is this for single women looking to get married?"

"No, sir. They're already married."

"Happily married or miserably married?" he asked.

"Miserably married."

"Adultery or no adultery involved?"

Irma thought that he was pulling her leg. "What?"

"Well, they've got books on what to do after a wife's affair, after a husband's affair—they've got it all."

Irma went on her gut with that one. In her years as a house-keeper, she had seen many things. Adultery peeks out of the trash can, the laundry, the sock drawer. "No, no adultery."

"Okay, here we go." Bob kneeled down to the bottom shelf of books in the women's section. His knees gave a loud creak and Irma wondered if she would have to help him back up. "'Titus2 Women's Ministry Series: Lord, Fix This Marriage!'" We've got one leader's guide and four group members' guides left."

"That's exactly what I need!" Irma gasped.

"I hear that all that time, ma'am. All the time," he smiled slightly. Bob grabbed the books in one hand and then stead-ied himself by holding on to a shelf, slowly resuming a stand-ing position.

Irma took the books from him and was surprised to find that they were booklets. Couldn't have been more than thirty or forty pages each, maybe a few more for the leader's guide. She hoped that the length was a sign that the information would be concise and concentrated for maximum benefit quickly. Neither Adrian nor Sonia had much wiggle room right now.

CHAPTER 17

Kennard spent another night in their bedroom and Sonia spent another in the guest room. The kids thought the whole arrangement was dandy, but their parents were biding time. Their words were clipped; not more than ten in a day's time.

Mid-morning, Irma called Sonia at work to make sure that she would be coming to the meeting later in the evening. "Yes, ma'am. I'll be there." Sonia suddenly remembered that she still had a few more verses to research. Between work, the kids, and Kennard, she had not spent as much time in the Word as she had hoped during the previous week. If she rushed to get the kids ready for her mother's house, she could get at least half an hour to study.

No sooner had Sonia set her mind to finish work a little early so she could get to the scriptures, her phone rang, bringing her news that cut her work day even shorter. "Mrs. Riley, Kamron is in the nurse's office. He lost his breakfast in the library, and he says that his stomach is still aching."

"I'll be right there." Sonia barely had the words out before she threw her purse over her shoulder. She stopped at her supervisor's office and respectfully informed him that she was leaving early. Times like these, Sonia didn't bother to ask for permission. "I'll take half a day of vacation," she told John.

He exhaled audibly. "We really need you around here, Sonia."

"I'll see you Monday." Sonia wasn't paying John any attention. If Elizabeth in public relations could take a month off for a tummy tuck and Don in public relations could have his entire schedule rearranged to accommodate his cat's radiation therapy, this mother could leave early one day to see about her sick child.

She had made it all the way to the parking lot on autopilot when she heard Morris, who was parked next to her, ask, "Early lunch?"

"No. My son's school called. He's sick. I'm leaving for the day."

"I'm sorry to hear that. I hope he feels better soon," Morris said, giving his regards.

"Thank you, Morris. I'm sure he'll be okay. You have a great time with your boys."

"Will do."

Sonia drove to the children's school and was immediately reminded of her last visit to the campus. Same bench parked outside of the main office, same glass trophy case displaying a copy of a check from the local Optimist club. The floor's white, shiny tiles reminded her of a hospital, but thankfully the faint smell of fresh paint and the steady hum of the children in the cafeteria put her at rest. Sonia hated hospitals ever since the touch-and-go days when the twins were born. She'd spent hours pacing, looking down at hospital tiles through the blur of her tears, and praying to God that He would spare her son. "Thank You, Lord," she said softly as she entered the school office. She thanked Him as often as she remembered how far the children had come.

After a thorough maternal examination, Sonia figured that Kamron had a virus. She checked him out of school and made a quick stop at the drugstore. She plopped Kamron on the bench near the drugstore's entrance and told him to wait while she gathered liquids, popsicles, applesauce, and something to relieve the stomachache. The items would cost a lot more here, but at least Kamron could stay in one spot and she could keep an eye on him via the security mirrors strategically placed throughout the small store.

After purchasing the items, they went on home. Sonia proceeded to park in the garage when she saw Kennard's Mustang again. Only this time, it was midday. *What is wrong with him?* Sonia couldn't imagine what he was up to now. She was bombarded with the worst thoughts. *He had better not be in there with that old crazy Victor. Ooh! And don't let me come up in here and find another woman. That's all I need to get my walking papers after I beat 'em both down.*

"Momma will be there in a minute, baby. Go on up to your room when we get inside, okay?" Sonia instructed Kamron as she helped him out of his seat belt. Sonia rammed through the door to her house like Rambo. And there Kennard was, busy trying to slay a giant green figure in a video game.

Sonia was both disappointed and relieved. A part of her had hoped that this was her chance at the last straw. But, amazingly, there was also a part of her that was glad to know that Kennard was still Kennard. Sitting up doing what he always did. "Kennard, why is there a big grown man sitting up in my living room playing a video game in the middle of a weekday?"

"They changed my schedule," he said as he jerked to one side to avoid an animated bullet.

"Since when?"

"S...s...since today," he stuttered through a response, his attention focused on the game.

"Exactly when will you be going back to work?"

He pushed the pause button and looked his wife square in the face. "What difference does it make? You don't talk to me, I don't talk to you."

Kennard had a point. Him being there didn't change anything one way or another for Sonia. She just didn't like the thought of him being there when she wasn't home, especially not if he was going to be playing video games all the while. He could do *that* at Victor's.

"Why are *you* home?"

"Kamron's sick."

"Oh," his voice trailed off.

"Is that all you have to say—*oh?*"

"What do you *want* me to say?"

"Say 'What's wrong with him?', say 'What can I do to help?', say 'Would you like for me to go pick up Kelsi at daycare so you can stay home with Kamron?' That's what you can say." Truly, none of those thoughts had come close to crossing Kennard's head. "Why can't you *think*, Kennard?"

"I *do* think; it's just not the same way that you think. If you left your job to go pick up Kam from school and you didn't call me to see if I could help you in any way, I figure you've got it covered," he shrugged.

"You've got all these strategies for this *stupid* video game, but you ain't got none for me and these kids. It's not that hard. Just look around and see what needs to be done and then do it."

"You're asking me to read your mind, Sonia," he said as he stated his own mind and resumed the video game.

"Do I have to spell everything out for you?" she asked.

"If you want me to do it your way, yeah."

"Okay, how about this: My mother will be keeping Kelsi tonight, but Kamron needs to stay home. Would it be possible for you to stay home with Kamron tonight?"

His neck snapped up. "Where are you going?"

"I have plans."

He paused the game again and looked at her with jealousy etched across his face. "What *plans?*"

"The same kind of plans you have—plans with other people."

"What *people?*"

"People that I know."

"Whatever, Sonia."

He turned back to the game, but he didn't push the button to continue playing. The idea of Sonia having plans and carrying out those plans while he was at home with their son was sinking into his head. Stay home with his child while his wife went out doing...doing whatever! Oh, no. That was not going to work. The men in his family had taught him better than to let a woman make a fool of him! Plenty of times, Kennard had listened to his Uncle Clyde and Uncle James while sitting out in the garage listening to Motown hits and playing dominoes. They had schooled him in the fine art of dealing with women. He could hear his Uncle James now, "I wouldn't *let* my woman run the streets while I was at home babysitting. You must be outta your mind if you 'gon stay home with these kids while she's out with some man—she got you lookin' like a sissy!'"

Kennard raised his head high and announced to himself as much as Sonia, "I'm not watching him tonight."

"What do you have to do?"

"I've got plans, too."

Sonia waited until he looked her in the eyes. "You know what? When you leave tonight, you need to take everything with you. Take your clothes, this video game, your DVDs—everything."

"Whatever."

"Whatever my foot! If you can't get over yourself and your plans long enough to help me, then I really don't need you." This was one of those moments where Sonia wished she had something quotable to say; something that would stay on his mind from this day until the day he lay on his deathbed thinking about all the mistakes he'd made in his life. She wanted it to stick to his soul and eat him from the inside out from this moment forward, but nothing came to mind and she was running out of time. *The Color Purple.* Sonia said, "Until you do right by me and these kids, everything you try to do is going to fail."

Kennard recognized the line. "Okay, Celie," he sighed and turned off his game. He left the house like a *real* man. His uncles would have been proud.

Sonia was all too happy to call Irma and inform her that she couldn't make it to tonight's meeting. *Maybe the prayer isn't working.* Well, then again, Sonia had to admit that she had not done as much praying as she'd hoped to do since the last meeting. When it came down to it, the whole truth was that the prayer wasn't working because Sonia wasn't doing it consistently.

No need in trying to show up at the meeting and act like she'd been doing all the right things. No need in discouraging everyone (particularly Adrian) with the fact that things had gone from bad to worse. Maybe if she could just get a week away from everyone, things would go better. Besides, she wasn't about to take Kamron out and get everybody sick. She laughed at the thought. Kamron would make everyone physically sick and she had the potential to make everyone spiritually sick.

Sonia knew better than to wish for Irma's voice mail. She'd have to tell her and have an answer ready for the question 'why?' And when Irma asked that 'why?', Sonia offered the only excuse that Irma might actually buy, "Kamron's sick, and I really don't want to get him out."

"Oh, baby, is he all right?" her voice a whisper of concern.

"Yes, ma'am, he'll be fine."

"Well, if you don't mind, I'll come by tomorrow and drop off a book for you so that you can be looking over things until we meet again. I won't even disturb you. I'll just put it under the doormat. Is that all right?" Irma asked.

This woman is determined to see my marriage mended! "That'll be just fine, Miss Irma. Thank you."

"Well, since we're going to miss you tonight, I'd like to pray with you."

Sonia had been trained to never turn down prayer. "I certainly welcome it."

"Father God," Irma began through the phone, "we bless You for who You are, and we come to You thanking You for all Your many provisions. Please be with Sonia this week as she seeks You for guidance and direction in this marriage. Let Your name be glorified as Your will is revealed in this situation. And now we come to You thanking You in advance for the healing of Kamron. Thank You that Jesus died on the cross to provide healing for Your children. Touch his little body and send him back to his usual rippin' and runnin'," she laughed gently. "In Jesus' name, Amen."

"Amen."

"We'll see you next time, hear?"

"Yes, ma'am. Good night."

The prayer that was intended to make Sonia feel better made her angry. Righteously angry because she felt the enemy cheating her out of this meeting, her last lifeline. The enemy, of course, had presented himself in the form of Kennard Riley who, with one selfish act, had turned what might have been an otherwise productive evening into a bust. Even with Kamron's illness, God had worked it out so that Kennard could stay home with the kids—but no! Kennard was too busy.

Sonia thought of calling her mother and asking her to come over to the house and watch both kids while she went to the meeting. Mrs. Gibson would have been glad to fuss over her grandbaby, but she would have questioned Sonia regarding her whereabouts. One thing would lead to another and Mrs. Gibson would have learned the true nature of the meeting and been terribly offended to know that Sonia was seeking marital advice from other women. Another can of drama waiting to be opened.

Sonia had enough working drama with Kennard at the moment. Sonia decided to go ahead and call her mother to say that the children would not be coming over.

"What's wrong?" Clarice asked.

"Oh, Kamron's got a little stomach virus."

Clarice's motherly instincts went to work. After interrogating Sonia about Kamron's symptoms, she gave her medical advice. "You keep him home 'til at least Tuesday. Bring him over here if you need to."

"We'll see," Sonia half-accepted the advice. Sonia wished that she could tell her momma what was happening in her life. Clarice could be so helpful when it came to her grandchildren. Why couldn't she help her own daughter? Sonia pressed her lips together to keep from crying.

"Sonia, you there?" Clarice asked.

Sonia responded before she had a chance to recover, "Yes, I'm here."

"Baby, what's wrong?"

Sonia regained the even flow of her voice and replied, "Oh, nothing. Kennard and I had a disagreement."

"Well, you know how men are," Clarice dismissed Sonia's concerns. "Sometimes you've just got to go with the flow. It's a small price to pay to keep the family together. Ooh, chile! I learned real quick—a man is gonna be a man. Baby, you hold on to the Lord's unchanging hand. He'll give you peace like a river. Peace that surpasses...."

Sonia couldn't take this farce anymore. "Momma, when was the last time you talked to Daddy?"

"Um...," Clarice tried to remember, "it's been...let's see, the other week...."

"That's what I'm talking about, Momma. You and Daddy have been married for thirty-five years."

"Thirty-*six*."

"Thirty-six," Sonia stood corrected. "I understand what works for you and Daddy. But I want something more. I want to *see* my husband and *talk* to him and *enjoy* him on a regular basis. I don't want what you and Buddy have. I want to break that mold."

Clarice clicked her tongue between her teeth. "It ain't a *mold,* Sonia, it's the way things *are* between men and women."

"Do you really think that's what God had in mind when He created marriage?" Sonia asked.

"Well," Clarice created a diversion, "there was only one perfect man who ever walked the earth, and they pierced Him in His side, put a crown of thorns on His head, and crucified Him on the cross. And He never said a mumbling word—just hung His head and died! Oh, but on that third day, He rose from the dead! All power in His hands!"

No disrespect, but Sonia had to bring this sermon to a close, "All right, Momma. I'll speak to you later."

"Well, at least I *did* teach you to call on the name of Jesus," Clarice said.

Sonia had to agree. "Yes, you did, and I thank you for that, Momma."

"Okay. Well, you take care of Kamron and let me know if you need anything."

Sonia hung up and vowed never to go there again with her mother. If Clarice was happy with her life, who was Sonia to point out the problems?

Okay, get back on track. Think. Think. How can I still make the meeting? There had to be a way to work this out. Praying with Irma and listening to her talk to the Lord despite the fact that Sonia herself wasn't doing right reminded Sonia that others were interceding on her behalf. Though Sonia was sure they would all understand her predicament, she couldn't help but feel that she had somehow let them down by first of all not praying, and secondly, by not showing up for the meeting.

Sonia had an idea: she could invite the women over to her home for the meeting. As long as she kept Kamron upstairs, the women would be fine. She could pop in a Disney movie and Kelsi would be set for at least ninety minutes. *Yes!*

As she prepared to call Irma with the proposal, Sonia prayed that her home wasn't too far out of the way for the ladies. Irma was thrilled with the idea and agreed to call Sonia back as soon as she got in touch with everyone else.

Irma started with the one who would be most opposed. "But, Bev, her son is sick! I'm not gonna argue with you anymore. You pray about it and I'll call you back in five minutes. If the Lord tells you not to go, then I'll accept that. Otherwise, I *do* hope you'll be more considerate."

Irma hung up with Beverly and called Rose and Adrian. They readily agreed to the change of location. As she promised, Irma called Beverly again in five minutes.

"Bev?"

"Yes."

"What do you say?"

"I *said* yes."

"Great. Be here at 6:45, please, ma'am," Irma teased.

"Bye."

Irma laughed at her friend as she set her phone on the receiver. In all these years, Beverly's attitude was still as stubborn as it had always been. Beverly could play a tough role, but when it came down to it, she'd do anything for you. Pray for you, cook for you, give you a ride where you needed to go, give you her last dime and never ask for it back. That's what love is all about—accepting people as-is, without a warranty. Thinking more about their good points than their negatives. Irma only hoped that she could help Sonia and Adrian understand this truth.

CHAPTER 18

Irma parked next to Rose. Then she turned off the engine and gave Beverly one last thank you for coming. Beverly bowed her head and thanked Irma for her persistence. "I need to be here as much as anyone else," she admitted.

"I know that's right," Irma rolled her eyes. Beverly slapped Irma's arm and they both walked to the doorway arm-in-arm.

Sonia met them with bare feet, so Beverly asked sarcastically, "Would you like for us to remove our shoes?"

Sonia gave a snarly smile and replied, "Oh, no. I have two kids—there's nothing they haven't already tracked into this house. I'm just barefoot for the sake of comfort." And comfortable she was with her Capri-length jeans and a faded yellow Gibson family reunion T-shirt.

When Sonia made no effort to take them on a grand tour of her home, Beverly sent her emotional guards home and allowed herself to get over the fact that she was meeting in this young woman's home. Sonia led them to the family den where Rose was waiting. As they finished their greetings, Adrian arrived at the door and the processional briefly replayed itself before they got down to business.

Irma opened the meeting with prayer and then Beverly led a discussion about the verses from the previous week. Both Adrian and Sonia were familiar with the verses, yet they both had to admit that they hadn't spent as much time in the Word as they'd hoped. Adrian had a busy week at work, and Sonia said something about being a "single parent" now.

Beverly rolled her eyes and said, "Those excuses are not acceptable." Beverly folded her arms, cocked her head to one side, and pressed her back into Sonia's couch. These girls were half-stepping. "If *I'm* giving up *my* Friday evenings to help *you* young ladies with *your* marriages, *you* need to do *your* part."

Sonia and Adrian sat like two children being questioned in the principal's office. Their reasons were completely valid, as far as they were concerned. Adrian shrugged and spoke for herself and Sonia, "Well, I don't know what else to tell you."

Beverly unfolded her arms and asked, "Did you go to the restroom this week?"

"Huh?" Sonia asked.

"Did you go take time out of your busy schedule to go to the restroom?" Beverly asked again.

"Yes," Sonia replied.

"And did you eat?" Beverly asked.

"Yes," said Adrian.

"Then you had time to meditate on the Word. I don't care if you have to take your Bible to the toilet seat with you, you do it. So long as you are still handling your basic biological functions on a daily basis, you have time to ingest the Word. It's that simple," she said point-blank.

Sonia and Adrian were dumbfounded. Talking to the Lord on the toilet seat?

"What Beverly means," Rose tried her best to translate, "is that you can't *make* time or *find* time to spend in the Word. You have to *take* time."

Though she was in her own home, Sonia felt like she'd just gotten a whippin'. Actually, she would have preferred a whippin' over Beverly's mini-lecture. These women were serious about this Word, and Sonia realized that if she wanted to hang with them and go deeper in the Lord, she would have to get serious, too. She felt like saying "Yes, ma'am," but uttered, "Okay," instead.

Adrian nodded, too, and added, "So that's the key, huh?"

"There's no substitute for studying and meditating on the Word of God," Irma said. "Absolutely no substitute for letting the scriptures wash over your mind throughout the day."

"I tell you what, though," Rose smiled. "Once you start spending that time with the Lord every day, you will wonder how you ever made it before. And during those times when you call yourself too busy for the Word, things will get so crazy that you'll *run* back to the Word."

"I know that's right," Beverly sighed.

Sonia and her guests heard tiny footsteps before they saw Kelsi's head above the stair rails. "Come on down, Kelsi," Sonia ordered. Kelsi happily flew down the last few steps and took center stage in the midst of the women's group. Irma was the first to get a hug. Kelsi was passed around the room like a trophy. Sonia was last in line, and she gave Kelsi a light pat on the behind, telling her daughter to stay upstairs unless she needed something.

"Well," Irma changed the course as she pulled booklets from the canvas tote bag she'd brought along, "I picked up something today that I think will help us along." Irma distributed the Titus2 books to the group and waited for their reactions.

"Oh! This is the one Deborah told us about!" Rose shrieked. "Oh, Irma, what do we owe you?"

Irma waved her hand. "Nothing, girl. It was my pleasure." Sonia and Adrian both tried to pay Irma, but she refused their money, too. Irma's payment would be to see their families whole again.

After they had all finished previewing the book, Irma flipped to the first page of her leader's guide and read the brief introduction to the entire group. Sonia felt as though she could have done a holy dance right then and there. Finally, someone who knew exactly what she was talking about. Someone who understood the sinking sensation of a marriage slowly going down, down, down.

Since this group was past the point of committing to honesty and confidentiality, Irma pulled out the index cards and had each woman answer the discussion questions on the last page of the introduction. The first question asked each woman to compare and contrast her marriage in the beginning to the present state of the marriage, starting with the older women. Since Beverly wasn't married, she volunteered to facilitate this part of the discussion. Rose went first, describing how she had entered marriage with little knowledge of what she was getting into.

"My parents had a good, functioning relationship and I thought things would be the same when I got married. But Theodore was in the military so our relationship was nothing like my parents'. He worked and he expected me to stay home and raise the kids, I think. That was a serious problem. I told my momma that Theodore and I were having religious differences—he thought he was God and I didn't!" Rose slapped her thigh, laughing along with the group.

"See, I had seen my parents work side by side all my life. But we butted heads for years about our roles. Now, I understand that we are a team even though we don't run a store together like my parents did. We ran a family. He worked outside the home, I worked in the home."

Sonia thought about Rose's situation and asked, "Miss Rose, do you feel like you gave up who you were in order to be this nice, sweet wife that your military husband wanted? Sounds to me like you gave up a lot of your ambitions."

"Well, my ambitions were to be able to have a nice home, a nice car, opportunities for my kids that I didn't have, you know. And God was faithful—He made a way for us to have all that on Theodore's salary alone. The Lord had me to remember the times I used to pray to God that He would let the store burn down just so my parents could take a day off from work and go to the park with us. One day I realized that God had made a way for me to have all the things I wanted, *including* a good relationship with my children. I began to praise God for giving me what I needed and some of what I wanted. I got rid of my prideful ambition, thanked God for providing for me and the kids through my husband, and began to take some pride in my role as a wife and a mother—which is something that I think this generation of women takes lightly, I might add."

Adrian let out a "Hmmm," and breathed heavily through her nose. "Must be nice to stay home and have your man take care of you and your kids."

"It most definitely is," Rose agreed. "Don't let women's lib fool you."

Sonia laughed and threw her hands in the air. "That sounds like primitive talk to me. I just wasn't raised like that."

"I wasn't raised like that, either," Rose reiterated. "I had to *learn* how to be a wife and a mother. It's a lost art, if you ask me."

"Well, I ain't trying to find it," Sonia said with a smirk.

Rose pleaded with her eyes. "But you *need* to find it, Sonia."

"Why?" Sonia bristled. "So I can be dependent on some man all my life? I don't mean to be disrespectful, Miss Rose, but that's just not me. I was raised to be independent and to be able to stand on my own two feet. I went to college so I could get a good job so I wouldn't have to rely on anybody but myself."

"No disrespect to you either, Sonia, but where has that gotten you in your marriage?" Rose asked.

Blessed silence. Rose hadn't intended to get so far up onto her soapbox that evening, but Sonia had pushed a button. All this talk about how oppressed women were back in the day was crazy. These young women might have had better jobs and might have had more opportunities as single women, but they were obviously no better off. They were popping Prozac and packing on pounds faster than any generation before. They were *not* fooling anyone, least of all the older women.

Rose continued, "God did not create you to be dependent upon yourself. He created Adam and Eve so that they could be a team. I hate to burst your bubble, but we as women are the ones who have come out with the short end of the stick with this I'm-every-woman thing. Nowadays, men feel like they don't *have* to work to support their families, they don't *have* to be the leaders, they don't *have* to do anything because you young women—with your independent, I-can-do-all-things-through-me philosophy—*can* and *will* bring home the bacon, fry it up, clean up the kitchen, and take out the trash in the morning for them if they don't. And you know who's suffering?"

Sonia could answer that one. "Women are."

"You got that right," Rose agreed. "God intended for men to provide for their families—it's just the way they're wired."

Adrian asked, "So where does that leave us? Somewhere in the background?"

"God made women to complete men. Neither is more important than the other," Rose explained passionately. "You do your part and let him do his part."

Sonia sat back, crossed her arms, and pouted. How *could* she let Kennard be the man when he wasn't acting like the man? This whole role thing was ridiculous. Their family would be a complete disaster with Kennard at the wheel.

Adrian spoke up for those in her generation who didn't feel the same as Sonia. "I, personally, would have no problem quitting my job and staying home to raise a family, even if it meant that we wouldn't always have the most fashionable clothes or whatever. But some men take their roles a little too seriously. It's his way or the highway."

Rose knew that she couldn't argue with Adrian; there is no substitute for the experience of what God can do with a surrendered will. "I'm tellin' you, you all are making your lives harder than they have to be. Just line up with the Word, honey, line up with the Word. God will move when you line up with the Word."

"I'd rather have a bossy man than a passive man," Sonia countered. She would trade places with Adrian in a New York minute even if it meant that she and Kennard would butt heads every now and then. "I can work with that."

"Irma, I think you can take this one," Beverly turned the conversation to the other older married woman in the group. Having known Irma and Harvey for many years, Beverly understood that Irma could relate to Sonia.

"My husband was not saved when we married. See, my family has a legacy of holy women marrying worldly men. I'm talkin' about the kind of men who'd be in hell in a wink if they died at the altar." Irma couldn't help but laugh at her family. "Ooh, Lord, I could tell you all some stories about no-good husbands married to saintly women that would make your heads swim. Everything from bustin' up in juke joints with Bibles to throwing holy oil on the other woman—you name it, some woman in my family has done it in the name of tryin' to save her husband from hell."

Sonia leaned forward now. She was ready to listen to this testimony. She should probably be taking notes.

"Now, Harvey was always was a hard worker, I can say that for him. He always had a day job, but that Harvey was a rascal and a hustler—bettin' on pool games, runnin' football pots. He even opened up a nightclub once. There I was, an usher in the church, seating some of the same folks that had been to my husband's club the night before."

Adrian interrupted Irma in disbelief. "Did you think you were going to change him?"

"*Yes,*" Sonia and Irma said in unison. The two women looked at each other with an understanding that only a woman in this situation could comprehend.

"So, there I was—a Christian woman married to a hustler who knew no boundaries when it came to the pursuit of money. Harvey didn't mind coming to church, but he was spiritually passive, which always upset me because I was the one always praying for us, always looking out for God's will in our home, and I felt like Harvey was undermining everything I was trying to do. He never would pray with me about the miscarriages; he would just run out, get absorbed in the clubs and the hangouts and leave me to deal with the emotional baggage all by myself. I understand *now* that he didn't know how to process his feelings, but that didn't help me *then*. He never saw a problem with our marriage. Things were just fine, so far as he was concerned. He had a respectable wife, a clean home, he had hot meals, he had sex—what else did he need?"

"He had his cake and ate it, too," Sonia summarized.

"Exactly. He did not need me to add to his troubles," Irma added. "And he was not willing to see about what I might need in return for all that I had put into the marriage."

"I'm with you," Sonia nodded. "So what did you do?"

"I got a life," Irma replied firmly. "I fixed up my relationship with God, repented to Him for marrying someone who didn't love Him passionately, and asked God to do His thing in our marriage. I started working, cleaning up homes because I actually enjoy creating and maintaining order. I know it's hard for a lot of people to understand, but I do like to clean. Harvey was never crazy about it, but he always let me have my space seeing as he didn't really want me in *his* space to begin with.

"For a while there, it seemed like we were just two people living in the same home. But after a few years, Harvey missed me—emotionally. And we started over again with this God that he had seen me praying to. One day he says to me, 'I've been watching you, Teacake. You really do have a relationship with God, don't you?' and I told him yes. And he just started asking questions, and I'd show him the answers in the Bible. Next thing you know he asks me how to get saved and I led him in the prayer of faith. We've been growing together in Christ ever since. God just kind of played out the clubs and Harvey's new spirit wouldn't let him rest in these ungodly places. I guess you could say he grew up after I stopped beating him over the head with the fact that he wasn't growing up. Harvey's still not big on church, but he does go to Sunday school regular 'cause he is a student of the Word. I wish he was a preacher, I wish he would reach out more to people, I wish that he would take charge and be more of a leader in our church. Nevertheless, God is still God, Harvey is still Harvey, and I have learned to let both be."

Beverly bobbed her head up and down. "Ooh, Irma, that was powerful. You have learned to let God be God and let Harvey be Harvey."

"Yes, Lord. And because God is God, even when Harvey is Harvey at his worst, God is still sovereign. That's how you can learn to let your husband take on his role. Not because your husband is so perfect, but because when you honor God, He will honor your obedience by moving in this union that He created."

By the sighs, wringing hands, and wrinkles in their foreheads, Beverly could tell that Sonia and Adrian had had their fill. Irma closed her leader's guide in accordance with Beverly's leading.

Beverly led them all in prayer, praising God for His majesty and thanking Him for their time together. She asked for the Holy Spirit to work in these wives and in these families for the Lord's glory and asked Him to show Adrian and Sonia where they had opportunity to spend more time in His Word. Everyone agreed with an "Amen."

As the women packed up their belongings, Irma reminded them all to read the first chapter in their books and look up the verses referenced. Sonia and Adrian readily committed, along with Beverly and Rose. The mood in the room became less intense, and suddenly Sonia found herself hoping that they wouldn't all leave so quickly. Though they had been through some powerful dialogue, the meeting had taken less than an hour.

"Wait a minute," Sonia kicked one leg over the other. "Miss Beverly, we didn't hear from you tonight? What happened when *you* got married?"

"The first time or the second time?" she laughed, pleased that someone wanted to know what *not* to do.

"Let's start with the first time," Adrian suggested, dropping her purse back onto the floor. Adrian planted her chin between her hands and gave Beverly her undivided attention.

"I tell you one thing, I was ready to divorce after the first night," she recalled.

"Be for real, now, Miss Beverly," Sonia harassed her. "The first night?"

"I didn't know nothin' about sex," Beverly admitted. "I was terrified and I thought, *If I have to keep doing this, I ain't gonna be able to make it.*"

Adrian and Sonia fell onto each other in disbelief. "Okay, how could you *not* know?" Sonia asked.

"I had some idea that something was going to happen, but things were hush-hush back then. People didn't talk about sex the way they do now. You didn't see all this kissin' on television and people touching each other in public. Things were more decent back then—people were modest."

"Didn't that lead to ignorance?" Sonia asked. "I mean, you need to know what's going on or you might find yourself pregnant without knowing why or how. I just can't imagine not knowing about sex before getting married. I really can't imagine not *having* sex before getting married. I don't know of anyone who was a virgin when they got married. I mean *nobody.*"

"Well," Beverly said, "that really says a lot about how times have changed. I don't think we had as much opportunity when we were growing up. We were always being watched at church, in the community, at school. And even though I'm sure people did it, they didn't go around *talking* about it."

"Okay, so what happened?" Adrian asked. "I mean, did you finally just start liking it or what?"

"I had a nice, long talk with Rose here."

Beverly patted her friend on the knee and Rose's lips turned up at the corners. She wasn't entirely comfortable with the conversation, but in the company of these women, she would allow it.

"She told me to relax and gave me a few pointers, and...let's just say that after a while, things got better. *Much* better. A *whole lot* better."

"We get the picture," Rose cut Beverly off. "And she's been a wild woman ever since!"

"Ladies, I have never had this conversation with my mother," Sonia admitted.

"My mother let me get married without so much as one word about sex."

"You ever asked her?" Irma asked.

"No way!" Sonia yelled.

"Well, I'm sure your mother can tell you about a lot of things if you'd just sit down and talk with her," Irma said.

"I can't talk to my momma about *that*. My mother was always too stuffy," Sonia said. "When I told her that I had gotten my cycle, she just bought me a box of pads and put 'em in my closet. No 'welcome to womanhood', nothing."

"Well, at least you knew what a cycle was!" Beverly hollered. "Ooh, chile, I thought I was dying!"

Sonia laughed and shook her head. "Beverly, you just didn't know anything, did you?"

"Sonia, they kept us in the dark about *everything* back then. I guess that's why I read so much now—trying to see what *else* I don't know."

They talked for another fifteen minutes about their generational differences—how they weren't allowed to wear nail polish, pads that had belts, the days when women had to quit their jobs because they were pregnant. So much had changed, and they had so much to learn from each other.

CHAPTER 19

Adrian let her jaws flap with the puff of air that she let out of her mouth. She said good-bye to her hotel room, grabbed her tote bag in her right hand, and pulled the larger suitcase with her left. After spending Friday night in the scriptures, Adrian was thoroughly convinced that she needed to go back home and allow the Lord to work things out between herself and Daryll. She didn't know how He was going to do it, but she knew that staying in some hotel across town in a stubborn fit wasn't helping anything. So, at exactly 11:59 A.M., Adrian paid her bill and left that hotel.

Daryll wasn't expecting her. Though they had talked recently, he hadn't been able to talk her into coming back home. When he heard her pull into the driveway, he dropped his cold sandwich onto the napkin he'd been using as a plate (since he was not one for cooking or washing dishes) and stopped for a moment to make sure that he was hearing what he thought he was hearing. His wife was home. He wanted to rush to the door to greet her like a puppy, but he didn't know if that was what she wanted. Was she just home to get more clothes? To ask for a divorce? He decided to just stay put at the table and see what happened.

The house was somehow different to her. Everything was where it should be, but there was a newness to the familiarity. Adrian wondered if Daryll would look new, too. She went straight to their bedroom, not even looking toward her silent kitchen.

Daryll watched her, saw the luggage, and smiled inside. His wife was home.

Adrian threw the luggage onto the bed, popped the lock on her suitcase, and began unpacking. She came across the white envelope with $1300 enclosed and wondered exactly what she should do with it. Adrian didn't want or need the money. Adrian wouldn't wipe her behind with that money. She thought of throwing that envelope in Juanita's face, but that wouldn't be very Christian-like. Maybe she could give it all in church, but that would start some speculation about how much money Adrian and Daryll were pulling in—a whole other bunch of church gossip waiting to happen. Adrian decided to give it to the money-hungry person in the house: her husband.

Daryll was still sitting at the table, barely breathing as Adrian approached him. She slapped the envelope on the table and said, "Here's the money your mother tried to pay me off with."

"Huh?"

"Oh, she didn't tell you that part?" Adrian folded her arms across her chest and read her husband's face. His questioning eyes said that he really didn't know. "She gave me this money to keep up the façade."

Daryll apologized for his mother's actions and said that he would return it to her as soon as he got the chance. "It's just her way of dealing with things," he excused Juanita's actions.

Adrian resisted the urge to let her husband know that Juanita had rubbed off on him, thinking that money was the answer to everything. Instead, she asked, "What makes her think that I am for sale?"

"According to my mother, everybody has their price," Daryll quoted one of Juanita's favorite sayings.

"I don't," Adrian disagreed.

"I know you don't," he said.

Adrian sat down at the table and eyed Daryll. "And when did you figure that out?"

He shrugged. "I don't know. Maybe at church. Maybe when I saw that you were willing to throw it all away for...for whatever you left for."

"You honestly don't know why I left?"

Daryll had asked himself that question for several days now and never could come up with a solid answer. Why would a woman leave a man who provided for her? Isn't that every woman's dream? Isn't that what a man is supposed to do?

When he couldn't answer the question, Adrian filled him in. "Daryll, I left you because I don't feel needed in this relationship. All I am is a paycheck to you. I feel as though you didn't marry to build a life and a family. You married me to build a portfolio."

Any other time, he would have dismissed her, but he remembered now how very sad she had been on Wednesday night. He remembered the ache in her cry, the despair in her praise. His wife needed something else—something that he truly did not know how to give her. If she would just tell him, spell it out for him in terms that he could understand, he would try. "Adrian, what do you want from me?" He had asked that question before, but he never meant it until now.

"I want to build a love and a life and a family with you, Daryll Wayne Jacobsen. That is all that I have ever wanted from you," she explained to him again.

"You say that like it's nothing," he said. "You are asking me to give up all of my dreams for you, throw away all the plans I had for us. All I ever wanted was to grow old comfortably and be able to provide for you. I don't mind building the love and life. To me, that's what a life is. Working hard so that someday you can enjoy the fruits of your labor."

"What about the family?"

"Kids would change everything. I'm comfortable where were are now."

"We can be comfortable as we grow old with a family, Daryll!" Adrian tried to reason by using his parents' example. "Look at your mother and father. They had three kids and they're still comfortable financially. They gave us this house, they go on vacations, and they evidently have thirteen hundred dollars to throw away."

"I just can't see it. Maybe we can think about it if the market goes back up after the next election." Daryll turned from his wife and looked down at his food again. He took another bite of his sandwich, though it had lost all taste at this point.

Adrian sat there and watched his every move. In the past, when they'd had these discussions, one or both of them would leave the room. Now, they sat there in silence and for the first time, she stopped, looked, and listened to Daryll's body language. Adrian couldn't quite put her finger on how she knew this, but immediately she knew that there was something racing through her husband's mind, something that he wasn't saying.

When Adrian was in elementary school, she got into lots of trouble for talking in class. Her teachers would send home notes saying that Adrian had earned herself a detention for excessive communication. It was Adrian's plan to keep those notes in her backpack and spring them on her mother the next morning before school so that her mother wouldn't have time to fuss at her and whip her before school started, but Adrian never made it that far. When her mother came home from work, it took her exactly two seconds to read Adrian's anxiety and say, "You might as well go on and tell me what happened. I can look at you and see there's something wrong." Now, Adrian was as sure as her mother had been: something was wrong.

"Daryll, what's really going on?" she asked him.

He overreacted, jumping and fidgeting in the chair. "What?"

Adrian's eyes narrowed and she fished his face for details. "What's on your mind, Daryll?"

"Nothing." He tried an angry pretense now, "Ain't nothin' wrong with me. I just don't have time for no kids, that's all." He got up and threw away the rest of his sandwich and the napkin. "If that's what you came back for, you should have stayed gone."

Those words bounced off Adrian like water off a duck. She followed him to the kitchen and back to their bedroom, declaring to him, to herself, to every demon and every angel within hearing distance, "I'm not going anywhere! You can say what you want to say, do what you want to do, I'm not leaving this house! I came back because I want to see what God is going to do in this marriage!"

Daryll started getting dressed, though he had nowhere to go. Adrian sat on their bed and watched him in amusement. He could leave if he wanted to; she'd be right there when he got back. "Daryll, I love you."

"I love you, too," he fussed back through clenched teeth.

"And I'll be praying for you."

"'Preciate it."

He left and Adrian got busy praying. Watching her husband squirm under the new declaration of their marriage wasn't only amusing, it was intriguing. Somehow, Adrian saw past her husband's mean words and realized that he was running from himself. He was afraid of something.

Daryll stormed out of the house and Adrian returned to the kitchen table. It was just her and that stupid envelope full of hush-money. Adrian looked at the white envelope. It looked back at her. Whatever was wrong with her husband, Adrian knew that Juanita had something to do with it. She was always pushing Daryll's buttons, always manipulating things and people in her favor. Well, Adrian was not one of her playthings and Juanita Jacobsen was not going to have a foothold in their marriage anymore.

Adrian grabbed the envelope, grabbed her keys and purse, and headed straight to her in-laws' house. It was the first Saturday of the month, so Mrs. Jacobsen was probably at the church feeding the homeless with a ten-foot ladle. Juanita had tried on more than one occasion to ax this ministry, but God's will always prevailed. And Juanita, being the head of the minis-ters' wives committee, begrudgingly showed her face, yet mumbled under her breath the whole time. It was just as well that Juanita wouldn't be there, Adrian thought as she drove to the Jacobsen home. Her anger had diffused a bit and allowed Adrian to think more clearly. She would just leave the money with Daryll's younger brother. Michael was one more unem-ployed and unmotivated young man, but he was no thief. He didn't have to steal because Juanita made sure Michael had everything he ever wanted.

When she pulled into the driveway, Victoria's Benz outshined every other car on the street. Adrian laughed now as she thought of how Daryll described his own sister—ghetto fabulous. He always said that Victoria was the last person on earth who needed to win the lottery because no matter how much she made, Victoria managed to live above her means. Even before she became a millionaire, Victoria always drove fancy cars, though it meant she didn't have $10 to put gas in the gas tank.

Adrian had hoped that Mike would come to the door, but she was unlucky enough to encounter Victoria instead. "Hey, sister-in-law," Victoria said, giving Adrian a fake hug and then inviting Adrian into the entryway.

"Hi, Victoria." Adrian could only take Victoria in small doses without Daryll around. Adrian quickly took the envelope from her pocket and handed it to Victoria. "Here. Could you please give this money back to your mother for me?"

"Oh?" Victoria asked, grinning like a Cheshire cat. She purred, "I knew that you'd lost your job, but I didn't know that it had come to *this*. If you and Daryll needed to borrow money, I would have loaned it to you, you know?"

Adrian's lips tensed as she considered exactly how much—if anything—she should tell Victoria. It would have probably been best to keep her mouth shut, but Adrian would not dare leave that house with Victoria thinking that she and Daryll had fallen on hard times. Adrian would never be embarrassed to borrow money because she had been needy for the better part of her life. Yet Daryll and Victoria competed like two athletes going for the gold. Victoria would rub it in his face and Daryll would have a conniption. After an enormous amount of thinking in a short amount of time, Adrian answered, "We didn't borrow the money. Your mother gave it to me, but I won't be using it for her intentions."

Victoria laughed to herself and spoke in a tone just loud enough to peak Adrian's curiosity, "Mother is up to her old tricks again."

"What tricks?"

"Buying people off to save her precious little Daryll's reputation," Victoria mumbled, still looking at the envelope, counting the money. When she finished, she said with a smirk, "Hmph. Whatever she asked you to do, she obviously doesn't care too much about it. Thirteen hundred dollars is a little low for Mother."

"Victoria, what are you talking about?" Adrian asked, wondering if she actually wanted the answer.

"Daryll's messes are always very costly, and you are not the first one that mother has had to clean up."

Adrian didn't want to hear anymore. Victoria was getting way too much pleasure out of this. Whatever this alleged mess was, Adrian wanted to hear it from her husband, not from her trifling sister-in-law. "Just give Juanita the money, okay? Can I *trust* you with that?"

Victoria instantly lost her bourgeoisie accent and went straight hood. "Look, I got more money than your whole little neighborhood back in Groverton, okay?"

Rather than laugh in Victoria's face, Adrian simply walked away, leaving her sister-in-law standing in the doorway with lips poked out and hands on her hips. As refined as Victoria tried to make herself out to be, it was clear that the Jacobsens were not too far removed from the wrong side of the tracks.

"Adrian," Victoria's properness returned.

Adrian tried to hide the smile from her face, but she couldn't do it quick enough. She stopped momentarily and turned back toward her sister-in-law, "What?"

Victoria was all too willing to wipe the smile off Adrian's face for her. "Her name was Tamisha Sneed."

When Victoria was certain that she had relieved Adrian of all cheer, she closed and locked the door to the Jacobsen home.

CHAPTER 20

Adrian could not wait for Daryll to come home. She needed answers now. Her first stop was Daryll's office. When she didn't see his car there, she went on to the church. The line of hungry people spilled out of the back door, and immediately Adrian's anger died down a notch. As bad as things had the potential of becoming, at least she had food. She forced a "Thank You, Lord," but that quick prayer of gratitude didn't make it past the roof of her car when she saw the rear of Juanita's white Lincoln Continental in the lot. What she saw next was Daryll and his mother standing to the side of the car engaged in a heated discussion.

With all the action taking place on the east side of the church, Daryll and Juanita were at liberty to have their argument on the west side. Heads were rolling, hands were flying. Juanita and Daryll were going at it. Adrian had never been so happy to own a hybrid vehicle. At a full stop, the engine was completely silent. She jabbed the button on her panel and the voices in the parking lot grew more audible with each inch of the window's retreat.

"Momma, I'm a grown man now. I don't need you in my business anymore." Daryll sounded more like he was pleading than commanding.

"Please, Daryll. If you had listened to me, you wouldn't be in this mess in the first place! I'm always having to chase after your silly behind and try to undo what you've done!" Juanita yelled. The tuft of hair at the top of her French roll wiggled like a rooster's red comb.

Daryll tried to take advantage of the pause in her speech. "Momma...."

"And this is the thanks I get for trying to save your marriage!"

Adrian watched with pride as her husband's jaw tightened. Adrian knew that look—he was about to go off on Juanita. "Momma...."

"I should have let that Tamisha just go ahead and have that shameful baby and ruin your life!"

Daryll's shoulders suddenly slumped and he seemed to shrink an inch. "Do you *always* have to bring that up?" Daryll lowered his voice a notch and visually searched the lot to make sure that they were still alone. Adrian didn't have time to throw her car in reverse, so she sat there and waited for the moment. When Daryll's eyes landed on his wife's eyes, he froze.

It took Juanita a few seconds to follow Daryll's gaze, but when she did, her eyes narrowed in disgust. "Well, I guess the cat's out of the bag now." Juanita threw her hands into the air and switched back into the church.

Adrian's eyes burned with tears. With each second that ticked away, Daryll seemed further and further away to Adrian, as though she was panning back with a camera. *A shameful baby?* Daryll's image blurred as the tears came. With her eyes still focused on Daryll's, Adrian placed her hand firmly on the gear, trying to decide whether to go forward or reverse. Daryll stepped from behind his mother's car and began walking toward Adrian. Adrian decided that she'd better go in reverse because if she went forward, she might run over him. *Shameful baby?*

Adrian peeled out of the parking lot and Daryll jumped into his SUV to follow her. In the interest of safety, Adrain obeyed the speed limit, though she felt like running every red light and stop sign in her path. On one of the two-lane streets, Daryll tried to pull up next to his wife, but she rolled her window back up and refused to look his way. The worst-case scenario ran through Adrian's mind: Daryll had had an affair, got another woman pregnant, and Juanita had paid the woman to...Adrian couldn't complete the thought. In the first place, it was too horrible to think of Daryll cheating on her. After all she went through for him! After all the ridicule from Juanita because Adrian was too dark to pass the "brown paper sack" test. And the baby! It's one thing to cheat—it's another thing to allow yourself to impregnate someone. *But he didn't want to have a baby with me! This girl must be a Wonderwoman! She can have him! I should have run him over!*

Her car came to a screeching halt in the driveway and Adrian jumped out just ahead of Daryll. "Adrian, wait!"

Adrian angrily swung the front door open, stuffed her keys into her pocket, and headed toward her bedroom with Daryll's pleas for her attention following all the way. Adrian felt like she was going in reverse as she repacked the suitcase she had just unpacked only hours ago. Daryll was just as busy lugging things out again. It looked like a scene from *I Love Lucy*. Finally, Daryll took his wife's shoulders into both hands and physically stopped her. "Adrian, stop! Listen to me!"

Like a madwoman, Adrian smiled softly, tugged one of the loose twists from her eyes and fell from her husband's grip onto the edge of their bed. Daryll almost wished that she would yell at him. Seeing her this way—breathing deeply with a perfect smile plastered on her face—was the calm before the storm. If she killed him right now, she could probably get off with a plea of temporary insanity. He chose his words carefully. "Adrian, it's not what you think."

At that moment, Adrian felt like this whole thing was a bad dream. It wasn't really happening. She was not sitting on the bed next to her husband who was about to explain that he'd had an affair, gotten another woman pregnant, and run to his momma to help him cover his slew-footed tracks. Adrian cocked her head to one side and spoke in the tone of a wind-up doll, "How would you know what I'm thinking, Daryll? Are you a mind-reader?"

Daryll had never seen his wife so off-key. Beads of sweat appeared above her top lip. Daryll held out both his palms toward Adrian, attempting to bide more time. "Adrian, I know you're angry...."

"I'm not angry," Adrian interrupted him, as she stuck her chin forward and spoke with professional coolness. "People from Pleasant Hills get angry. I'm from Groverton, remember? I don't get angry, I get *mad*, Daryll. I get really, really *mad*."

"Adrian, listen. All of that happened a long time ago, okay? Before I ever met you."

The thought of this occurring before they met had not entered Adrian's mind. She let the possibility sink in for a moment. With this new information, Adrian was able to take another breath. About a quarter of her senses returned, setting up hope that her husband was not the evil man she'd billed him to be in the short time since they'd left the church parking lot.

Daryll watched as his wife's stare softened a bit. The fact that Adrian was still sitting next to him on the bed and had not yet scratched his eyes out gave him encouragement to continue speaking. The brother had to talk fast. "I dated a girl named Tamisha Sneed my freshman year in college. Within a few months, she got pregnant, and...."

Adrian recognized the name Victoria viciously uttered. "So, you *got* her pregnant, right?"

Daryll bowed his head and rearranged his words. "Yes, I got her pregnant."

"Get it right, then."

"Okay," he agreed. Adrian was now the second person—after Juanita—whom Daryll had admitted this to. "I explained the situation to my mother. I didn't love Tamisha and she did not love me, either, but I felt sorry for her because she didn't have a family. Tamisha was an only child, her father was dead, and her mother was incarcerated. I told my mother that I cared about Tamisha and that I would do anything to make sure that my child was taken care of and Tamisha didn't have to drop out of school. I was willing to drop out myself, or go to school part time so I could get a job if it meant that my child and my child's mother would be all right in the long run."

Hearing Daryll say the words "my child" broke Adrian's heart. She had never heard him speak so fondly, so proudly of the prospect. Though his confession was heartfelt and Adrian was glad to know that Daryll had proper intentions, she could not help but be jealous. He had created a life with someone else first.

Daryll kept going. "After I told my mother, she asked me how she could get in contact with Tamisha and said that she would take care of it. I thought she was going to see about finding a doctor for Tamisha, finding out if there was a way for me to keep part of my academic scholarship if I was a part-time student." Daryll gave a dry, humorless chuckle now and looked down at his empty hands. "I was so naïve back then. I always let my mother handle everything—she filled out my college applications, she signed my name to all kinds of documents. I trusted her so much. I mean, she's my mother, you know?"

Daryll looked to Adrian for support. She had nothing to offer except silence. Daryll gulped to stop his Adam's apple from bobbing and then contined. "Well, she took care of things all right. She talked Tamisha into aborting the baby and leaving the university. She actually paid for Tamisha to attend Jackson-Wiley College, which is near Tamisha's hometown, Caney Creek. I don't know if she ever graduated or not. It was as though my mother just made her disappear." Daryll balled his fists and then quickly flicked all of his fingers forward in a magical move. "Poof."

"You never heard from Tamisha again?" Adrian asked.

"No. When my mother wants someone to disappear, they disappear."

"Daryll, I'm sorry, but your momma is crazy." Adrian had said it before, but she meant it this time. "What happened to Tamisha? How do you know she's not *dead* somewhere, thanks to Juanita?"

"My momma's not *that* crazy."

Adrian looked him up and down. "I wouldn't put it past Juanita."

"I wouldn't put it past *you*, Adrian."

"Don't," Adrian warned him, raising one eyebrow.

Adrian jumped back to her feet and stood over the suitcase again. It was empty now and Daryll stood at her side, ready to remove any stitch of clothing she attempted to pack. He was not going to let the life of this marriage be terminated by his past or his mother. "Adrian, I'm sorry." They stood there side by side, facing their headboard. Two defendants standing before a wrought-iron judge.

"Exactly what are you sorry for, Daryll?" Adrian asked for clarification. "Sorry for lying? Sorry for keeping secrets? Sorry for letting your mother run your life? Which one of these things are you sorry for—A, B, C, or D or all of the above?"

"D and E," he replied in a wavering whisper.

"What's E?"

Daryll's voice did not crack—it split open with the weight of a tearful apology. "I'm sorry that I made you pay the price for my ignorance and guilt."

Adrian turned to look at her husband now. She needed him to connect all the dots for her. "What are you talking about?"

"After all I did—after I stood by and let my mother go to bat for me and pay someone to kill my child, I don't think I deserve to be a father. Every time you brought it up, it reminded me that not only was I irresponsible enough to make a baby with someone I wasn't married to, I was not man enough to personally see to it that things were taken care of the *right* way. I never dreamed that my mother would pay to kill my baby—her grandchild."

"Well, what did you think your momma was gonna do—throw her a shower?" Instantly, Adrian wished that she could take it back, but it was too late. Daryll was down and Adrian was kicking. *Lord, for the next five minutes, please don't let me say another stupid thing, okay? Just five minutes.* "I'm sorry."

"No, I deserve it. I deserve everything you say, everything you do, and more," he wagged his head from left to right and poured his soul into his wife's heart, hoping that she would punish him more so that he wouldn't have to keep doing it all by himself. "I always wanted to be a father, Adrian. When Tamisha told me she was pregnant, I was scared and I knew that it would be a huge disappointment to my family. They were all counting on *me* to be the successful one because, by that point, it was obvious that Michael and Victoria were not going anywhere with their lives. I was the first and last hope, so I knew they would be angry.

"That next year, I met you, Adrian. I decided to put it all behind me. I decided that from then on I would handle anything else that came up. Plan things out, you know, have money on hand to address any issue. Even still, the fact remains: because of my irresponsibility, a life was created and then snuffed out. Not just any life—the life of my son. I know it would have been a boy. I just know it. He was going to look just like me, and we were going to name him Daryll Jacobsen III. Call him D3, for short," Daryll smiled now with the painful memory.

Adrian listened to her husband as though she was listening to an alien. All this talk of fatherhood, all this mention of his son. *D3.*

Once the stream of tears had dried from Daryll's eyes and Adrian's cheeks, they each took in the first lungsful of air in the clearing atmosphere of their marriage. The weight of Daryll's sin was greatly reduced, and Adrian felt like she had some answers. Being from Groverton, she wanted to ask, "So what was the big deal about all that, Daryll?" She'd seen many a person go off to college and then come back pregnant or kicked out or both.

But as she watched the pain in her husband subside, she realized that it wasn't just about the baby. It was also about his integrity and his mental well-being. Even things that start out as innocent mistakes can weigh a person down with time when the enemy makes the mind his playground. Daryll had taken a beating on that playground, and Adrian understood now why his attitude had deteriorated over the years.

It was silly, but once when she was in junior high, Adrian and some of her friends had stolen several of her algebra teacher's Gimme-a-Break coupons from the teacher's desk. The coupons could be used to add points to low scores. Over the course of the following three weeks, Adrian and her friends made nothing but high grades thanks to those coupons. At the end of the six weeks, Adrian had the highest class average—a 97. The algebra teacher recommended Adrian for student of the month for the entire eighth grade, due in great part to her unde-served high grade. There were other kids in that class who deserved the honor much more than Adrian, and when those deserving students clapped at the recognition, Adrian felt sick to her stomach. She told her algebra teacher, Mrs. Miller, that she would not be able to attend the Student-of-the-Month PTA cere-mony because her mother was ill. "Oh, she would have been so proud!" Mrs. Miller had said.

But Adrian wasn't proud. For the last two six-week sessions, whenever Adrian earned Gimme-a-Break coupons, she refused to use them. In fact, she had even sabotaged her grade a little to try and bring her average down, negating the extra points she didn't deserve. If she felt that badly about stealing algebra points, she could only imagine how badly Daryll must have felt about inadvertently stealing a life.

With great and deliberate force, Adrian swallowed her anger and finally spoke to her husband. "Daryll, it wasn't your fault. You never meant for...her...to have an abortion." She thought about blaming Juanita, but since Juanita didn't impregnate anyone, the blame didn't rest squarely on her shoulders. It was just a bad thing all around. When Adrian took a step back from it all, she realized that it was all the work of the enemy. He was using something that happened eight years ago to ruin her present-day marriage.

Adrian was not having it. "Daryll, I am highly upset and I cannot even begin to sort through this all right now, but I do love you no matter what you've done. And in God's timing, I believe that you will be a great father to our child."

This time, Adrian's talk of a child sounded like music to Daryll's ears. When it came down to it, Daryll wanted a son—when the time was right. But, until now, he'd never found the opportunity to deal with his feelings. "Thank you, Adrian."

"You're welcome."

Adrian and Daryll got their first taste of what it means to be a team; to be partners in the 3-legged race called marriage where, if one falls, the other has to slow down and help the other one up lest they both tumble or one be worn out from the struggle of trying to drag the other one along. In the years they had been married, Adrian could not remember a time when Daryll leaned on her for strength, and Daryll could not remember a time that he had turned his heart inside out and shown Adrian his true, tender self. He tried to appear large and in charge for everyone else, but underneath it all he was just a preacher's kid who tried with all his human strength to be everything his brother and sister could not. All he wanted was to be a respectful son and a provider to his wife and keep all this dignity afloat in a boat that had a gaping, growing hole in the bottom.

Exhausted from exposure, Daryll took off his clothes and crawled into bed. He beckoned for Adrian to join him, faintly hoping that maybe they could start working on that child, but she instead kissed his head and told him she'd be in later. "Just get some rest."

Maybe she was wrong, maybe she was being stubborn, but the last thing Adrian wanted was a guilt-baby. She wanted to make sure that Daryll was ready to stand up to his mother because she was *not* going to have Juanita's nose all up in her business when it came to the baby. Adrian laughed to herself now. She could already see Juanita examining the newborn's ears and fingers to see what it's "natural color" would be. Juanita wouldn't give two cents for the baby if it had a dark complexion. On the other hand, if the child had Daryll's complexion, she envisioned Juanita telling the child to come in out of the sun before he ended up looking like his mother. No, Daryll needed to get some things straight with his mother before Adrian could proceed with the baby-making plans.

She didn't have much of an appetite and she didn't want to talk to Daryll anymore, so Adrian went to the computer to check email, something she hadn't done much in the past week since she'd been at the hotel. She had a message from Camille. The newlyweds were somewhere in Georgia for a dentists' convention. There were pictures attached. Evidently, they were having a great time in the months before the baby arrived.

There were two more messages: one for breast augmentation and the other for diet pills. As Adrian backed out of her email, a flashing announcement bombarded her: "Find Anyone in the USA!" *Find anyone. Find Tamisha Sneed?* It was probably wrong, she knew. Adrian knew that Daryll had sown a few oats before they married, so there was no need for her to trip now. He had already said that he and Tamisha didn't love each other. But they must have at least been friends, obviously, and he had cared enough about her to volunteer to drop out of college for her well-being. *Tamisha Sneed.* Adrian clicked on the advertisement and immediately found herself amidst a quick scam to pay $39.99 to search for this woman.

"I don't think so," she said out loud. It wasn't that serious, but her curiosity had been aroused. Maybe she could take a cheaper route. She went to *Google.com* and typed in the words "Tamisha Sneed" in quotes. No hits. Next, she tried "Tamisha Sneed" without the quotes. 211 results. "Tamisha Sneed Texas"—123 results. "Tamisha Sneed Jackson-Wiley College"— 4 results. Adrian scrolled down through the results and found one that might match. Adrian followed the link and opened the .pdf file for a recently posted internal newsletter for a hospital in east Texas. This Tamisha Sneed's picture showed an attractive, vibrant woman with a warm smile. If she had entered college with Daryll, she should be around 28, but this Tamisha looked older than 28, with fine lines beneath her eyes and a crease at the corner of her lips. Nonetheless, she made for a beautiful woman who had probably earned that smile.

Adrian read the adjacent article out loud. "Tamisha Sneed is a graduate of Jackson-Wiley College, where she received her degree in nursing. As a new staff member, her warm smile and comforting nature has quickly made its way into the hearts of families whose children are suffering from terminal illnesses. When she's not working at Liberty Medical, Tamisha enjoys reading, writing, and spending time with her 7-year-old daughter, Darellyn."

"Daryll! Come here!"

CHAPTER 21

It was Saturday evening, but somehow Kennard was still home. She wasn't going to sweat it. Sonia had moved all of her necessities upstairs so that she wouldn't have to see Kennard's face. Besides, Kamron needed her upstairs so that she could respond to his calls. At this point, Sonia could tell that Kamron was recovering, but she still didn't want Kelsi around him.

While the video games played downstairs, Sonia read chapter 2 of the Titus2 book and tried her best to keep her sniffles silent. She grabbed her Bible and looked up the referenced verses and answered the questions as well.

Since Sonia had already surrendered her marriage to the Lord, these first chapters served to confirm that she had done the right thing. Beyond that, she was reminded that this battle was the Lord's. A part of her cried because she knew she'd have to let go of her pride in order to move forward. Letting go of her pride meant letting go of her control and position in this family. She would have to surrender to the Lord through surrendering to her husband, and that was a problem because Kennard was a mess.

While Kamron watched *The Incredibles* in his bedroom, Kelsi lay on the love seat to the left of her mother, watching *Finding Nemo* and mouthing every single word right along with the characters. Sonia stretched out on the den furniture and positioned herself so as not to allow her daughter to witness how often Sonia's hand swiped away tears.

At the end of chapter 2 in the book, there were several questions, including, "Have you ever loved someone but disliked their actions? Describe that relationship. Does it parallel the relationship between you and God?" In the space below the question in her book, Sonia wrote:

I think that I love my husband even though I do not like him very much right now so I'm not dealing with him. I don't want to get hurt again. I don't think that parallels with my relationship to Christ in any way because He still works with me regardless. He does not love all of my actions, but He shows love for me no matter what happened the day before, the week before, the year before.

Just as Sonia was getting ready to get into forgiveness mode, Kennard's angry voice barreled up and over the balcony, "Can you turn that durn TV down? Dang!"

Kelsi's movie had been playing for at least forty-five minutes and now, suddenly, it was too loud. Sonia's first instinct was to holler back and tell *him* to turn up *his* TV if it was causing such a problem—not that one *needs* to hear in order to play video games. But for the sake of peace, Sonia lifted and tilted her head up over the arm of the sofa and said to Kelsi, "Turn it down, baby."

"But, Momma, I won't be able to hear," Kelsi whined.

"You heard your daddy," Sonia reiterated.

Kelsi looked at Sonia as if to say, "What have you done with my mother?" She was shocked to hear Sonia actually stand behind something that Kennard said. Still sulking, Kelsi lowered the volume exactly one bar.

"A little more," Sonia pushed.

Another blue bar disappeared from the television screen.

"How is that, Kennard?" Sonia yelled.

"Yeah," he replied.

A little thank you would have been nice.

Kelsi crossed her arms and complained, "I can't hear the movie now."

Sonia laughed at her daughter. "You don't need to hear. You already know the words!" Kelsi continued sulking but gave it up when Sonia clearly ignored this mini-tantrum by returning her attention to the book.

With the simple forgive-and-forget attitude of a child, Kelsi scooted herself off the love seat and knelt down at her mother's side. Sonia smiled inside, glad to be so close to her daughter and thankful that, at least for now, Kelsi still loved being in her mother's presence. With Kamron out of commission and the movie apparently out of her hearing, Kelsi pushed her elbows onto the cushion and plopped her head between her hands, planting herself right next to Sonia. "Momma, what are you reading?"

"I'm reading a book about marriage," Sonia replied.

"But you're already married," Kelsi said.

Sonia laid the open book on her chest and looked at her daughter now. Kelsi's deep brown eyes viewed the world in black and white. So innocent, so vulnerable. As Sonia used her nails to comb back the stray hairs that had come loose from the child's ponytail holders, she responded, "I want to learn how to make our family better and how we can bring God more glory in this family."

"Oh." Kelsi's eyes drifted away from Sonia's. While her little body fidgeted, her mind scampered to make sense of this. "We don't have a good family, Momma?"

Sonia wished that she could say, 'Oh, sweetie, our family is great!' but she couldn't. Kelsi was locked onto Sonia's eyes for an answer in the native language of emotion—the language that every human knows before ever learning to speak; the language in which children are still very fluent. Finally, Sonia answered, "We're going to let God make our family better, Kelsi."

Kelsi's eyes fluttered now with excitement and Sonia realized how much this meant to Kelsi. *This girl loves her daddy.* "How's God going to do that?"

Sonia picked up the book again and gently tapped Kelsi on the head with it. "I don't know. That's why I'm reading this book, Miss I-gotta-know-everything!"

"Well, when God changes our family, will *that* be a miracle?" Kelsi asked.

Sonia held her breath to keep from crying. "Yes, baby, it will be a miracle."

Smiling, Kelsi pushed herself up by her toes and then crawled toward the television screen so that she could hear the movie.

Sonia's maternal instincts got wind of the situation and fussed, "Kelsi, sit back from that screen 'fore you blind your eyes out!" *Oh, my goodness! That sounded just like something my momma would say!*

Kelsi rolled onto her side and faced her mother. "What?"

Sonia could only laugh at herself, and Kelsi joined with giggles of her own. "What did you say, Momma?"

"I don't even know *what* that was," Sonia laughed, placing her fingers at her temples and wondering where that one had come from. It had to be a mixture of "put your eye out" and "you gon' go blind."

And then Sonia heard Kennard's laughter come from below, "That was wild, Sonia."

Kelsi ran to the balcony and asked aloud, "Daddy, did you hear what Mommy said?"

"Yeah, I heard it."

And then all three of them laughed again.

⁓

Sonia grabbed the nearest pen on her desk to sign off on a set of purchase orders. One of these days, she'd have this job down pat, but today was definitely not the day. Earlier, John had come in and dumped a stack of files on the corner of her desk and asked Sonia to go through a stack of work that had obviously been sitting on the corner of somebody else's desk for quite some time. The first half of the month was always busier than the last, and Sonia expected that. What she didn't expect was that the "other duties assigned" would be duties that someone else was being paid to tackle.

"John," she asked her boss for some clarification, "when do you need these back?"

"I needed it done yesterday, but I'll take it first thing in the morning," was his reply as he closed the door on his way out.

The second knock on her office door was a nuisance—especially when she considered that it might be John, returning to give her more work. "Come in," Sonia huffed.

To her pleasant surprise, it was Morris. He was dressed in a metallic, pewter shirt and deep gray slacks. Between those two, he wore a simple black belt that confidently outlined the widest part of his body. His jewelry, minimal, was silver. Shoes were black, fade was tight, and cologne was kicking.

"Hey, Morris," Sonia greeted him. "How was your weekend with the boys?"

He took a few more steps into her office and leaned on the back of the guest chair. "We had a blast—race cars, video games, pizza, a whippin'...."

"A whippin'!"

Morris's eyes hit the floor and he raised a hand to his heart in mock sadness. "I had to lay it down on my youngest son. Now I understand what my momma meant when she said 'This is gonna hurt me more than it hurts you.'"

Sonia had to agree. "It does hurt to have to discipline your kids. But you know what they say, if you don't do it...."

Morris cut her off with his bugged eyes, leaned forward, cupped both hands around his lips and whispered, "The white man will do it for you!"

Sonia hadn't heard that one in a long time. She busted out laughing. "You are crazy! That is *not* what I was going to say!"

"Okay," Morris leaned back again, placing his manicured hands on top of the chair, "what were you going to say?"

"I was going to say...see, you made me forget!"

Morris laughed now, and Sonia couldn't help but notice his stomach heaving up and down in the process. The belt buckle was the catcher. It jerked up and down like the marker on a polygraph machine. Sonia had an instant, intruding thought of what Morris must look like naked. Not a pleasant thought, but nonetheless intriguing. Were there rolls of fat or was he solid and thick underneath that heavy fabric?

Stop it! Sonia felt a flush of embarrassment. And though he didn't say anything, she knew that he'd seen her watching his belly in motion. Hopefully he thought she was only noticing his fat which wouldn't be nice, of course, but it would be better than him thinking that she'd thought of him naked, which was the fascinatingly inappropriate truth. *Stop it, Sonia!*

When Sonia's eyes met his again, he still wore a smile on his face. Maybe he was used to people gawking at his frame. Maybe he was proud of his stature; he sure dressed like it. Whatever the cause for Morris's inexplicable level of comfort in his own skin, Sonia liked the fact that she didn't faze him. That takes confidence. Character. As if to spare *her* further discomfort, Morris changed the subject, "I just came by to see if your son was feeling better."

"Thank you, Morris. That's so nice of you to ask." It occurred to Sonia that most people in her corner of the office must have known that she left early on Friday to tend to her son, but Morris was the only one who'd asked about Kamron's condition. "He just caught a little 48-hour bug. He's fine now." She genuinely appreciated his inquiry.

Morris stepped toward the door now, heading back to his work presumably. "Hey, I was thinking of going to that Italian restaurant on the corner for lunch today. You game?"

"No, I can't do it today, my brother." Sonia used her eyes to point at the stack that John had put on her desk. "I got some extra work piled on me today."

"I understand," Morris said. "You want me to bring you something back?"

"Um..." Sonia thought about it for a second. She would, eventually, need to nibble on something. "Yeah. I like their grilled chicken Alfredo." Sonia reached down and pulled her purse from the bottom desk drawer to give Morris some cash. He came back into her office for the moment. To her dismay, she had only two one-dollar bills and some change. "Dang, I don't have enough cash on me."

"Oh, don't worry about it. I've got you," Morris backed away from her.

"Here," Sonia handed him the two dollars, "use this for the tip at least."

"Cool." He took the bills, folded them neatly and tucked them into his pocket. "I'll bring it back by 12:30 or so."

Sonia returned to the pile on her desk with thoughts of how nice it was to have someone go pick up lunch for her when she wasn't able. The fact that Morris had taken the two dollars rather than insist on paying for her lunch in full proved to Sonia that he was not looking for anything more than a brief, casual work relationship. Not that she needed to convince herself of this. Or did she? There was never a hint of anything other than a professional acquaintanceship until she sat up there and undressed the man with her eyes. Morris hadn't done anything wrong. *Why am I even thinking like this? I have never been attracted to overweight men.*

The work on her desk was tedious and confusing. If she didn't know any better, Sonia would think that the person who had those files must have already put in his or her resignation because, despite the number of unfilled back orders and unresolved issues, the accounts did not show corresponding notes in the computer system. "This is a mess!" Sonia said out loud as she picked up the phone and made a call to Kennard. His new schedule (whatever it was) might allow him the opportunity to pick up the kids from daycare so that Sonia could attempt to finish her work.

She would have to leave a voice message, but hopefully Kennard would get it before too long and return the call with a yes or no. An hour later, Kennard called her back and said that he couldn't pick up the kids.

"What time do you get off?"

"I can't leave here until four-thirty at the earliest," he said.

Sonia let her neck settle to one side. "The daycare stays open until 6:30. I'm pretty sure you could make it if you *wanted* to." Then she remembered—she was trying to save this marriage, not doom it. She aligned her body language with the words that she would force to come out of her mouth. Neck back on straight, attitude in check. She closed her eyes and tried to remember how she used to talk to him before they married, before they had kids. Back when she adored Kennard and he adored her as well. The words came out Smokey Robinson smooth, "Kennard, I've really got a lot of work to do and I would really appreciate you helping me by picking up the kids."

"I just don't think I can make it in time. I've got some other things to do when I get off work." He had added an addendum to his excuse.

Sonia kept her professional timbre, "You know, Kennard, the other day you said that if I let you know what I needed from you, you would do it...."

"Sonia, I would if I could, but I can't so I ain't," he restated one of his Uncle James's favorite lines.

Sonia closed her eyes and gave an answer that surprised even her, "Okay."

Kennard waited for a second and then asked, "Is that it? *Okay?*"

"Yes," Sonia said, feeling herself grow stronger in kindness. "If you say that you cannot help me with the children because something more important has come up, I have no choice but to accept that. I'll see you later." Sonia folded her cell phone, tossed it into her purse, and got back to work.

Morris was back a little after 12:30. The fresh-baked bread strung garlic-scented reams down the side hallway and the aroma hit Sonia's office before he did. "Hey! One grilled chicken Alfredo coming up." Morris set several sacks down on the side table and looked for the one bearing Sonia's name. Sonia noticed that there were two other sacks—one marked Alex (from accounts receivable) and one that read Evelina. Sonia didn't know Evelina, but from what she'd overhead at the water fountain and what she'd read in an internal email that was sent to her by mistake, Sonia gathered that Evelina was one wanton woman. A twinge of jealousy caught Sonia off guard. Well, maybe it wasn't jealousy. Maybe it was disgust. What kind of man associates with a woman whose promiscuous reputation precedes her? And how often did Morris find himself in *that* woman's office? *He's just delivering lunch, Sonia! Besides, what do you care?* Sonia resisted the urge to question Morris. She had no right.

Sonia seated herself at the side table, deciding that there was no way she could manage to maneuver this potentially messy meal while attending to the documents. Morris asked her if she was going to take a break, and when she said yes, he asked her if she would mind his company. "No, I don't mind. Come on back."

"Let me go deliver these." He spoke under his breath as he read the names on the last two bags, "Alex...Evelina. My, my, my—let me dab some olive oil from one of these rolls so I can pray for Evelina. She needs some deliverance."

Sonia's laughter carried out into the hallway. Morris took her *way* back with the reference to what was commonly used as blessed oil. Only someone raised in a holiness church would catch that one. Morris was definitely the son of a preacher.

"Better yet, you got some blessed oil in your desk, Sonia?"

"Naw, I ain't got no blessed oil in my desk!"

He poked out his lips and gave her a scornful, holier-than-thou look that was often passed around the sanctuary when a well-known sinner had the audacity to get up and testify in church. "You ain't *saved* like you say you is."

"Get out!"

Sonia laughed the whole time he was gone to deliver the lunches. As rude as it was, she had to start eating without him. Morris brought back two bottled waters to go with their meals. He bowed for a second and blessed his food, then started on his stuffed manicotti. It was a heavy meal for a lunch. Sonia knew that she'd be stuffed for the rest of the day if she finished the entire entre. With her fork, she marked a line in the middle of the dish and pushed half of the meal to the side, resolving to save it for dinner.

"What are you doing?" Morris asked.

"Oh, I'm going to save this for later," she said.

He nodded. "Is that how you skinny folk do?"

"I am *not* skinny, Morris."

He looked her up and down and remarked, "You certainly aren't fat."

"I cannot eat all of this," Sonia got back on course. "I'll eat half now and half for dinner tonight."

"Hmmm," Morris took a deep breath. "That'll be me in a few weeks. I'm having lap band surgery."

"Really?" Sonia shrieked. "Morris, I'm so excited for you!"

He muttered in obvious disappointment, "I don't really have a choice. Blood pressure up, cholesterol up, knees are bad—it's a miracle I don't have diabetes yet."

"Well, thank the Lord for preserving you up until now," Sonia said as she tried to cheer him.

"Mph," he rolled back, as though Sonia's statement had physically impacted him. Then he said in all seriousness, "He definitely upholds me with His right hand of righteousness. I am thankful."

Sonia recognized this verse from the Bible. It occurred to her then that Morris was so completely out of place in SAIT. Sure, he had the technical know-how to write and evaluate software, programs, and implementation. But he also had the gift of making people feel comfortable. For all his joking and imitating the saints, there was no mistaking Morris's calling.

Morris cleaned his plate "for old times' sake" he said. Then he helped Sonia clear the small table and they both got back to work only twenty minutes after she'd first begun to eat.

Five o'clock had come and gone, and Sonia knew that she'd be pushing it to get to the daycare on time. At 5:30, she decided that John would just have to get over himself. The more she delved into the task, the more comprehensive it became. It was unreasonable of him to ask her to complete all of that work in one day. Maybe after SAIT completed their upgrades, she would be able to access the network from home and do things like this after hours, but until then she could only do so much between the hours of eight and five.

The thought of SAIT completing the task was bittersweet. Sure, it would allow Sonia to do her job with more ease, but when the job was complete, that would be the end of Morris.

Sonia smiled as she allowed the cinema of her mind to play a short flick. She saw herself on a tropical island—no. Scratch that. She wanted something more practical. She changed the setting. This time she was at the grocery store, casually pushing a cart wearing form-fitting jeans, a red tank top, and simple flip-flops. She was probably fifteen pounds lighter and (though her face had not aged a day) Sonia imagined herself old enough that the twins would have graduated by then because she was sporting the short afro that she promised she'd give to herself when she turned fifty. Kennard was nowhere to be found and she conveniently decided to fast forward through any explanation of whether or not she was still married to Kennard. Sonia was writing, directing, and viewing this daydream. She could do what she wanted in her own mind.

As the scene continued, she saw herself bent slightly at the waist, searching through a pile of tomatoes for the ripest selection when suddenly she heard her name.

"Sonia?"

Slowly, she turned toward the handsome man who was calling her name. The voice was vaguely familiar, but she couldn't quite place the face. Her eyes narrowed, begging for him to help jog her memory.

"It's me—Morris Dupree. We worked together on a project years ago...."

She suddenly remembered him. "Morris! Oh, my goodness! Look at you!" Gone was the roll of fat beneath his chin, the tire around his waist, the slight rasp in his voice. All of that replaced with absolute fineness to go with the face, aura, and fashion sense that had always been attractive to Sonia. He approached her for a purely innocent hug and Sonia was pleasantly surprised by the tone of his muscular torso. Unlike some of the other bariatric patients she knew, Morris's body was tight. She felt his hard body against hers—could have bounced a quarter off his chest. She exclaimed again, "Morris, you look so good! It's so nice to see you again after all this time!"

Fast forward again to a coffee shop where she and Morris sat talking, catching up on each other's lives. He was a preacher, she was retired. His boys were doing well, and so were Kelsi and Kamron. They laughed about how tough it had been to put their respective children through college, but it had all been worth it. Somehow Sonia knew, by this point, that they were both single. They would have to be because she didn't want this to be a sinful movie.

"Ma'am," a young man's voice abruptly cut the film tape. While Sonia had seen his silhouette in her range of vision, his presence had not entered her consciousness.

Sonia literally shook her head as she snapped back to reality. She wondered how long she had been in the trance but found the word to respond, "Yes?"

"I need to empty your trash."

"Oh my gosh!" Sonia gasped. She figured she must have been sitting there daydreaming for some time because she rarely saw the custodial crew. She quickly grabbed her purse and whisked herself out of the office as she said good-bye to the young man who appeared to be wondering if Sonia was psycho.

CHAPTER 22

Thursday morning, John immediately logged on to his computer to pull the updated reports he needed for his 8:30 meeting with the powers that be. As the papers began spewing out of the laser printer next to his desk, John visually skimmed the reports to get a feel for the bottom line. The Kingsford account—still in the red. Humectra account—no change. In fact, very little had changed since he gave the responsibility to Sonia. His blood pressure quickened and pumped him all the way to Sonia's office. "What happened to the updates?"

Unaware of the knot in which John was tangled, Sonia rolled the chair back from her desk, turned her right palm up and, like a game-show hostess, waved her open hand across the four stacks of folders on her desk. "I'm working on them right now, John. Ooh-la-la."

His lips tightened and his skin deepened another shade of red. His butt was on the line and there Sonia was acting like this was some game. "Apparently, you did not grasp the urgency of the situation. When I said I needed this finished the day before yesterday, I meant it."

His attitude took Sonia by surprise, but she was not short on words. She cocked her head to one side and gave him a get-real look. "John, there was no way on earth that I could have finished all of this work yesterday. It took me half the morning just to make heads and tails out of these records. This is *at least* a three-day job."

"Well, maybe if you hadn't spent so much time laughing through lunch with your SAIT friend, you could have gotten more work done," John accused.

If Sonia could have turned red, she would have done so, too. Sonia set her eyes dead on John's, her left eyebrow pointed toward the ceiling and she tilted her chin to her neck. "You are out of line, John. If you want to get angry with someone, get angry at the person who *didn't* do the work before you gave it to me."

John huffed and puffed but relinquished his verbal assault. "How much longer, Sonia?"

"All day today and tomorrow, at best."

John would have to face his superiors with inconclusive data and beg for a few more days to get things done. Push come to shove, he would pay overtime for someone to come in on Saturday and finish whatever Sonia couldn't. "Fine. Let me know where you are by noon tomorrow."

"I can do that."

John left without another word. No apology, no acknowledgement of the fact that his request had been excessive, no acknowledgment of the fact that he was wrong for busting up in her office all big and bad. He just left like he was in the right all along. *Actin' like Kennard.* And what was all this nonsense about Morris?

Sonia didn't have time to entertain John's fantasies. She got back to her work—or someone else's work —and didn't look up from her desk until well after 2:00. Morris barely cracked the door long enough to say hello in passing. Sonia quickly motioned for him to step inside and close the door behind him.

"What's up?" he asked.

"We're being watched."

"Who?"

"Me and you."

"By whom?"

"My boss, John," Sonia informed Morris.

"Oh, he's on the surveillance team, now, too?"

Alarmed, Sonia asked, "What team?"

"You're on the late show, my sister."

"Morris, what are you talking about?"

"We'll have to discuss this someplace else later. Blinky's Burgers—after work?" he suggested.

Sonia wanted to know about this team of people watching her. "Okay," she agreed, "but I can't stay long."

Morris quietly opened her door, looked both ways out into the aisle as though he was crossing the street, and then looked back at Sonia showing all the white of his eyeballs. "I'm feelin' like a runaway slave."

Sonia couldn't hide her smile. "Steal away," she whispered.

Throughout the rest of the day, every time Morris walked past her office, Sonia could hear him humming *Swing Low, Sweet Chariot* and *Down by the Riverside* with his acutely tuned voice that strummed up her memories. As crazy as Morris was, his singing carried her back to the days when she performed with the children's choir at church. Their church always put on a special program in honor of Black History Month, filled with reflections from the past and projections for the future. Those were the good old days.

These days, she wished she could go back to the last time she sang in the choir, the last time she gave an Easter speech, the last time she complained about the white ushers' gloves. If she could have gone back to that last time, she would have done things differently. She would have kept her mind on the Lord and gotten to know Him and herself better instead of being side-tracked by Kennard's good looks and boyish humor. She would have dated some of those "good guys" that she threw away because they weren't "adventurous" enough. And last, but not least, though she could not imagine her life without the twins at this point, she might have waited to have kids if she had known that Kennard would remain such a big kid himself. Shoulda, woulda, coulda.

Sometimes Sonia felt as if she'd cheated herself out of so much. And yet, the women in the Titus2 group seemed to think these feelings were a normal part of growth and change. Before marrying Kennard, Sonia wanted someone to make her laugh and to give her space. Now, however, what she needed was someone to be there more often than not, help with the awesome task of raising children, and laugh with her at the end of the day. If he couldn't do the first two, there was no need to bother with the last one.

A snack pack of graham crackers from the vending machine held Sonia's appetite at bay while she put in a full eight hours on John's impromptu project. John was throwed, but he was still "the man" in the truest sense of the word. Though her work environment was not volatile, Sonia knew better than to risk baring her neck to the corporate ax by letting it be said that she didn't come through as promised—especially not after what Morris had said.

At 5:17, both she and Morris pulled into the parking lot of Blinky's Burgers. She recognized the BMW right away and walked toward him as he hoisted his heavy body from the vehicle. Like an elderly driver, he held on to the frame of the door for support and balance. Sonia felt sorry for him, but that pity didn't last long in light of his upcoming surgery. She imagined that in another year or so, Morris would glide in and out of

BMWs with ease. In an instant, she wished that she could keep in touch with Morris so she could see him after his weight loss. It was just a thought.

Sonia's cell phone rang and she slowed her pace toward Morris's car when she saw Kennard's name on the panel. "Hey."

"Yeah," Kennard said, "I'm getting off a little early. You want me to pick up the kids?"

Sonia stopped in her tracks in the middle of the parking lot. She resisted the urge to be sarcastic by asking, "Is this Kennard?" Instead, she jumped at the opportunity. "Yes. Actually, that would be great."

"All right." Then he held on to the phone for a second longer.

"Okay," she concurred.

"All right, bye."

As she hung up with her husband, Sonia realized that the pause at the end of his conversation was probably his way of giving her a chance to thank him for picking up the children. *Whatever.*

Sonia spent the next hour and a half with Morris at Blinky's despite the fact that there were two distantly familiar faces from work also seated in the restaurant. Blinky's was always loud, always busy—the perfect place to get tucked into a corner and lost in the crowd. Morris assured her that those two were not on "the team," as he referred to the office spies. Sonia listened and learned the identities of charter members of the surveillance team: Jack from public relations; Steven McAllister; and a recently demoted administrative assistant named Lois, whose cubicle was positioned within view of Sonia's office door. Jack was upset because Morris was not gay, Steven was evidently offended that Morris did not frequent the hot spots with SAIT, and Lois was the one who told both of them that Morris couldn't be gay nor did Morris have time to fool with the SAIT lunch crew because Morris was too busy flirting with Sonia during their alleged two-hour lunches.

Sonia hurriedly swallowed the gulp of her virgin daiquiri and slammed her glass on the table. "What two-hour lunches?"

"Don't get upset," Morris calmed her by leaning his back against his side of the booth. "It's nothing personal. This kind of thing happens everywhere we go. People are bored around the office. They have nothing better to do, so they make up things about the visitors in order to have something to talk about. People like drama. It's kind of funny to me."

"It's not funny to *me*," Sonia said. "I mean, you get to leave and go on about your life. I have to work with these people day in and day out. I don't want my name in a bunch of office gossip."

"I wouldn't worry about it," Morris said, attempting to lighten the mood again. "In my experience, when petty people like Steven and Jack and Lois start talking, anybody with any kind of sense knows to consider the source."

When their meals arrived, Sonia blessed the food and they had a less intense conversation about how quickly he thought SAIT would wrap up its work. Morris said that it wouldn't be more than a couple of weeks.

"Where will you go next?" Sonia inquired.

"I've got a week-long project in Memphis, and then I'll take time off for my surgery." Talk of surgery seemed to sink his spirits.

"Aren't you excited?" Now it was Sonia's turn to change the tide. "This is a whole new life for you, Morris!" Sonia reached across the table and slapped him on the shoulder.

Morris flashed all thirty two and bowed his head for a second. "I've got a wonderful job, two healthy sons, and I keep in touch with my college friends. My life is pretty good right now."

Sonia nodded. "I'm sure it is, but you're reinventing your-self. It's like you're getting a new start." Sonia wished like crazy that she could have one of those new starts.

Morris sat back against the bench again and thought for a second. Then he said, "You know what really bugs me?"

"What?"

"I'm not going to be happy if people suddenly start warming up to me, you know? All these people who wouldn't give me the time of day when I was fat and then—bam—all of a sudden I'm socially acceptable. I don't want people to treat me any differ-ently than they would if I was fat."

Sonia let her chicken sandwich droop down between her hands. "Morris, please. Men are not held to the same standards of physical excellence as women. You could weigh ten times what you weigh now and women would still want you because you've got a good personality and you're in a pretty good tax bracket." Then she added something she'd wanted to say since the first time she heard him sing. "Plus you're a preacher. God's got somebody for you."

Morris coughed and beat his chest with his fist. "Watch-o mouth," he struggled to say while taking a sip of his drink.

"You know you're supposed to be somewhere up in some-body's pulpit. It's written all over you, clear as day." Sonia took another bite of her sandwich, ignoring the look of shock on Morris's face.

When it was clear to him that Sonia was not going to take the words back, Morris's shoulders collapsed in capitulation. He wiped the corners of his mouth and nodded. "Okay, okay. You got me on that one."

"You gonna eat all those fries?" Sonia asked, pointing at his basket.

He shook his head no.

Sonia thanked him as she reached over and grabbed a few.

"How you just gonna *tell* me I'm a preacher and then ask me for my french fries?"

Sonia laughed through her explanation, "I'm telling the truth *and* I'm hungry. I worked all through lunch trying to finish that thing for John."

"Go on, then. You just took my appetite away with that declaration of yours."

"That's 'cause it's true."

Morris took another long sip while his eyes focused on Sonia's. He smoothed away the moisture from his lips by pursing them together for a second. He asked, "How do you know so much about me?"

Sonia swallowed her food and returned his gaze, bringing laced fingers to her chin. "You can take the boy out of the church, but you can't take the church out of the boy."

"I can appreciate your honesty. You want to know what I know?"

"What?" Sonia squinted her eyes, just waiting for him to say something comical.

"I say this with all respect."

"Okay?"

"Your husband is one lucky man."

All of the heat in Sonia's body rose to her face and she felt as though she might rise in the air, a balloon filled with helium. She could not remember the last time she'd received a genuine compliment from a man. Sure, the occasional stranger tried to make conversation in the grocery store, and every so often a truck driver would honk at the aerial view of Sonia's honey-brown legs, but she'd heard nothing this meaningful in a long time. At that moment, it didn't matter that this man's belt buckle was probably on its last notch. Morris's compliment watered a neglected garden of womanly desire.

Sonia's lips curled to a warm smile. "Thank you, Morris."

After her spontaneous dinner with Morris, Sonia floated home a little after seven and Kennard abruptly popped the bubble. "Where have you been?"

As she descended back to earth, she determined to keep her voice level. She had to phrase her response just right. "Some of my coworkers and I decided to go by Blinky's after work."

"Since *when* do you go to Blinky's after work?"

Sonia asked, "Since *when* do you have a problem with the concept of hanging out after work?"

"I've been here with the kids for *two* hours!"

"Okay," Sonia shrugged her shoulders as she walked toward their bedroom slipping off her shoes, one in each hand. The carpet welcomed her feet after a day in heels. She heard the rumble of the twins' activity upstairs and asked, "Have they taken their baths yet?"

"Baths! We ain't even *ate* yet!"

"Why not, Kennard? You've got two hands. You know how to make sandwiches and warm up soup. Matter of fact, there's some leftover spaghetti in the refrigerator; you could have put that in the microwave." Sonia sat down on the bed now and finished undressing. In her flustered state, she had forgotten to utilize the guest bathroom.

For Kennard, it was a fortunate mistake. Seeing Sonia undress right before his very eyes quickly diverted Kennard's attention. Beneath the black skirt and form-fitting maroon button-down striped blouse, Sonia wore black, lacy boy-cut briefs and a matching bra that pushed her breasts to the brink of exposure when she bent over to pull a pair of pajamas from the bottom drawer.

Kennard licked his lips and took a deep breath. He weakened with each gentle sway of her frame. He could not even remember the last time he and Sonia had made love. "Sonia," he said finally.

Sonia stood upright and faced him. "What?"

He wanted to say some of the things his uncles had taught him to say, but now was not the time. He thought about arguing some more, but it was obvious that Sonia would not reciprocate. Left with nothing more than the discomfort of his vulnerability and a burning desire to experience his wife intimately, Kennard spoke his heart.

"Why did you do that?"

"Do what, Kennard?"

"I tried to do something to help you with the kids, and then you just ruined it." He turned his eyes heavily toward the floor. Kennard didn't know how to say that Sonia had ignored his attempt at active fatherhood.

Sonia tried her best to translate and came pretty close, figuring that she had hurt his feelings. "I was not trying to *ruin* anything. You offered to pick up the kids and I took you up on the offer."

"But you didn't come straight home," he spelled it out for her. "How was I supposed to know you weren't somewhere in a ditch?"

Sonia bounced down at the foot of the bed and raised her knee onto the bed in a ninety-degree angle. Kennard thought he was going to pass out from her beauty.

"You could have called," she shrugged.

"That's not the point."

Sonia tried to remember her Smokey-Robinson-smooth voice. "As I see it, Kennard, the problem is not that we weren't in touch. The problem is that I did exactly what you do, and you couldn't handle it. This feeling you're having right now is the same one that I have every day. You can't stand the taste of your own medicine."

Kennard placed his hand on his forehead and then rolled that hand to the back of his neck. He stretched his neck to the side and pulled until his vertebrae popped. Sonia patiently waited for him to finish his shenanigans. He looked like an athlete warming up for a competition. Actually, Sonia noted now that his body looked strong enough to compete in any event. His legs, exposed from mid-thigh down, thanks to a pair of denim shorts, still retained the muscular curves and definition of a sprinter. It's not every day that a man's legs command attention, but Kennard was an exception. His chest muscles made stiff, clear-cut mounds beneath his T-shirt and, though his stomach was no six-pack, she'd settle for his four-pack any day.

Today would be nice.

When Kennard had run the full gamut of stretches, he finally spoke again. "Look, I don't appreciate you taking advantage of the situation."

She could think of a million reasons why Kennard had no right to complain. Sonia knew that she was right. The only question was whether or not she wanted to prove it to Kennard. One line in the Titus2 book came to her now: *Start with you.*

Sonia made the conscious choice to relinquish her rightness in the name of peace and said, "I'm sorry."

For the second time in two days, Kennard had to wonder who he was talking to. The Sonia he knew would never offer an apology—not without a sarcastic tail on the end of it. He stood there waiting for the rest of the statement. "That's it?"

"Yes," she repeated, "I'm sorry. I can run out and get something for you all to eat. Just let me finish changing clothes."

Clone-woman aside, the last thing Kennard wanted was for Sonia to cover her body before he got the chance to touch her. "I...I'll go get something in a minute."

"Okay? It's almost seven-thirty. The kids should be pretty hungry by now."

He blinked, stopping his eyelids half of the way back up. "I'm hungry, too."

Sonia read his expression and remembered: *Your husband is one lucky man.* She felt attractive. Sexy. "How hungry?"

This whole thing was too good to be true. In the time it took Kennard to turn his back, walk to their bedroom door and lock it, Sonia unhooked her bra and let it cascade down her arms and to the floor. Now she stood before Kennard wearing only the sexiest pair of panties he had ever seen. He didn't know if these panties were new or if he just hadn't seen Sonia enough lately to have the opportunity to lay eyes on them.

Kennard pulled his shirt over his head and walked toward Sonia with the purposeful, calculated steps of a lion sneaking up on its prey. He kissed her neck first. Then her chin. Her nose. All places where she could not reciprocate. She could only receive. When he finally landed at her lips, Kennard subdued her eager kisses by gently stroking her arms with his fingertips. She might as well slow down because he was going to take his time. Sonia enjoyed this kind of play: following his lead, surrendering herself, panting at the mercy of Kennard's expertise.

Sonia wore a damp smile as her pulse returned to its resting rate. Kennard kept his promise to go get dinner. Sonia lay in bed thinking of what had just happened. She had made love to her husband partly because she had been...well...aroused by another man.

Sonia took a shower, rinsing her mind of both Kennard and Morris in an attempt to prepare herself for Bible study. She was determined to get in all her time with the Lord this week. No more letting Him down, herself down, or even Beverly.

CHAPTER 23

Irma had not called Harvey's attention to the table in the east corner of Blinky's restaurant because she didn't want Harvey to have a reason to discourage her from meeting with the mentoring group. Harvey had a habit of supporting Irma until she got "too involved" in her hobbies. Perhaps the better way of explaining it would be to say that he got jealous every now and then. Irma also kept the secret to herself because she didn't want to hear Harvey fuss at her about jumping to conclusions.

Maybe Irma *was* jumping to conclusions. Maybe the gentleman with whom Sonia dined over in that back corner of Blinky's was a relative. Maybe this was a business meeting. Irma focused in on the body language. Smiles. Lingering eye contact. There, Sonia touched the man's arm as she laughed.

This was all bad news to Irma. Bad news. She didn't know what to do then and she still wasn't sure about what to do now as the women arrived for their third meeting.

Adrian had not been able to sleep or eat well since learning that Daryll was a father. "I can't believe this is happening," Adrian had said one night as they lay in the heavy silence of their bedroom. Though it had been at least fifteen minutes since turning off the lights, she knew that Daryll was not asleep.

He swallowed a few times. "You have every right to be angry, Adrian."

"I don't know if angry is the right word." She fished her brain for the right term, but came up empty. "I don't think a word exists for what I'm feeling right now. Embarrassed, hurt, jealous and fooled all at the same time. What's the word for that?"

"B...th...da," Daryll stumbled and settled on, "I don't know."

Adrian jumped outside of her circumstances and asked, "Is this the kind of thing that couples refer to when they say, 'We've been *through* a lot'?"

Daryll rolled onto his back now and faced the ceiling beside his wife. "I guess," he answered.

"I always thought *through* meant stuff like job changes and the flu and money problems," Adrian somehow laughed at her innocence now.

Daryll chuckled, too. "And I always thought that as long as we had money, there would be no problems."

Though she could barely see his outline, Adrian turned her head toward her husband. "I guess we were both wrong, huh?"

"Guess so," Daryll agreed. Then he asked for Adrian's hand in marriage all over again. "Adrian, will you go *through* with me?"

Adrian surrendered with a sigh, "I'll try."

"That's all I'm asking for."

⁓

When Sonia arrived, Irma led her into the gathering room where the others were waiting. Since Rose was leading this meeting, she called them all to order with prayer and a review of the previous week's reading. Then she forged ahead into the third lesson. Throughout the evening's meeting, Sonia felt Irma's glance and Irma quickly redirected her gaze to someone else in the group. She did it so quickly that Sonia figured that she herself must have been imagining things. Maybe she was paranoid, especially considering the topic: Closing Yourself Off to the Enemy. Though Sonia had indeed skimmed through the pages to prepare herself for the meeting, the message hit home harder now in light of Morris.

At first, Sonia thought the topic was just about the usual taboos: gossiping, watching bad television, hanging around with people who meant them no good. Having come from a Pentecostal church, these came as no surprise to Sonia. But the final section of the chapter stepped on her toes as the authors explained the importance of taking control of the thought-life. With her busy job and her busy twins, Sonia didn't have time for talking on the phone, laying up on the couch watching television, or running with her friends. Really, she had not talked to her best friend Gina in weeks. For all she knew, Gina could be off helping villages somewhere in Africa. No, Sonia's problems weren't on the exterior—they were interior thoughts and fantasies that took center stage by storm.

She imagined running into Morris at the children's college graduation. His youngest son, who had waited to go to college, finally went back after several years' hiatus and now, he was in Kelsi and Kamron's graduating class. Morris looked good and he told Sonia that she looked good, too. Somehow, miraculously, they were both single and available. He made her laugh again, made her think again.

Every once in a while, when the fantasies started to include sweet nothings and private touches, Sonia found the need to reason with herself, "Everyone has fantasies. Besides, I'm not attracted to large men in real life." Until tonight, Sonia never realized that the fantasies had dangerous potential. Sonia squirmed under the microscope of scripture.

The message in the book and in the Word was clear: she had to cut it off with Morris. But she wasn't exactly sure of how to do that seeing as they hadn't actually *done* anything. She couldn't very well go up to him and say, "I can't see you anymore because I've been having inappropriate thoughts about you." That would sound silly. Aside from that, Morris was on his way to the pulpit. If she was honest with herself, Sonia had to admit that Morris had not done anything entirely inappropriate. If he had made any advances, Sonia would have kicked him to the curb for disrespecting the institution of marriage by coming on to a married woman. No, Morris wasn't the problem. *Sonia* was the problem.

Adrian had some imaginations of her own to conquer before tomorrow's drive out to meet Darellyn, Tamisha, and Tamisha's fiancé, Robert. Adrian's mind had run the full gamut of scenarios: Darellyn might be a spoiled brat that Adrian would loathe; when Daryll met Tamisha, the old flame might spark again; Adrian had even gone so far as to hope that, in person, Tamisha would not be as pretty as she appeared in her online photo. Petty. It shouldn't have mattered. Still, Adrian scheduled an emergency appointment with her hairdresser and made sure that her nails and toes were tight. One can never be over-prepared for a meeting of this nature.

She and Daryll had talked calmly and extensively about the situation and agreed to welcome Darellyn into their lives and do their fair share of supporting her financially. Adrian herself had talked with Tamisha and she seemed cordial. The legalities of it were all very cut-and-dried: Daryll had a child and he wanted to be a part of her life. Adrian, Tamisha, and Tamisha's fiancé, Robert, were in agreement. Those were the facts. Still, Adrian felt duped. She wanted to be a *birth* mother, not a *step*mother. She realized this was not entirely Daryll's fault. She understood it. Didn't mean she had to *like* it.

This week's lesson, however, calmed Adrian's nerves a bit. The Word gave her the assurance and the tools she needed to conquer the worst-case scenarios that had kept her awake at night. It enabled Adrian to focus on the good that would come of this. Daryll would get the chance to make amends. Juanita's spell would be broken. And a little girl would now get to know her biological father. In fact, this little girl would have two fathers, because evidently Robert treated Darellyn as his own. And although Tamisha had asked Daryll if he would object to Robert's presence at their first meeting, her question was more a matter of courtesy than a request for permission.

The Bibles and books were hidden back in their zipped conference bags and canvas totes as Irma prepared to bring the meeting to a close. She asked for special requests and Adrian thought this was just as good a time as any to tell the group about Darellyn. They were all aware of struggles in the Jacobsen household and Adrian felt their prayers working in her home. It could not hurt to bring them into the fold about this. More than anything, Adrian needed to get this off her chest, split the load with some other godly women.

"I have a request," Adrian said. She stopped and waited for an acknowledgment of the request, but in that instant, the dimples appeared in her chin, her checks, and between her eyebrows. She was flooded with emotion and Sonia reached out to hug her sister. Strengthened by Sonia's embrace, Adrian continued, "We learned the other night that Daryll has a child already...with a woman he dated briefly in college and...we're going to meet Daryll's little girl and his...ex-girlfriend...and her fiancé tomorrow. Pray that everything goes well. And pray for my attitude 'cause it's bad right about now."

Beverly drove the fingertips of her left hand into the center of her right hand, signaling time-out. "Whooow. Slow down."

"I know, I know," Adrian sat upright now.

"Well," Rose interjected, "the way I see it, God's just cleaning things out before He makes His next move. You know? Getting it all out in the open so you two can deal with it before you add something else to the plate."

Adrian nodded and raised both eyebrows. "Yes, I do believe you're right."

"It's going to be all right, girl." Sonia squeezed Adrian again, though Sonia couldn't imagine how things can be all right when you find out that your husband had a baby—even if it *was* before he met you.

Once they had all assured Adrian that they would stand in agreement with her and pray according to Romans 8:28, declaring that good would come out of this situation, Adrian could breathe again. Irma had a prayer request for Harvey, whose knees had been bothering him. Beverly requested prayer because she was going to have a LASIK operation performed on her eyes the following week. Rose requested prayer for her sister's son who was facing some legal battles.

It was Sonia's turn now to request prayer. She thought about confessing this whole thing with Morris to the group, but it was too embarrassing. How was she going to explain it to these women? Her mentors? All they had to complain about were bad knees, minor surgery, and…well, the legal thing sounded serious. Matter of fact, that was so serious that Sonia felt silly about the thought of revealing this frivolous matter before her group. Sonia decided to go generic. "Just continue to be in prayer for my family."

After closing prayer, Irma offered them fresh-baked cookies before hitting the road. The women were happy to partake of anything from Miss Irma's oven.

Beverly remarked, "Irma, girl, you put your foot in these!"

"Thank you, Bev."

Mid-cookie, Beverly asked Adrian, "So, now, Adrian. I have to ask. How did you find out? What did Daryll say?"

Adrian didn't know where to begin. "It all happened so fast!" Adrian explained the sequence of events as Sonia and the mentors listened in amazement.

Beverly asked, "Have you all considered the specifics—you know, child support, visitation."

Adrian nodded. "Yes, we're ready to talk through all of that tomorrow."

"That's good," said Rose. "I think it's really great that the two of you are going down *together*. That says a lot about the priorities of you and Daryll. Let's the mother know that you two have a sense of family."

"That is so true," Irma echoed.

Beverly added, "The other thing is, you and your husband should clearly present yourselves as a unit. You don't have to be rude or ugly. Just let Daryll facilitate so that the lines of communication between all adults involved are open. No 'This doesn't involve me' on your part, no 'I can't leave the message with you—I have to talk to him' on her part. The more open things are, the less tension there will be, and the better things will be for the child."

Adrian took a deep breath and received this advice from her big sisters in Christ. In Adrian's experience, she had a hard enough time dealing with her blood relatives—let alone outsiders. Adrian made up in her mind then and there that Darellyn would not become an additional source of stress in her marriage.

They shared a little more about tomorrow's meeting and even got down to what Adrian would wear. Adrian didn't want to seem silly, but she wanted their advice.

"Look *married*," Rose said.

"Look like you'd be a great role model for her daughter," Irma advised.

"I think you should look like you got it going *on*," Beverly laughed as she repeated something she'd heard one of her nieces say. "I mean, if I was going to meet my husband's ex-girlfriend, I would be looking like a million bucks."

Rose rolled her eyes as the ladies laughed. "Don't pay her no mind."

Sonia had to agree with Irma. "I know that if ever I found myself in a position where another woman might become involved in my children's lives, I could not care less about her beauty. I would want to be impressed by her sense of compassion and understanding. *That's* what would make *me* feel comfortable about forming a relationship with her and allowing my child to spend time in her company."

Irma nodded, "My thoughts exactly."

"It won't hurt to look good. That's for *you*, not her," Beverly said.

Rose shook her head and smiled to herself. Beverly always had to have the last word, God bless her. "Well, I think it's about time I headed on out."

"Me, too," Beverly rocked herself up from Irma's sofa. She took a few wobbly steps, allowing her legs to take note of the change.

Sonia grabbed her purse and stood, too. As she resumed an upright position, she felt a sudden heaviness in her bladder. Since having the twins, it seemed that her bladder gauge had two settings: empty and bursting. There was no in between. "Miss Irma, may I use your restroom?"

"Sure. Down the hall, second door on your left."

Irma said her good-byes to everyone and waited for Sonia to return so that she could send her off with a warm adieu as well. As Adrian, Beverly, and Rose pulled out of the driveway, Irma wondered if this time alone with Sonia was one of God's divine appointments.

Sonia flattened her blouse as she came out of the restroom. "Well, Miss Irma, I look forward to another week in the Word and in the Titus2 book."

"Me, too," Irma smiled, wringing her hands. She followed Sonia back into the living room where Sonia collected her belongings. Time was slipping like water between her fingers, and Irma's heart burned with conviction. She had to say *something*. "Sonia...wait just a second, sweetheart. I want to talk to you."

Sonia's purse slid from her shoulder to her hand where Sonia quickly caught the strap before setting the purse on the floor and her body back onto the couch. "Yes, Miss Irma?"

Irma's search for tact was unfruitful. She had hoped to have a hypothetical conversation, but that wouldn't do. "Sonia, yesterday Harvey and I ate at Blinky's and I...saw you with a gentleman and...it concerned me."

Now it was Sonia's turn to fidget. "Oh, Morris?" She overreacted, throwing a hand to her heart and leaning back. "Oh, no! He's just a coworker of mine, Miss Irma." Sonia had never lied to Miss Irma before and, technically, she wasn't lying now. *So why does it feel like a lie?*

Irma placed a hand on Sonia's jumping knee. "I'm not accusing you of anything. I was just concerned." Irma's hand settled back onto her own lap and she contemplated her next words. She had gathered the group to help Sonia and Adrian stay married to their husbands. She had come out of pocket, out of time, out of energy. Now it was time to bring some skeletons out of the closet, too. Or at least crack the door open long enough to expose the ugly truth of infidelity.

Irma smacked her lips and bared herself for the sake of the Rileys and her commitment to the Lord that she would do His will as she worked with this group. Irma closed her eyes and spoke. "A long time ago, I met a man. He was a door-to-door encyclopedia salesman. Back then, salesmen came into neighborhoods to sign people up for different products and to collect payments. Harvey met him once, during his initial sales pitch. After that I was the one who met him at the door when he came to deliver new editions and collect payments. The first month that he came by, we talked at the door. The next time he came by, we had coffee. We had such a nice, fine conversation that he stopped by the following week when he visited other families in the neighborhood. I didn't think anything of it because he was just so nice and friendly and I wasn't doing anything wrong— though he never seemed to drop by when Harvey's car was in the driveway. Before long, we were seeing each other every week, sometimes two and three times a week."

Sonia held her breath. She wasn't sure if she wanted to hear Miss Irma confess to having an affair with Encyclopedia Man. "Miss Irma...."

"No, let me finish. Please," Irma stopped her.

Sonia exhaled.

"When people say 'one thing leads to another,' they mean it, Sonia. It doesn't matter what your intentions were or how innocent things were in the beginning." Miss Irma narrowed her eyes and peered straight into Sonia. "Before you know it, you could be doing things you never imagined yourself capable of."

Sonia closed her eyes and then opened them again, looking at Irma's textured ceiling. Then Sonia gave herself away and whined, "But, Miss Irma, I haven't *done* anything."

Irma smiled, knowing that these were the same thoughts she herself had had when justifying the growing attraction to the salesman. "But you have done things in your mind, haven't you?"

Sonia bowed. "Yes."

"And that's where it starts—in your mind. For us as women, especially, it's not always about the physical connection. We can have an emotional affair without ever touching the other person."

"An emotional...affair?" Sonia sputtered.

"Same as a sexual affair—getting emotionally involved with another man," Irma explained. "It's a lot of things—giving another man the emotional position that rightfully belongs to your husband, letting the other man support you emotionally, giving him the tools to support you by sharing your deepest thoughts, sharing your joys and your pains with him. By pouring out your emotional self to him you'll look up at some point and find that you have shared so much of you with this other man that you have become emotionally vested in the relationship whether you touched him or not."

Sonia set her elbows on her knees and thought for a second. Already she had indeed begun to think of how she and Morris might keep in touch after he left. They could always do email. Email is safe, isn't it? "Miss Irma, what about just being friends? Can't men and women be friends? I mean, who's to say that Morris and I won't just be friends for the rest of our lives?"

"Well," Miss Irma gave Sonia the benefit of a doubt, "would it be a friendship that you would be able to discuss and share openly with Kennard?"

"No," Sonia answered quickly.

"Then the answer to your question is no."

"But Kennard is not open-minded enough to accept that I could be friends with a man," Sonia argued respectfully. She felt warm suddenly.

Irma pursed her lips and gave Sonia a prim and proper smile. "The problem is not Kennard, Sonia. If you are willing to risk your marriage to pursue a secret, platonic relationship with another man, trust me, it ain't platonic."

Sonia surrendered with a sigh.

Glad that she had broken through to Sonia, Miss Irma built her younger sister up again. "Honey, I know it's tough sometimes. I know that when you meet someone new, things seem fresh. You're learning new things by talking to him, he's intrigued by you. Feels like you're falling in love again and that *is* exciting. No doubt about it. Everyone wants to feel like they're falling in love.

"The falling-in-love grass on the other side is *always* greener. Reality cannot compete with fantasy. But if you take that same energy that you use to look for greener pastures and use that same energy to take care of your *own* grass, it can be just as green. You can even plant some flowers and vegetables if you'd like. I can't guarantee you that you'll feel like you're falling in love every day, but God'll give you rain and sunshine. And in their seasons, those flowers will bloom and those vegetables will ripen and you'll get the smell and the taste of your labor and His love. Nothing smells sweeter, nothing tastes better. Now *that's* the good stuff that marriages are made of."

Sonia's eyes were brimming with tears as she gave Irma the biggest smile. Irma returned the smile, showing off the gap between her two front teeth.

"Thank you, Miss Irma." Sonia seized Irma's neck in a tight embrace.

"You're welcome, baby, you're welcome."

CHAPTER 24

It was a 3-hour ride but it felt more like a day's journey. Daryll drove the whole way, listening to smooth jazz and whistling every now and then. Their conversation was sparse for the first two hours, but when Adrian saw the sign that said Caney Creek 39 miles, she had to speak to prevent exploding.

"Did you tell your mother?" she asked.

"I haven't had time," was his excuse.

"Well, when do you plan on telling her?"

He shrugged.

Adrian turned toward her window and looked out at the bluebonnets that lined the Texas highway. Here and there, cars were pulled over and small children posed in the patches of bluebonnets as their parents took pictures of them in this naturally beautiful setting. Maybe one day Adrian would do this with her children.

As they approached their exit for the town of Caney Creek, Adrian retrieved the directions to Tamisha's house from her purse and Daryll followed her instruction without question. They pulled up to 6298 Houston and took in the neighborhood. The first thing Adrian noticed was the mature trees overhead, giving almost every homeowner shaded lawn areas fit for swinging benches. The homes were at least twenty years old, old enough to have been run down but, obviously, the homeowners in this area were too proud to let their properties deteriorate.

Adrian lowered her shades as she got out of the car. Daryll met her at the passengers' door and helped her onto the sidewalk. Directly before them was the quaint, one-story brown brick home where his daughter lived. Already, Daryll felt relieved to know that his daughter was not living in squalor. A wind chime seemed to announce their arrival with the breeze.

Daryll rang the doorbell and within seconds appeared the face of the woman Adrian had seen online. She looked the same except for her hair. Instead of the wedged bob, she wore bone straight micro braids pulled back into a simple ponytail. Tamisha's face was lightly dusted with makeup, her eyebrows arched, and she wore a touch of lip gloss. Her clothes were unassuming—a red stretch tank T-shirt with rhinestones lining the rim, khaki cargo pants with ties, and bronze flip-flops.

Tamisha unlocked the screen door and welcomed them by extending her hand first to Adrian. "Hi, Adrian. It's nice to finally meet you."

Adrian nestled her shades back into her afro and shook Tamisha's hand. "Same here."

Then came Daryll. They shook hands and exchanged smiles. "Hey, Daryll. It's been a long time, huh?"

"Sure has," he said.

"It's nice to see you again."

He returned, "Same here."

Robert came from a hallway to the left, introduced himself to both Adrian and Daryll. Robert was tall and broad, with cornrows and a pair of hoop earrings. *Perhaps a corporate thug, perhaps trying to hold on to his youthful hip-hop days,* Adrian thought to herself. Either way, he wore it well.

Adrian tried to categorize the smell of the home. Laundry detergent? Oranges? Febreze? Whatever it was, it registered pleasantly and Adrian wondered if Tamisha smelled like this wherever she went. Some people *always* smell like their homes.

When they were seated in the living area, Tamisha answered the question that was on Adrian's mind. "Darellyn is at cheerleading practice, but she and my grandmother should be arriving any minute now."

Adrian nodded silently as an awkward silence set in.

"May I get you two something to drink?" Robert offered. "Coke, water, juice?"

"I'll have some water, please." Adrian wanted to make him feel useful since obviously no one else was useful at the moment. Daryll declined but thanked Robert anyway.

Robert asked Tamisha, "Baby, you want something?"

"Uh, bring me a Coke." Robert moved past her toward the kitchen, leaving Adrian, Daryll, and Tamisha alone for the moment to engage in idle chat.

Robert returned with drinks for Adrian, Tamisha, and himself. Again, there was silence, like they were waiting for someone to say the word "go." They took long sips of their beverages and Tamisha got up from her seat two times to look outside for her grandmother and Darellyn, as though they could possibly forget which house was the correct one.

Finally, she plopped down on the sofa across from Daryll and Adrian and started the conversation, "Daryll, I want to explain some things to you." Robert put his arm around Tamisha's shoulder and rubbed her bare arm, a gesture of encouragement. "I always felt badly about what happened, but as a single mother and as a woman, I did what I had to do. Things haven't been easy, but I wouldn't trade her for anything in the world."

"Back up a second," Daryll gently directed her. "That was all my mother's doing. I never dreamed that my mother was going to ask you to have an abortion, and I *never* said that I didn't want the baby."

Tamisha leaned forward in shock, "What?"

He repeated, "I never wanted you to have an abortion."

"But, but," Tamisha stammered, "I have letters from you. You said…,"

"*All* my mother," Daryll interrupted her. "I should have handled my responsibilities myself. And for that, Tamisha, I do apologize."

She took a deep breath and it appeared to Adrian that Tamisha was rearranging the shelves in her mind. She was making room for Daryll's confession while sliding old cans of anger and hurt aside. Tamisha was about to respond when she noticed the glare from the sun's reflection on her grandmother's car as it pulled into the driveway. "Oh, here they come."

Everyone stood, Tamisha opened the door, and Darellyn rushed past her mother to Robert, oblivious to her guests. The child hopped up into Robert's embrace and hung onto him as she slid back down to the floor. "Hey, Daddy! Guess what? I learned a new cheer today! You want to see it?"

Robert bent down, kissed Darellyn on the cheek, and then whispered something in her ear.

"Oh," she said as she turned to include the rest of the human population in her daddy's-girl-world. When she faced Daryll and Adrian, there was no denying her lineage. Forget Daryll, forget Tamisha. From her squared nose to the dimple beneath her eye to the streaks of light brown hair, this was Juanita Jacobsen's granddaughter all the way.

Tamisha took Darellyn's hand and together they walked the four feet from Robert to Daryll. Adrian noticed the pained expression on Robert's face. She recognized it from weddings—a father giving the bride away.

Tamisha introduced them, "Darellyn, this is the nice man I told you about. This is Mr. Daryll."

"Hello, Mr. Daryll." Then she remarked, "Your name is almost like mine!"

Daryll leaned over to shake his daughter's hand and look closely at her little face, "Yes, it is."

"And this is his wife, Miss Adrian," Tamisha continued.

Adrian smiled at her stepdaughter. She was a beautiful, dainty little bundle of energy, wearing pink shorts, a pink "Princess" shirt, and pink butterflies throughout her naturally wavy hair. All she needed was a tiara. "Hello, Darellyn. It's nice to meet you."

"Hi, Miss Adrian."

After dispensing the required number of handshakes, Darellyn abruptly ran back out to the car to aid her great-grand-mother. "Granny G bought me some new shoes, Momma!"

Tamisha rolled her eyes and said to Adrian, "Ooh, my grandmother cannot go *anywhere* without getting something for Darellyn."

"Come see, too, Miss Adrian!"

"That's what grands are for," Adrian guessed as they both followed Darellyn outside to the car.

Daryll and Robert were seated again in the living room. Robert stated the obvious, "We haven't told her yet."

"I understand," Daryll nodded, though his head seemed to rattle from the shock of seeing his seven-year-old daughter for the first time.

"Quite frankly, we don't know how. Darellyn was two years old when Tamisha and I started dating, and...I love that little girl." Robert stopped speaking long enough to regain control of his voice. "I love her."

"I didn't know...."

"I know," Robert interrupted Daryll, "I know you didn't know. I'm *glad* you didn't know because I don't think I could sit alone in this room with you if you hadn't just explained yourself to Tamisha."

Daryll nodded again, swallowed his pride (something he had done more in the past two days that he had done in all of his life), and said, "That's fair, man. That's fair."

Darellyn's hands were filled with cheerleading gear, so she used her foot to push the front door open. "I got everything, Daddy," she announced, ignoring Daryll completely.

Tamisha followed, laughing with Adrian about Darellyn's sense of independence. "She's seven going on twenty," Tamisha said.

Tamisha's grandmother, Geneva, remarked, "Well, she got it from her momma."

Tamisha closed the door after her grandmother entered and introduced Daryll to Geneva. "Grandmother, this is Daryll. Daryll, this is my grandmother, Geneva."

Daryll held out his hand to greet Tamisha's grandmother, but the woman refused. She kept her wrinkled hands at her side and stared at Daryll so hard for so long that he could see the gray outline of her brown eyes.

"Grandma," Tamisha nudged.

Geneva spoke words she'd been holding inside since the day Tamisha came home from college distressed and pregnant. "You and your family caused my granddaughter a whole lotta pain.

Tamisha struggled to get through school and make something of herself. I know ya'll gave her that pay-off money, but it wasn't enough to pay for her schoolin' and half the daycare and all the little knick-knacks that come along with having a baby. I just thank God for sendin' Robert to be a *real* man in Tamisha's life!" Though she was several inches shorter than Daryll, Geneva somehow managed to look down on him.

"Ma'am, I didn't know about Darellyn. I thought...."

Geneva waved off his explanation. "I don't want to hear your *words*. I'll listen to what you *do*, not what you *say*." Geneva pulled her handbag closer to her side, turned up her royally wide nose, and left the room without looking back.

Tamisha slapped her hands on her thighs as she sat down again next to Robert. "That's my grandmother."

"She has every right to be upset," Daryll pleaded Geneva's case.

The Jacobsens took their places again on the love seat. "Well, since it's on the table, I would like to go ahead and try to get some kind of child support arrangements set up. If you'll give me the name of your attorney, I'll have my attorneys contact yours as soon as possible." Adrian had hoped he wouldn't be so forward about things, but that was Daryll for you. He had no problem discussing money, his domain.

Tamisha and Robert looked at each other for a moment and then Tamisha spoke. "We're doing fine so far as her day-to-day needs are concerned, but we don't have much saved for college. That is where we could really use the most help."

"I'll be sure to let my attorneys know," Daryll concurred, and then he laughed proudly. "Darellyn is obviously very bright."

"*Very* bright," Tamisha agreed, "with *very* big dreams." Then Tamisha asked, "What are your thoughts about visitation?"

Daryll answered for himself and his wife, "We were hoping to participate in her life. I know it's a lot to think about right now, but I would like for her to know who I am, when we all agree that the time is right."

Robert looked away from the Jacobsens now. Tamisha squeezed his hand. "Darellyn knows that Robert is not her biological father. We told her last year when she was in kindergarten. She asked why her daddy didn't live with us like the other kids' fathers and why we all didn't have the same last name."

Daryll asked, "Did she ask about me?"

"Yes. I told her that you lived far away." Tamisha laughed a little. "What she wanted to know more than anything else was if she had brothers and sisters."

"Hmph," Daryll shared her laughter. "Nope. No brothers and sisters on this end."

Adrian forced a smile to match Daryll's.

Robert cleared his throat and said, "I'll go get the phone numbers you asked for." He excused himself and left the room.

Tamisha gave him a sympathetic nod and then looked down at the floor as she said, "Please understand, Robert is very upset right now. He was planning to adopt Darellyn after we get married next month."

Daryll rolled his lips between his teeth. He could not believe how stupid he had been. Stupid enough to allow another man to take over his responsibilities. Sitting in the same room with Tamisha, her warm smile and her easygoing nature, the sense of caring that drove her to a career in nursing, Daryll could have kicked himself. He figured he should have known that Tamisha wouldn't go through with an abortion. "Tamisha, I can't tell you how sorry I am for not stepping up to the plate."

"And I'm sorry for not giving you the opportunity to step up."

As she watched the sincerity written on Daryll's face, Tamisha realized that she should have trusted her instincts about Daryll. In fact, her instincts had been talking to her when she named the newborn after its father. Deep down inside, she had doubts about the messages Juanita relayed "on behalf of her son," but Tamisha was too devastated to process her true feelings back then. She was eighteen, pregnant, back home less than a year after graduating from high school, witnessing her life's dreams swoosh down the toilet while a church full of whisperers and a neighborhood full of haters watched her belly grow larger month after month. By the time the baby was born, Tamisha had almost convinced herself to get in touch with Daryll again, but she'd sold out already. Contacting Daryll to let him know that the baby was alive would have meant the end of tuition, paid courtesy of Juanita. Then where would Tamisha have been—a teen mom with a baby and no way to afford college? Not to mention the risk of having Daryll reject her and the baby in his very own words. Eight years ago, Tamisha had cut her losses and moved on. A bird in the hand beats two in the bush. Thinking like a mother, Tamisha took the money and ran with her baby.

Robert came back into the room and exchanged cards with Daryll. When Robert didn't sit down, they all took it as a sign that this meeting was officially over. "I'll go get Darellyn so that you can say good-bye."

Within seconds, the sprite young lady bounced back to the living room and stopped just shy of the threshold, painting the room with her innocent radiance. She stood there with her feet perfectly still, but her body rotated impatiently. Darellyn did not appreciate being pulled from her dolls to be a part of what appeared to be grown folks' business.

Tamisha instructed Darellyn to say good-bye to Mr. Daryll and Miss Adrian. As rehearsed, Darellyn thrust her hand forward again and shook the strangers' big hands, "It was very nice meeting you."

Both Daryll and Adrian returned the compliments and Darellyn skipped back to her bedroom. Tamisha and Robert walked the Jacobsens' to their car for another round of handshakes and good-byes.

As Daryll was making a U-turn at the dead end, Tamisha ran toward them, her hand flagging them down. Daryll pulled back to the curb and slowed to meet her.

"Here's her first grade picture," Tamisha said as she handed Daryll the photo of a grinning Darellyn. No one could ever accuse this little girl of being camera-shy.

"Thank you," Daryll could barely speak.

"You're welcome. Y'all have a safe trip back."

Adrian was the first to comment as they drove away, "She looks just like your mother."

"I know, huh?" Daryll gasped. "It's almost scary."

"You've got to tell her soon, Daryll," Adrian shook her head.

All the way home, Adrian listened to him replay the thirty minutes they'd spent at Tamisha and Darellyn's home. Adrian couldn't count the number of times he said "smart" and "pretty" from Caney Creek to Dallas. "Did you hear when she said my name sounded like hers? She's pretty articulate, huh?"

And Adrian could only reply, "Yes."

Adrian blinked to stop the tears from breaching the dam of her eyelids. This entire situation was bittersweet. Daryll's paternal passions were flowing and he was probably more likely than ever to have a child with Adrian. But why did it have to come to *this* for him to see that children are gifts from God? It didn't